Taken for a Ride

First published in the UK in 2003 by
Dewi Lewis Publishing
8 Broomfield Road
Heaton Moor
Stockport SK4 4ND
+44 (0)161 442 9450

www.dewilewispublishing.com

ISBN: 1-899235-89-2

Cover Photograph: Neil Roland
Design & artwork production: Dewi Lewis Publishing
Printed and bound in Great Britain by
Biddles Ltd, Guildford and King's Lynn

9 8 7 6 5 4 3 2 1

Taken for a Ride

Neil Roland

DEWI LEWIS

PUBLISHING

I am hugely grateful to
Richard Gallagher, Michael Schmidt and
my agent Bruce Hunter of David Higham Associates
for their enthusiasm, support and friendship
as *Taken for a Ride* evolved.
Thanks, too, to Sara for her opinions and
for laughing in all the right places, and to Felix
for not arriving until it was all written.

For Ruth and Theo, my exceptional parents.

One

I flick to the end of *Cold Sun in Spring*. Leaf slowly backwards the three, four pages of *'Other titles from this publisher'* bit. Irresistible, that last page. Like an opened box of chocolate truffles to a diet. A blink in a not blinking contest.

The air in the second-hand bookshop is as thick and textured as corduroy. It torments me, its pleasures beckoning and always just out of reach. How can anyone absorb so much pleasure between the covers? I have to be out of here within seven minutes, but I can't settle on one I want.

Something to get me through the afternoon. My fingers hold the thinnish volume, and I glance for a moment at the cover, a '50s line drawing of a woman. I think she looks a bit like me. In her thirties, shapely in the way women were and I, it seems, still am, and alluring in the way I seem to manage to be only for men who don't interest me. She looks puzzled. Bemused. A bit cross. As if she just can't get into the novel pressed behind her title page.

Even before I've been fully seduced by the hero – when I'm only a few pages in, I have to search out that last page. The one blistered with ink just across the top third, the rest blank with that after-book nothingness of cream, blind paper. I don't want to ruin it for myself – who would? But I need to see if my hero is still speaking – is still alive – at the end. And then I hate myself. The truffles all gorged. The blink blinked. I've destroyed it all for myself. But it's not a choice thing. It's what I do. Like trying to out-wit the 'fridge light.

I can tell you now, that I'm still here at the end of this book. No need for you to sneak a peek. I don't do myself in with pills on page 147. An elderly Volvo estate doesn't surge from nowhere on page 155, its ancient owner lost in a reverie, her foot finding the accelerator instead of the brake. There's no squeezing of hands over the coverlet of a hospital bed on page 208 (is there a page 208?) as I declare yet again my adoration for Blue, who will be in the world alone as an untimely disease whisks me to eternal calorie counting in the sky. No, it's ok. I said that doesn't happen. Anyway. Who's Blue? And whoever he is, I'm not saying that he doesn't meet a disturbing, undignified end by the early pages of chapter eight. Possibly, even, at my hands.

Actually, I don't know him myself yet. I'm about to see him for the first time in three or four minutes, but that's in a page or two. Unless, of course, I've already flicked forward. No willpower. That's my problem.

Immaculata, her hair, like cascades of liquorice, and now mostly on the floor, raises one pencilled brow to a circumflex, and gazes in the mirror.

'And you think Silvano would've stayed if I had looked more like... a man?'

'They're all £1, that lot.' I look up at the bookseller who sweeps his arm to indicate that pretty well anything would be £1 if I'd just care to buy something.

I take his point, and replace the old novel. I have to admit, I'm a bit intrigued as to why Immaculata's lover would prefer her if she looked more like a man. But not enough. Still, I've got to pick something.

We're what Mr. Clegg calls 'a bit flat' in the office. Not that property isn't booming here in Manchester's leafiest suburb, but there are one too many estate agents in Didsbury, and Anthony Holland and Clegg Can-I-Just-Put-You-On-Hold? seem to be that one. Should a real person come into the office, Mr. Clegg has shown each of us how to press the hash and star buttons in one move so that the other telephones ring all over the office and Trish or Pam or the trainee, who looks about twelve, can tell the fresh air behind the receiver that they've received an offer at the full asking price and is it convenient to come in to sign non-existent forms. Mr. Clegg enjoys believing this will help business.

The bookseller goes back to his cataloguing, and I pick up the novel again. There is a picture of the author on the back cover. Immaculata's creator. Square necked dark crêpe dress, a sole row of pearls hemming her throat. Each pearl is repeated in the slightly smiling mouth of little neat teeth. The author is described as 'London born and now living in Rome with two daughters.'

Of course, she won't be living anywhere now. She was probably Immaculata herself. All that energy. Frustration. Thwartations – that really should be a word. Joys. All for £1, and I don't want it even for that. I do feel a bit pressurised to make my choice. Anything. I've been in this second-hand bookshop for over half an hour, but nothing quite fits the bill.

'Sorry. I'm not feeling very decisive today,' I offer the bookseller. He's very charming. Tells me it doesn't matter if I buy anything or not. I picture myself back in the office for an afternoon of tedium with Trish and Pam who disguise their weary dislike of each other with random compliments about each others' appearance. There's a predictability about their routines which, for me, is beginning to spill into bold splashes of pure irritation. I know just how the afternoon will begin.

I give it five minutes before Trish says 'Sweet enough eh?' to Pam's refusal of sugar in the mug with the smirking pig on it. Pam will chuckle a feigned Lancashire 'Oh-aye' though she knows Trish means 'Fat Enough?' and is hurt by it every day. This is all followed by three and a half hours in which the two of them will 'at-the-end-of-the-day' and 'to-be-honest-right?' me into day-dreaming about punching them.

Didsbury has two second-hand bookshops. It's that sort of place. Full of people who read. Rich people who buy second-hand because of the feel of it. And that sizeable stratum, the not-so-nouveau-pauvre in big houses empty now of dead husbands and nest-left children who make occasional valiant efforts to clear some of the debris of livelier decades past so they can sell and move smaller and live more comfortably off the proceeds.

Then there are the thirty-somethings like me, who've stayed on after the student years, carefully avoiding London's lure in order to bask in the pleasures of Didsbury's giant park-style horsechestnuts and limes spreading above the streets like half drawn chenille curtains, their roots bunyoning the tarmacked pavements beneath.

And then there's that special breed. The aging Didsbury ladies, who have made a vocation of eccentricity. They are second-hand bookshop users. Impossible to know if they're going to be donors or buyers. One's in right now. Emerald green woollen cape, black, high crowned hat with black ribbon trailing down the back like a 1920s' pall-bearer and, as always, those patent beige, square toed boots. The sort where you can see the stitching where the shoe ends and the boot part begins. Circa 1973.

You only have to say 'green cape', and anyone in Didsbury knows who you mean. They can picture her buying her lone Arbroath smokie from Evans the Fishmongers, or recovering her breath on the low wall of Peacock's Funeral Directors or commenting cheerfully on the tête-à-tête daffodils to the drunks on the steps of the octagonal library. But they know little more than that. Didsbury is like that too. Its own, self-contained village, but part of a wider picture. Part of the city. Besieged but aloof. Threatened but defiant. Cautiously smug.

I've only got three minutes till I'm expected back. I scan the old orange-back Penguins he keeps in three wooden troughs near the door in case I've missed one. No. It looks as if Immaculata with the liquorice locks is going to be my companion for the afternoon.

'Have you ever been in one of these places when there wasn't a single Edna O'Brien novel in this section?' I look up from the trough and feel a surge of excitement as pure and perfect as panic. When I look back in the book you're reading now, perhaps from my vantage point of the sixth chapter, certainly by the tenth, I'll never remember exactly what it was that made me know that the man standing next to me, flicking the pages of a paperback and not looking back at me at all, would have such an effect on my life.

'Yeah – I know, or an H.E.Bates,' I answer, smiling, wishing I hadn't just picked up a 1961 *Guinness Book of Records*. I slip it back onto a low shelf and feel it slide in with satisfying ease.

He's smiling now too, and looking at me. 'And always a range of Lynn Reid Banks,' he adds. Can he be unaware of the blast of thrill I'm feeling? Someone who knows the old orange Penguin shelves like I know them. Someone who has actually noticed that every second-hand bookshop in Britain, no matter what else it stocks, always has these authors shoulder to shoulder with each other. Always the same titles – O'Brien's *Girl with Green Eyes* or *August is a Wicked Month*, always one or other from the Reid Banks trilogy.

It's nothing so remarkable in itself. Lots were printed. Were read in their time. Why not? But for someone – a man, no less – to recognise what I've recognised is like a delicious conspiracy.

'And that Miss Read,' I go on. 'I've never read those – I think it's the inverted commas round her name. Seems so tongue-in-cheek.' I stop speaking. The discovery of shared views is so precious. So exciting. And nothing ruins it all more than the sudden introduction of something unshared. But he grins.

'Know just what you mean. Amazing. I've never read one either.'

I want to ask him how come he's so familiar with these yester-decade books – he's younger than me. Can't be more than 28 – 30 at most. But he nods his head and laughs at the pleasure of these last few moments and tells me he'll catch me. For a moment, the doorway of the darkish shop is filled with the cinnamon suede of his jacket, the stripe of worn denim as his legs leave, and the dull glint of a silver earring. And then I'm left alone, with Sarah Vaughan's *What Kind of Fool Am I* like a vapour in the air. I could race out of the shop and reach him. But this is page nine. I know nothing more of him. I wouldn't know what to say. I don't have that sort of confidence. I don't even know his name. He's uncatchable, but will catch me. Said so.

Two

Two hours and three minutes till *Countdown*. Good god. What's it all come to? Ah. A knock at the door! How exciting. Must be Federal Express with that 'blanket of youth' I ordered. Simply remove all the packaging, open it out, place over head (diagram one), making sure it covers all parts of decrepit old body (diagram two), and count to twenty. Remove Blanket (diagram three), casting it onto the floor, and hey presto, you'll have shed fifty years (diagram four) and are now ready to place two fingers up at matron and march haughtily out of the Sidney Fleiss Home for Bewildered Driftwood (diagram five). I must learn to control these fantasies. They won't bring me lasting pleasure.

'Come in!'

'Hello Mrs. Laski. How are we today?'

'Ah Penny! Yes. Penny. Oh what a lovely jumper. Is it new? Now, let me see if I can remember. You are Penny – not Penelope, but Patricia which – yes that's it – your father liked, but you never much cared for him because he left you when you were – now what was it? eight? and your mother remarried and lives in – urm – Llanelli – and you are studying midwifery at Glamorgan and you are engaged to – to – to – Justin, who does something quite fascinating with seal pups on the Farne Islands.'

'Oo Mrs. L, you know me better than I know myself. I'll have to come to you to remind me who I am when I'm your age, won't I?'

'What a perfectly dreadful thought!'

'What is?'

'Oh – you ever being like this, I suppose. Wouldn't wish it on my worst... and you're certainly not that. You're the only one who remembers I like Earl Grey in bags, not loose.'

'Mrs. Lustig prefers them loose.'

'Yes, well, what does that tell you?'

'Oh, you've lost me Mrs. L.'

'What a funny thing to say.'

'What's that then?'

'Well – that I've lost you, when that would mean that I have done the losing – while all the time, it's you who's lost. Not me. Do you see dear?'

'Can't say I do. You're too clever for me, Mrs. L. Now. Have you had that tablet?'

'Yes dear. All done.'

'Well what's it doing on your table then?'

'Ah – that's tomorrow's. Nothing like being organised.' Penny stares at me as one would an intelligent but wilful infant.

'Yes, I'm quite sure dear,' I return, meeting her gaze.

'You've still not said what Mrs. Lustig preferring loose tea bags says about her.'

'Not very much I suppose, dear. Mrs. Lustig isn't the sort of person about whom one can say very much is she. Still, I could tell you rather more.'

'About her loose tea?'

'About *her*, Penny.'

'Go on then.'

'No. It wouldn't be fair.'

'Oh – all's fair in love and war, Mrs. L.'

'Penny dear. I am not at war with Mrs. Lustig, and I can categorically inform you that I am not, repeat not, in love with her. If I declare one or fall in the other, you shall be the first to know.'

Exeunt Penny, unconvinced I've taken my tablet. Alone again in my thirteen by eleven foot castle. She's sweet really, Penny, though not tremendously bright. And I do wish she could run to the whole name – everyone who comes in with more than one syllable has them all confiscated but for a sole initial. And mine, bearing in mind that aitches seem only to exist to be dropped like spiders, except for the letter itself, which the staff all call Haitch, leaves me as Mrs. Hell. Which I suppose I am to some of them.

There's only one hour and thirty seven minutes to *Countdown* now. I mustn't switch on before. That would be the beginning of the end. Or perhaps a little further on than that. Why doesn't someone ring and want to come and see me?

* * *

13

Pam is bemoaning the fact that John Lewis seems to think that if you're a sixteen you'll only want to wear floating kaftans in varying shades of mud. Trish, perhaps out of spite, but perhaps not, volleys back that she has just spent the whole of her lunch hour trying to find a skirt in the same 'sort of bluey green' as the jacket she bought in some unlikely sale, but when she found exactly the right one, did they have it in an eight? No they didn't.

I don't think it's possible Trish really doesn't know whether Pam takes sugar. I've only been here for three weeks, and I suspect Pam's refusal of sugar is a newish thing, but I'm not sure I can bear to hear her ask again. And – there she goes again 'Sweet enough?' I try and sink unseeing and unseen into the life of Immaculata. But I can't.

It's the image of that man in the bookshop. He said he'd 'catch me'. But he can't have meant that. I mean, there was nothing to stop him asking if I'd like to get a coffee with him. Or perhaps that would be unreasonable. Maybe he was just a really friendly guy making light conversation.

Men with eyes and cheekbones like that shouldn't make idle conversation if they don't intend to spend the rest of their lives with someone. Or at the very least just touch every inch of them at least once. Not fair. Maybe he's gay. That would explain him knowing all about those authors. All women authors. Perhaps he's a regular at that bookshop. I could take all my four weeks' annual leave at once and camp out at the shop until he comes back.

'You having a brew love?' It's Pam's turn.

* * *

Sidney Fleiss Memorial Home. Room 6.

'Hello. Yes. I'd like a bouquet sent please. No carnations. What? No – I said no carnations. Urm. Lizianthus. Lizz – i – ann – thus. Yes you do dear. You always have. Well perhaps you could ask someone who does. And whatever those lilies that look like trumpets – I think they are called that. Trumpet. No! Am I coming out faint or something? I hardly think tiger sounds like trumpet. Anyway. Definitely not tiger lilies with lizianthus. Purple and orange? I rather think not. Now. A note. 'To my dear Rhona, with my love as always.' Yes, that's fine. My credit card? Oh yes. It's visa – Barclaycard. The name is Rhona Laski. No, SKI. Now, is it the long number in the middle you want? Yes? And the expiry date. Oh dear. Could you wait a moment, I've dropped the card that these – urgh – these bars of soap I call my hands won't seem to hold. Ah. Good. We're in luck. It's on my glasses. Thank heavens for senility strings.'

So. I dial the number I know so well. Speed-dial number 1. My friend Sylvia. Dialling involves all sorts of concentration it shouldn't nowadays. My fingers really are quite hideous, swerving eastwards at an obscene angle after the first knuckle. I'm in no pain though. None at all. It is regrettable that my fingers, which used to type so fast, look as though they've been caught in a hurricane.

Marie, who has the unenviable task of making us all beautiful on a Tuesday and Thursday morning – Marie who had an abortion at 19 and has never told a soul who the father was – Marie, who is 24, and already divorced and enrolled on a creative writing course at whatever the Polytechnic calls itself now – well she insisted on painting my nails 'winter garnet'. It's actually newly dried blood, but as it's what she uses on herself and I've grown so slow-witted, I let her do it. I'd have chosen colourless every time. I hardly want to draw attention to – Oh well. Never mind.

Howard, only and ever considerate son, brought this phone up when I first moved in. Big buttons, like something a child would use. Wonderful really. I just bash at it with my silly, painted paw and the right number comes up. Howard's on speed dial. He's number Two, after Sylvia. He hasn't been able to visit recently.

When I get through to Sylvia, I will say 'Hello dear, it's Rhona. How are you? No – I'm absolutely fine. I want you to come to lunch. Perhaps tomorrow. Splendid!'

I will of course be able to relate exactly what is said by Sylvia. I am, after all, listening at the other end of the phone and you are reading my side of things. But I won't. I will tell you that I want Sylvia to come to lunch with me at the Sidney Fleiss Home because I want her to sell up and join me. She's not as bad as me, of course. She can look after herself perfectly well when she chooses to, but you see she could have a flat here. Complete independence but help when she needs it. And a very good one has just come up. Well – it will very soon.

Old Joe Shabalan died last night, and his has a delightful view of the park and a separate lounge. Nobody knows about Joe yet. Only me, because I was just making my way back from what they fondly call dinner, as he was being brought down in the coffin lift. There's a special lift they only use for the newly dead (the Home likes to call it a 'goods' lift, which they think has us quite fooled).

Penny (not Penelope but Patricia) was just helping to wheel him in with Barry from maintenance, when she saw me. She'd never have told me – I think the staff imagines that the concept of someone dying never occurs to us, which is touching in an ironic sort of way. I knew she wouldn't say, so I asked if it was Herta Fox who had died. As Penny had just served both Herta and I with our apple strudel, she was so taken aback that I should imagine her dead and ready for burial just minutes later, that she blurted out who had actually died. So, I know, and now you know.

Essie Shabalan, Joe's wife for fifty-six years, doesn't know. She doesn't know if it's Tuesday or November. Poor Essie. Mind you, I don't always know the day or the month or the year. It seems a silly test of sanity. That's how they put away Vivienne, you know, the wife of T.S.Eliot. But why should one know whether it's Thursday or Sunday in a place like this. Knowing whether you've got children is a better test by far. And poor Essie, when asked tomorrow by the new nurse, will say she's not absolutely certain. Essie will be asked about the funeral. So of course, I don't know yet that she will have forgotten she has very ugly twin daughters who remarkably both found presentable husbands. But I will know in a few pages, so you might as well know now.

I knew Essie Shabalan when she was Essie Glick. Not aesthetically blessed, poor Essie. Navy black frizz of hair and quite enormous hooked nose, with no neck to speak of. The frizz is still there, but dyed a rather alarming marmalade which only takes in bits over what's now gun metal grey, but just as thick at eighty-six as at sixteen. A bit like an old Brillo pad. The nose was one of the first I knew to be done. Awful little coathook they made of it. I'd have wanted damages, but she was very pleased with it. I am a terrible old bitch, aren't I?

Now – I've digressed outrageously. That's what age does. Age and sitting all day every day surrounded by beige velour and waiting for *Countdown*. I am, you may just remember, telephoning Sylvia.

As I do, I am suddenly brilliantly aware of how dark it has become in here. My favourite darkness. Inside, late afternoon, when the sky bloats out in an old fashioned, monochrome bruise and turns my world – all thirteen foot by eleven foot six of it, into plum shadow. I look around and feel so grateful for my very good eyes. I have eyes that see and ears that hear. That is most uncommon here. Would I trade them – either of them – for fingers that could feel or legs that could walk? Well. It's difficult to say. But no. I don't think I would.

So, I look about me, enjoying the blunting away of all the straight lines. My escritoire – Country Georgian flame mahogany – that I've had since I was a girl. So familiar, its corners are smooth to me whether I can see it or not. My photograph of Number 3 in the burr walnut frame. Still my home when I close my eyes, though now – irony of ironies, a luxury residential home for the elderly. Better than this, though – the sumptuous darkness in my room rubs away all the 'things'. The bright, plastic things which are so hard to my very good eyes, but make life so much easier for my feeble legs and foolish fingers. There are buttons and cords, grips and switches. They are hard, beige, plastic. I am a sensible woman. I would not want to do without these things. Yet – in my head, as I telephone Sylvia – I have what I've come to call one of my wardrobe mirror visions. Images from the past as fleetingly crisp and as soon soggily lost as lettuce.

When my husband, Gussu, had left for work, I would lie a few minutes in bed and gaze at the copper beech tree in our front garden. But I saw it in the wardrobe mirror, reflected back so I was never sure if it really looked as it did, or the opposite. It was magical, that mass of moving rust-purple foliage, filling the oval glass, the bevelled edges making rainbow blisters in the morning light. As if, perhaps, there would be no tree at all if I ever looked out of the window directly, as if my wardrobe mirror image was special. Just for me. Reflecting a tree that had died and been chopped down long ago.

Right now, telephoning Sylvia, my wardrobe mirror image is of the inside of my kitchen cupboard door. How the mighty have fallen! The door, butter yellow, of my old Wrighton units, and inside, a row of blue, plastic tea towel holders. Blue plastic circles, scored through with a cross which held towels like a terrier's teeth. What a stupid, pointless thing to think of. That kitchen's been ripped out now of course. Perhaps I am beginning to lose it, like poor old Essie Glick. But those were *my* tea towel holders, and they were in *my* kitchen, which I haven't seen for nearly five years.

If I don't pull myself together, I might cry, and that would never do.

It is not kindness which makes me want Sylvia to put in an offer for Joe Shabalan's flat. I am not kind.

Three

There is something direct, cheerful and honest about Mr. Clegg. It makes him come across as direct, cheerful and dishonest. You can see from his canine smile why Mr. Clegg ended up on his own, and Mr. Anthony and Mr. Holland escaped together into a rival firm. I would like very much to like him very much. The smile may be that of a killer alsatian, but it's also the alsatian pup when it wants to be. I'd love the sort of relationship where, in thirty years' time, he's my final guest on *This is your Life* and I can thank him, my eyes glistening with gratitude as we hug in front of the millions. I know, though, that this is unlikely to happen. And not just because my heart is already dribbling out of the job. He takes Trish's "to be honests" a block further. No working day has gone by without me trying to block out Mr. Clegg's "If I can just be frank", and no working day has gone by without the buttock-clenching predictability of Pam's "You can be anyone you like with me love" in reply.

The difference, though, is that Mr. Clegg is thinking. Has intentions. Ambitions. Greed. Pam is not thinking. She has dreams, a weight problem and a charge-card that she's not afraid to use. I can breathe easier with Pam than with Mr. Clegg.

Immaculata, late of the liquorice locks, is a tedious creature indeed. How she ever appealed to the publisher is beyond me. I flick to the back, to the author photograph. Her smile is just like that of Mona Lisa. Neither seem remotely enigmatic to me. Bored, perhaps. Absent. Not enigmatic. I've stopped seeing her face anyway. I see the eyes of the man who you know is called Blue. I suppose my saying this means you know that I will see him again. Well – why keep you in the suspense I'm in. I know I'm going to see him again. I just feel it. No god could make me meet someone, make him make me feel like screaming with excitement and glee, and then not put us together to see it through. Having said that, God is quite capable of making him gay or married or partnered and oddly, seeing as how it's God – he seems intent on never making me meet anyone Jewish. How could I explain to mother that God appeared to me and told me to marry out? Who mentioned marriage?

I flick to the front of *Cold Sun In Spring*, and read *to Keith. Xmas 56. Doris*, in brown ink. What was Doris thinking giving this stupid book to Keith. Perhaps she didn't like him very much. In a different pen, is written *B.M. – crap.*

I'm going to nip back to the bookshop. Just in case. Maybe the owner will say "there's been someone looking for you". Mustn't think that, though, or it won't happen. Just now a man has come in to the shop (I think of the estate agency as a shop). He's been browsing at the massive old mansions section, the ones at over half a million. Reading the particulars about elm panelled hallways and gazebos in huge, majestic gardens – drooling over the many original features retained. But I know the sort. At best he's an extended East Didsbury semi with off road parking. More likely, a tasteful second floor conversion with four piece luxury bathroom suite in obsolete champagne.

I'm wrong. He's walked out.

* * *

Sidney Fleiss Memorial Home. Room 6.

I don't know why they call these "panic buttons". "Saunter-across-when-you're-good-and-ready" would be more to the point. I could be being raped in my bed. I am not, actually. Any rapist would faint in the heat of this place. But I telephoned through to the kitchen umpty five times and have now resorted to good old fashioned panic.

Eventually, Siklunli appears. Twenty three, Hong Kong born – mother from County Wicklow and father an engineer. Has to put up with Herta and Hettie at my table calling her 'Sick Loony' which is the best grasp of her name they can manage.

'Siklunli dear. I would like lunch for two tomorrow. Something cold is fine, but not those rather appalling vol-au-vent affairs. Just ask cook to poach some salmon fillet. Could you tell her to wrap it in foil, bring it to the boil and give it no more than two minutes, then let it go quite cold in the pan. No dear, I'm perfectly alright, but no one answered when I called. Yes dear, I know, but it *is* an emergency in a way. Besides, I really don't need to justify myself to you dear. That's a very pretty blouse. Suits you perfectly. Oh – and baby new potatoes. And white wine. Just tell cook to let me know the cost. Thank you so much dear. Yes, do run along. I'm sure you're terribly, terribly busy.'

* * *

'Anyone want a sandwich?' I ask, trying to adopt a tone just north of repellent. Pam does, but says she does not. Trish, though, asks where I'm going. This necessitates the reply that it doesn't matter – any of the sandwich shops to facilitate her. This necessitates Trish choosing smoked chicken on a ciabatta – no tomato salsa – from the shop most inconvenient to the bookshop.

I resist asking Mr. Bookseller Man if a man with amaretto latte eyes has been in twitching with fear at the thought that he's lost me forever. For his part, Mr. Bookseller Man resists telling me this time that everything is £1. Perhaps he's just glad to see the back of Immaculata. I stand around, picking up a cookery book showing an insane-looking Fanny Craddock, in full evening dress and an apron, gloating over a Charlotte Russe. I look back at the orange-back Penguin trough, and notice more acutely than ever before, the presence of Lynn Reid Banks and Edna O'Brien and H.E.Bates and Miss Read, swathed in her inverted commas as if they were sable stoles. I open a couple of old novels I know I've read before, and feel odd to have so few memories of the characters.

Will you, it makes me wonder, remember me in years to come?

He's not coming. Obvious really. Enough second hand fiction reading has made me wonder if he'll appear just as I'm on my way out. But that's someone else's story. I walk out into the village on a mission for smoked chicken ciabatta. No beautiful young man. And, I remember now, no tomato salsa for Trish.

* * *

The Sidney Fleiss Memorial Home. Dining Hall (Progression!)

One does not expect to suffer whiplash within the Sidney Fleiss dining room confines. Matthew – trainee assistant, a little effeminate and more than a little dim – is trying to change all that as he wheels Mrs. Susskind quite violently into Mrs. Katz. I am at my usual table, and relieved to be here, though my table-mates and I have reached a new ebb in levels of dislike. I am relieved to be here because just minutes earlier, as I found myself in my wheelchair in the lift with Mr. Sappirstein, I had been a prisoner.

The lift operates purely between the ground floor and the five steps up to the dining hall, but it might as well be the Empire State Building for the trouble it causes. In my chair, I am around three foot four high and cannot be expected to reach the button for dining hall. At six foot one, Mr. Sappirstein also cannot be expected to reach it. He has quite lost the plot. Terribly sad, as he was once the mouthpiece of cerebrovascular disease in Manchester.

And so I sit, and he stands, and the lift remains quite still. Mutually useless. I could see he was agitated by our inaction. His eyes tell me that buttons will not be pressed.

'You were born in Glasgow, Mr. Sappirstein,' I said.

'No.'

'Ah yes. You were. You lived in Queen's Park and your father came from Konigsberg.' He smiled at me then, a truly beautiful smile revealing exquisitely matched dentures, tinted to original hues. Such a tonic. Almost violent in its intensity.

'My father was a wonderful man,' he said, and I smiled up at him and took his large, once clever hand in my stupid one.

'Did you know him?' he asked me.

'No, but I believe he had a great brain.' He smiled more then.

'He was a genius,' he said, and I beamed up at him, like a grotesque heroine in an old film poster.

'Perhaps you could press that button, the red one,' I say, and without a moment's hesitation, he does, and we climb the five steps which have been, for these past minutes, our Kilimanjaro.

* * *

I feel somehow unprofessional walking straight into a meeting at the office while holding sandwiches. As if the sort of people who get on in life are those with attaché cases which click open to reveal electronic gadgetry and papers to sign. Not those with a ciabatta in a bag and the jamless remains of a jam doughnut between fingers. Trish and Pam seem to have gone home, and Mr. Clegg is sitting astride the edge of my desk, with his back to me, one leg swinging, and revealing a little swathe of leg as pale as raw chicken.

He's telling the man who'd been in earlier looking at the biggest houses to 'see how it goes, but don't do anything that could link...' at which point, the stranger smiles rather too eagerly at me, and says 'And so say all of us' while nodding at me. His clumsy attempt at letting Mr. Clegg know that I've walked in is enough for Mr. Clegg, who pivots in what looks like a most uncomfortable manoeuvre while saying, 'And really Gavin, at the end of the day, that's just the way the cookie crumbles.'

These two bizarre statements are followed by a silence which makes me think of forgotten lines at an amateur dramatic production. Mr. Clegg then grins at me and says, 'So, the prodigal daughter returns then.'

So, am I about to be fired? Why change the topic so suddenly? It makes me feel queasy, the thought that I am someone whose presence inspires this silence. Am I the cookie to be crumbled? I fill my mouth with the remains of the doughnut, letting my saliva act out the part which jam had played, and I wonder if being fired would be such a bad thing.

Walking home involves passing the bookshop. The really cheap unreadables are left out in the sheltered entrance, and I peer through into the silent word-yard behind. Didsbury is packing up for the day. Within an hour or so, the new crowds of revellers will begin their invasion, filling the main street with brake lights and bare legs tottering on suede heels and unrich men in expensive shirts leaving beer bottles on the chalky ledges of the elegant Rhodes memorial clock and slinging cans in its smooth old watering trough.

For now, daytime Didsbury is winding down. The great marble slabs are rinsed and rubbed in Evans the fishmongers, as the shiny, blues, blacks, silvers and corals of the gleaming sea life are wedged in ice. The frumpy shoeshop blinds come down, revealing last week's 'Fuck the Reds' graffiti, and the French patisserie is all bare formica shelves like arms in a sleeveless dress. Only the *Cheese Hamlet*, lit softly by the refrigerator glow, keeps its plump richness, yellows and cognac browns like raw amber piled in milky rolls swathed in pungent mould.

I walk with purpose towards my flat just a few streets away up Barlow Moor Road. The village centre is lost at night. A commercial vampire with neon blood on its teeth sinks into what used to be near silence. Not for me. I wonder if that guy is still in Didsbury, or if he's moved on. Away. I feel I have to know. I don't need him. Just need to know who he is. Whose air he's breathing. Too bad you can't tell me.

* * *

Sidney Fleiss Memorial Home. Back in Room 6.

Why do I so want Sylvia to live here, among all these poor souls who would share so many happy memories if only they could remember where they'd put them?

We wheeled our babies together through the park, the Marie Louise Gardens. We sat in our kitchens, she in mine, I in hers, and laughed. At least, we seemed to do a lot of laughing then. We made our friends young, and stood close to one another at their burials, whispering irrelevant asides to one another to stop ourselves concentrating on what was happening.

More important than half century friendship, though, is the thought of a sensible human being to sit with for dinner. Not that Sylvia could be described as sensible, exactly. But she is so much a human being, and that sets her in quite a different category to my present table partners.

Yes. I know, I know. They think far worse of me. They believe me an unutterable snob (because they're too stupid to see I'm not), and they think I make fun of their narrow, smug lives. Well, so would you if you had to sit with people with whom you share nothing but an ever growing knowledge of falling to pieces. It's really not enough of a binding agent.

We nurture our friends through life – cut off the dead-heads (stop inviting the dullards to coffee), water them (dinner parties, god knows how many) and train the creepers (unfortunate term) to cover all one's waking surfaces with their conversation. Their secrets. And as I wait for Matthew to bring the peach slices in jelly, I think how few of my friends are still in bloom. Still there, but empty pots in a pointless row.

I am not becoming maudlin. I really am perfectly content. Perhaps, when Matthew shunts me back to my room, Howard's number will be on my 1.4.7.1. I don't like to call him first, he works so hard, and Elaine would say he's under a lot of stress. The stress, of course, is being married to Elaine, but I've never once said so. She's very pretty in her own way. Very English. Of course, she lacks grace and charm of any kind, but she's adaptable as women are. Howard wasn't an easy boy, I suppose. Still, I should like to tell him about old Joe Shabalan. He and Sylvia are the only two who will remember him sensibly.

Gussu, of course, spent so much time with Joe – those hikes in Derbyshire, picnics at Alderley Edge. But I'm forgetting that Gussu is dead. Later on, when Penny has finished fussing with me and the room is dark, I may tell him anyway.

1.4.7.1. does not show Howard's Hertfordshire number. That crisp computer voice tells me that Sylvia's number has called me back. I do not have an answering machine. Hardly need one. Perhaps Howard called before Sylvia. Never mind. Perhaps he will call again.

Four

I'm waiting for change for my smoked mackerel fillet when he says 'I like the kind with the dill bits on', behind me. Seeing him at Evans' buying fruit and fish, makes me want to burst with joy. For a moment, I just stand there, unable to reach across the counter for my 38p change lying in the fishmonger's large dry palm.

Blue (so strange that I don't know this name yet) is grinning at me. I take in his thin, white tunic-shirt made of that feeble Indian gauzy stuff that I can't wear as it makes my bra stand out. I notice his corduroy trousers. A very narrow cord in an unlikely emerald green. Tight around his thighs and loose towards his ankles. I'm about to take in his boots, but my mind bubbles up like boiling milk. I want to tell him that I've thought of nothing but him since the bookshop – twenty two hours ago – I want all manner of things – to cliché myself into a chocolate oblivion with him. But stabbing at my sweet, hot thoughts is grandma's friend Millie Grodski from the Old Home who is kneading a hake fishball as if it were raw dough and asking in her distinctive way – a sort of athletic whine – whether they are today's (she always asks, and they always are).

And the fishmonger is looking like a window mannequin with his hand outstretched with my change and as I battle to make time stop and bring something useful to my lips, Blue says, 'Well, see y'about' and as the following seconds trickle through time, he's left.

I would love to say that I ran out into Wilmslow Road and our faces, glistening with mutual magnetic attraction and a fortuitous downpour that causes advertisement couples to throw their laughing heads back, meet and kiss. I would love to relate this in the diary unfolding as you read, but I cannot. I can record only that I am again offered my change, and that Millie Grodski rejects the fishballs for no good reason. God is working in his famed way. Or perhaps he is on sabbatical.

* * *

Sidney Fleiss Memorial Home. Room 6.

Sylvia is not coming. At least, not for lunch today. The morning is bright as new paint outside. Early rain has made a brilliant white gloss through my window which makes my whole room look as if it needs a lick of life.

I should like very much to rip this page out and rewrite it beginning with Sylvia's 'Oh Rhona, I'd love to!' But these pages seem to print themselves with no input from me at all. I am here to watch, it seems. It's all a game of musical chairs and I... ah, my morning drink.

'Hello Mrs. Laski. Would you like some tea? Orange juice?'

'Ah Penny. I think I'll have some tonic water. Yes, that beaker's fine. Thank you so much.'

It is quite remarkable that despite being perfectly surplus to the needs of anyone at all, and not really requiring any attention from anyone, there is a constant state of interruption here. It is as if I am the director of a multinational company.

Sylvia cannot come, because 'some people are coming' to see her. No one is coming to see her, you understand. We have known each other for the best part of sixty years. If real people are coming, they have names. Stories are told about them. Their appearance commented upon and usually shredded. It's what holds us together in a way.

I don't know why she won't come today. But tomorrow. Well, the salmon will keep a day. It hits me now that lunch shall not, after all, be at the table overlooking the Myrna Weinrich Camelia garden with that beautiful north light coming in from the big bay window. No – lunch shall be with Hettie Oppenheim and Herta Fox. Hettie is like an American chocolate brownie – very rich, rather dense and always surprising one with nasty little hard bits which would be better not there.

Herta, a week-old Victoria sponge, is fluffy, easier to digest at first, but one can't help feeling that if steeped in wine might improve no end. Prettily iced, she is dull inside – but no more so than one expects. Ah, you ask – and what am I? I don't suppose I'm cake at all. A gherkin, perhaps!

I shall call SupaKars. Rebwar is my man. My escape. His Nissan Bluebird motorcar is my white steed (it's metallic green, but we at the Sidney Fleiss overlook such things). He drives me just 500 yards from here, in perfect secret, whenever I choose. Once, sometimes twice, a week. He drives me to Eden.

* * *

Battles are being lost and won in Didsbury.

Another big Victorian villa has been ripped down. Civic Society and Real Didsbury folk nil – developers one. The old house, once home to a cotton baron and built close to the end of the 19th century, was so Didsbury, you hardly noticed it behind all the glossy rhododendrons that turned its frontage into an explosion of nail varnish pinks each May. Standing at the bus stop, you could see the gateposts – great sandstone phalluses carved with the name – not the usual 'Silver Holme' sort of name, but a mystical one – 'Davrach'. Not 'house' or 'lodge' or 'villa'. Just Davrach.

The twist in its wide driveway meant you couldn't see the house itself, but from the bus stop, round spire turrets pricked out above the giant chestnut trees which umbrella'd the gardens. You could see attic casement windows with leaded eyebrow roofs, the curves looking somehow questioning, a little melancholic, out of the lower sweep of dark slate. If you wandered up the potholed drive – as I did when the mood took me and I'd just missed a bus, you could see the garages. Not any old garages, but great coach house jobbies with tudored gables and vast panels of leaded lights glinting with stained glass tulips. I mean big, century old tulips bowing in their leading lit by the sky, hidden all these years by the sweep of a drive.

Of course, the house had been too big to live in as a house. Must have had a good fourteen bedrooms. A big, crudely painted road number had been daubed like graffiti over the engraved 'Davrach' – the same sky blue paint they used to daub the same number on the five wheelie bins which huddled near the end of the drive like women waiting to collect their children from the local school. Once I walked right up to the front porch, where there were twelve doorbells. The oak door was the original, as were the Moorish tiles across the porch, but only one pane of stained glass remained. And, as a Jew intrigued by Jewishness if not by Judaism, I had looked up as we seem trained to do, to above the right-hand side of the door, and made out a *mezzuzah*, smooth and submerged by decades of coloured gloss.

Who had lived here in recent years was hard to tell. A couple, or two, sharing a living room made from the ballroom, with a bare 100 watt bulb hanging from a hugely ornate ceiling rose. A turquoise bathroom partitioned off in the corner, cutting into the coving of plaster fruit, almost puréed by a hundred years of distemper and emulsion. Single people with yellow formica kitchenettes wedged beneath the eaves of servant quarter attics. Lavatories with high box cisterns and lead pipes elbowing through the walls.

Well – no more. HouseBryte Homes (the name you can trust) have wiped it all into memory with a bulldozer and the promise of yet another rash of two bedroom luxury apartments with a choice of bathroom fixtures and brushed aluminium kitchen appliances by the most costly German manufacturers.

The tragedy is felt by Mr. Clegg. He could not have cared less about Davrach (despite what he said to the old man who came in to tell us Didsbury is not what it was). His misery is due to learning that Anthony Holland & Clegg has not been chosen by HouseBryte to be sole selling agents for 'Windsor Court', described in their blurb as 'a truly aristocratic phoenix rising from the ashes of a fine old mansion.'

Mr. Clegg is holding another meeting with the man who was in the other day, when I had returned with Trish's sandwich and silenced them. I boil the kettle and spoon Nescafé into a mug (Pam's pink pig mug – I'm feeling rebellious). A note has been sellotaped to the coffee jar suggesting we keep the screw top screwed tight. I screw it back up, though the saving in instant coffee won't go far against the loss of the HouseBryte Homes account. I detect signs of crumbling throughout this high street cookie.

Five

Rebwar takes my cardigan over his arm, but we decide against bothering with the frame. He wheels me, with so much more care and success than Matthew, along the corridor to the entrance. I can see his car, passenger door already open, through the chicken wire glass of the entrance. A cashmere wrap – a birthday present from daughter-in-law Elaine when she thought it might sweeten me into leaving them the best of the furniture, is soft and warm around my knees.

The green velour wingback chairs which line the Sidney Fleiss entrance lobby are half full of inmates. I can admit to you, that I rather like to be seen going out, though I do my best not to meet envious eyes. I fuss with the wrap as if it takes all my powers of concentration. Certainly, the fact that Rebwar is so good looking does make me feel I am being taken out in style, but I've no wish at all to rub it in to, say, Lily Feigenbaum who is shaped like an 'S', never goes anywhere and has been widowed, childless, since 1938.

Herta Fox is a different matter altogether. She is sitting there, legs too fat to close together, a great wedge of Victoria sponge filled with far too much butter-cream, iced with blandest white and topped with her ever moving glacé cherry mouth. She is waiting for her family to arrive en masse. Seven of them. And not only is she waiting for them along with everyone else, but from experience, we all know that they not only exist, but will actually come.

'Hello Herta dear – you're looking very summery today – family about to descend? I do hope the weather keeps.' It has been lightly spitting rain for some time already, so Herta does not know what to make of my wish for her and her family. This is perfectly intended.

'Off on one of your jaunts dear,' she stabs back with a calorific smile. 'Your friends?' she goes on with impressive disbelief. 'Trudi and Max is it?'

'They've invited me to lunch in town.' I become charmingly bashful. 'I'd sooner they came here, but people are so very keen on restaurants nowadays, aren't they?'

'Well you enjoy yourself Rhona,' says Herta. She says it so

pleasantly, with the wealth of having her family making her magnanimous, I half believe she means it, and feel a touch sorry that we dislike one another so much. I smile back and raise my hand in goodbye. Trudi and Max always invite me to restaurants. They never choose to dine with me here in the Sidney Fleiss. They lived in Southport when we were young, and were killed outright when the small, private plane in which they were travelling crashed over Rhodesia on a beautiful day in July 1951.

* * *

Success (a small dose of). A Mrs. Webster, who had been umming and erring about an over-tarted up terrace in the village centre, has at last had her offer on it accepted.

All the usual games were played – the silly initial offer last Thursday, the splutteringly angry response from the seller, Mr. Moyne, who only a week before would have been happy to have accepted such an inflated price before we suggested a new one. Mrs. Webster's twenty thousand pound hike in offer, despite her protestations that ceilings had been reached. Mr. Moyne's 'I'll have to confer with my wife' followed by Mrs. Webster's sweaty extra four thousand on condition that some frightening curtains and an inappropriate crystal chandelier were included.

My constant telephone calls between the two felt voyeuristic as they both worked themselves up into an almost sexual frenzy of double bluffing and desperation. With Mr. Moyne achieving only £500 off the asking price, he shouted 'And tell her I'm throwing in the garden furniture' in rather the way of someone declaring their love for a virtual stranger just as he swerves towards orgasm. The tension was palpable, and I could almost see Mrs. Webster and Mr. Moyne lying back, sharing a cigarette after their great success.

'Tell Mr. Moyne he's very welcome to leave anything he wants in the garage until he's found a new home for it,' said Mrs. Webster breathily on hearing about the garden furniture. She had become all generosity, a woman sated, turning lazily to her lover and offering to cook breakfast as she runs her fingers through his chest hair.

I am just filling out the contract form and thinking how odd that after such intensity, Mr. Moyne and Mrs. Webster still do not know each

31

other's first names — Selwyn and Alison — when Blue (still quite unnamed to me) opens the door and strides inside making the world a silent, electric place I want to inhabit.

* * *

Sidney Fleiss Memorial Home. Room 6.

Rebwar has been driving for SupaKars for six years since coming from Kurdistan. I have tried to look up exactly where his family lived in my World Atlas, but cannot find it. He is married to an English girl, a nurse from Todmorden, and they have a small and very lovely looking little boy (he keeps pictures in his wallet). His features are certain and beautifully carved, like Edwardian mahogany, and he has vast, glittering eyes as dark and glossy as liquid chocolate.

For a long time he was very secretive about his background, and I wondered if he disliked spending time with old people. But that wasn't it at all. When I had asked his name, he had just said it was enough to call him SupaKars. I told him it might be enough for him, but not for me, and he smiled and laughed, spilling all the anguish and torment in his fine features into a wondrous warmth. Rebwar — a name easily remembered as Rebel Warrior. And he is mine. When I telephone SupaKars, they know to find me Rebwar, and he knows exactly where I will go.

He hears me describe Trudi and Max as he pushes me through the lobby. He hears my mention of hotels and restaurants, sometimes in town, sometimes in deepest Cheshire where I am supposed to be eating. He knows that we will first drive to Chorlton (two miles away, but another continent to those at the Sidney Fleiss), where he will jump out of the car, which he will leave on a double yellow line, and buy me a piece of cake from Barbakan, the wonderful Polish bakery on the borders of Whalley Range, wrap it in tissue, and leave it in his glove compartment until he wheels me back into the Home at the end of the afternoon.

He will hear me tell Hettie or Herta that this was the dessert I hadn't been able to manage after a huge meal, and would they like it. He will hear. He will understand. He neither thinks it is funny nor sad. He never questions me, but he makes himself there for me. When he lifts my fragile frame into the deep seats of his Nissan Bluebird motorcar, his face reflects that he is handling what he must see as a bird-skull – yet he is not only gentle. He is kind, too.

I recognise this, even though it is not in my own nature. Once I am belted in, a cushion beneath me so I can see over the dashboard, we collect the cake, and then return to Didsbury, Rebwar driving slowly down the private unmade-up road which leads to my favourite spot, to the Marie Louise Gardens.

There is an entrance with a terraced slope, ideal for wheelchairs, but there is always the risk of straying Sidney Fleiss inmates there, so Rebwar lifts me, in my chair , which he brings from the boot, up the stone steps until we reach... but we are not there yet. Please wait a page or two.

Today, as we return from the Polish bakery with a large slice of baked cheese-cake (he picks whatever he feels could most easily have been served for lunch with Trudi and Max) I see an alarming sight. Yes. Quite alarming. I see the home of my first boyfriend has quite simply disappeared.

'Gracious Rebwar – could you just stop the car a moment. I... I, well... I don't quite believe it. We are on Palatine Road aren't we?' I know perfectly well we are. It used to be known as Palestine Road ever since the Sephardic Jewish cotton merchants from the Arab countries built their big houses here. Edward Marcatta lived with his parents in a glorious house here.

He was the first boy to kiss me. The Jews of Syria and Egypt and Persia all flocked to Didsbury when Manchester beckoned as a world centre of cotton trading. They had as little as possible to do with us – the Ashkenazim from Europe. When I was a girl, Didsbury's Sephardim and Ashkenazim walked on different sides of the street. We called them Yakipaks. They called us Ash-cans. All that didn't stop Edward and I meeting at the Kardomah and rather falling for each other. We had been dancing round and round their wonderful drawing room – it was a sort of ballroom really – and he had kissed me quite suddenly on my mouth. I thought I was going to faint. Later, when the evening light sent the stained glass flowers into an autumn of maroons and bottle greens, we had been upstairs together in the attics. Goodness knows where his parents were. It was, I feel now, an almost impossible thing to have happened, but it did. I see the room quite clearly in my wardrobe mirror eye. A sloping ceiling with this eyebrow window in it, throwing light in boxes onto the floor. And the bed. There was a sort of painted frieze along the wall and he smelled of sweet smoke.

'I know the house too,' Rebwar says unexpectedly.' I am looking at my hands. 'My wife and me – we lived in that house when I first came to Manchester. A top room in the roof. It was small, but you could see many miles around.'

We both stare through our very different eyes between the gateposts named after David and Rachel Marcatta – Davrach – past the dusty rhododendrons, to a nothingness where spire turrets no longer rise from a dark, slate roof, and the attic windows we both knew are in our two, close-together heads. And they are nowhere else. Smashed somewhere.

'Perhaps you should not look, Mrs. Laski,' says Rebwar. I am amazed at him. He does not know – cannot know – of Edward Marcatta.

'Oh, it was only a building – everything must have its day,' I say. And I dislike myself very much for selling Rebwar short. He sees I am saddened.

'We will be late for Trudi and Max,' he says grinning. To hear the names of those two, who were dead years before Rebwar was born, makes me laugh aloud.

'Yes, yes. You are quite right. And that would never do, would it!'

Six

'Hello!' I say (it can only be moments before I find out his name).

'Hi. This is a surprise. I'm Blue,' he says (at last!). He makes to shake hands with me, which is so not what I had imagined would happen. His hand is a pianist's. Long fingers, a silver ring, a narrow leather strap knotted around his slim wrist. Flat but unbitten nails, a couple of clever veins beneath the tan.

'I saw you in the bookshop.' he says, and it occurs to me that he imagined I might not have noticed him.

'I've thought of nothing else.' God! Why do you let me say such things? How could you script me to let myself down like that. How humiliating – although, deeper inside, I'm rather thrilled that I have just said this. Short cut through the social dance hall.

'Excellent – that's so sweet,' he says. I am both relieved and not best pleased with sweet.

'Did you find what you want?'

'Oh yes!' I gush. My mouth forms its own words with no reference to my sense of dignified restraint. Something makes me wonder if I actually want to embarrass myself. 'Very much so.'

'I mean a book – your Penguin books.'

'Oh urm. Yes. Well, no.' I can hear babbling begin in my throat, and know it is working its way to my tongue.

'A story about this weird woman in Rome who tries to make herself into a man coz she thinks...'

'Immaculata with the hair like liquorice,' he breaks in. 'I know. It's shit, isn't it. I bought it myself and gave it back to them. I usually give a one word review in the front, but I don't know if I bothered with that one.'

I lift the book out of my bag and open it. *To Keith from Doris, Xmas '56.* And then I see again. *B.M. – crap.* 'So that was you?' I know I'll keep this book forever.

'So what brings you into Anthony Holland & Clegg? Can I interest you in a house?'

God, who had so recently let me down has come to my assistance, sending Trish to Boots for Tampons and Pam to the loo to stare herself slim in the mirror (I've seen her at it).

'Actually yes. I'd like a house – or a few houses, more precisely.

Urm, can I explain over a coffee – I mean, that isn't meant to sound like it does.' A slight trickle of confidence allows me to say,

'Oh well, maybe I can change that'.

'Great,' he says smiling, but I'm not clear which he finds great. He has good teeth. God is thanked, cautiously, again.

'When?'

I look round the office, the hessian screens of house details ranging from one beds in neighbouring suburbs masquerading as Didsbury by the door to the big villas (actually, we've only got two on our books right now) near the door through to the bathroom. I'm reminded that Pam is in there, smoothing her hands over her hips, willing them down.

'If you'd be interested in an immediate viewing on – this,' I select an awkwardly shaped flat made out of the wing of an old consulate in West Didsbury.

'Sure. Sounds good,' he says. I had hoped it would sound great. Terrific. Wonderful. But good is not bad. For a start.

'Just doing a viewing – this gentleman needs to see No. 7 and he's only here today,' I call through to Pam. I hear the flush which she always pulls despite the seat-lid being down, and beat a retreat with Blue before she can offer to accompany him herself. She's not beyond that.

'I'm a...a photographer,' says Blue as we walk to "Jem & I" on School Lane, my absolute favourite café with the very best comfort food in Didsbury, 'which is why I need houses,' he adds.

It doesn't seem too logical, but I don't care. My amaretto latte is hot, sweet and sipping it is like sipping him. His espresso spills onto the details of the deceptive garden apartment (unsellable converted basement) at No. 7.

* * *

Marie Louise Gardens – a few minutes, and a world, from the Sidney Fleiss Memorial Home, Room 6.

There is not so much which brings me near bliss nowadays. Where I am now is the closest I know. Rebwar has left, having wheeled me into the old bandstand in the park. Best of all, it has begun to rain – a hard, definite rain which crashes onto the roof of the old wrought iron-fronted shelter and spins whole voile sheets around me as if I were in a four poster bed surrounded by billowing drapes.

My back is to the obscene graffiti informing us all that Julie is a fit slag. I am cocooned, and I shiver, snuggling my cashmere wrap around my legs and my thick cardigan around my shoulders. Matron would be perfectly furious – but she must know that it is my death which will catch me and not the other way around.

This is where I come to dream – to stare out at the graceful trees, the grass, the squirrels and magpies and more than anything, the sky. At the moment it is graphite shot through with seams of butter. It is here, away from the tablet taking and do-I-want-a-cup-of-tea-Mrs.-Laski – away from those awful old women who talk about nothing because it's easier to chatter to the end than wait for it in silence, here, sheltered by the bandstand in the Marie Louise Gardens, I have my best wardrobe mirror images. Here I talk to my husband. I reflect on the goings on in my tiny world, and remember those in a bigger one.

My wardrobe mirror reflects old Joe Shabalan now. I do not close my eyes. I see the great cedar and the flamingo leg of the silver birch trunk, but I also see Joe reading poetry to me in the coffee rooms in town. He had a wonderful voice, full of fruit without being overly dramatic. We drank coffee at the Town & Country Club, while his parents played cards.

The thought of Howard taking a girl to anywhere where Gussu and I were spending the evening would have been quite inconceivable – but Joe was very close with his parents. They had a most modern relationship. They lived as friends off Wilmslow Road in a most peculiar house called *Maplehurst* – all dark corridors and Gothic windows. I remember a black and white chequered hallway and a minstrels gallery around the hall. It was perfectly square, the hall – the only room that was. He told me he'd never marry anyone if he didn't marry me. I told him he'd be a bachelor then as I had no plans to marry anyone. Dear Joe. Essie Glick snapped him up as if he were on special offer.

His parents died within a few months of each other just before the war. Nobody expected Joe to stay in Manchester, but he did. He stayed in his parents' house and he brought Essie there. They were known, rather unkindly, but perhaps with reason, as Beauty and the Beast. Not quite accurate. He was even featured. Not really beautiful.

The curtains of rain are still keeping me in my four poster bed. I was right about what would happen when Essie was asked about what she wanted as funeral arrangements. I had already flicked forward to this page when I told you she would have forgotten she had twin daughters. Well, Matron knelt by Essie this morning, and took her rather large hand in both hers, and gently told her that Joe had 'passed on' in great peace and with equal dignity in the night.

'Why?' asked Essie. Matron said 'Because it was the right time. The right time Essie.' For once, she dropped the 'Mrs. Shabalan' rule. Essie nodded and said 'There was a time, you know, when we were very young, when I could have married him. Will he be at the funeral?'

Matron called one of the ugly twins at 10 o'clock and she called her sister who was in the Algarve. The funeral will be tomorrow to give her a chance to get back. I will not go. It is too much trouble for people to negotiate me into cars and I don't want Rebwar there. Besides, neither Joe nor Essie will benefit from me being there, or even know if I am. Sylvia will go, of course – these things hold a strange attraction for her, though she'd never admit it.

And I shall use my not going to have her come to lunch and tell me about it. The funeral is at noon at Southern Cemetery, the Sephardic section of the Jewish. Doubtless the usual gaggle will be organised into the Sidney Fleiss mini-bus. Southern Cemetery has become like a charabanc excursion to the seaside for some of them. I'm sure Essie won't know the difference. She might quite enjoy herself. Which is not so bad, really.

A figure runs, at first indistinct, in the rain. As it nears, I see it is Rebwar. He is soaking wet, but his concern is me. Not, however, that I should *not* be out in such weather. He understands perfectly that I have a right to catch my own pneumonia if I choose. He has been sitting in his car smoking, and looked up, as he explains, to see Herta Fox, surrounded by three generations of overweight descendants, wobbling into the Marie Louise during a let up in the rain. I shall leave Rebwar something. A brooch, perhaps, he can give to his wife. Or perhaps £500. Is that enough, or too much, or not enough?

Heaving me down the steps, chair and all, he cuts a most romantic figure, his hair glinting black and plastered around his neck. Edward Marcatta had once carried me through a muddy field in the rain like this, except my arms had been wrapped around his neck, not clasped uselessly in my lap. And of course, there had been no wheelchair.

* * *

I remember that Edward, Rebwar and myself have all lived important bits of life in the attic rooms of Davrach.

£1,000, I decide. Yes, at least £1,000.

Seven

Blue has been commissioned, he tells me, by *The Independent* or is it the *Independent on Sunday*, to make a photo documentary about disappearing lifestyles. It's 'on the back of' (his words) a book of photographs called *Tomorrow Lost* – endangered urban environments, which was published a few months ago.

'I'm always fascinated by things in danger,' he says, tipping the last of his espresso back while I wonder how to make myself look in danger. 'I always was. When I was a kid,' he says, and I wonder how old he is now, 'John Craven's newsround said that ospreys were an endangered species. I organised a school raffle to raise money for them – I've got a certificate somewhere from the RSPB thanking me for three pounds eighty six. Then I remember being told there'd been some brilliant breeding programme thing, and ospreys were appearing all over the place. Lost interest just like that.' – his fingers click with a simple elegance of an Italian movie star summoning a waiter. And Tim, the manager-cum-waiter does appear at that moment to ask if we want anything else. I feel a rush of excitement at his power, even though I know it was coincidence that Tim came after Blue had clicked his fingers.

'So what I need,' he says, leaning forwards and weaving the fingers of both hands together, his elbows on his knees 'is to get inside some big old Didsbury houses – the sort that are still houses, and take pictures of the gardens through stained glass, and old plaster work and kitchens with wooden drainers – that sort of thing.'

Has he noticed me at all? I want to help him, but I want him to want me. To be indebted to me. Not very nice, am I?

'Well, all our viewings are accompanied,' I say, taking a little envelope of sugar and squeezing it absently. 'And we've only got a couple of really good ones, but I don't think it should be a problem.'

'Maybe you'd like to see some of my pictures,' he offers. Are these photographs really etchings? Do I want them to be? Would I be disappointed if they're no good or non-existent? There's a narrow band of hair above the slash neckline of his t-shirt and his Adam's apple bobs like a buoy in his throat.

'Yeah. I'd love to.'

'Tomorrow? Say seven?'

'In the evening?' I ask stupidly – my confidence is ebbing now. I need confirmation of everything.

'Seven in the morning really isn't my time of day,' he says laughing. 'Seven p.m. it is then.'

He leaves, and I'm left to pay. Hardly a problem, but it makes me think. I'm not sure if I'm pleased or not.

Trish says, 'There was a call for you just now,' when I get back to the office a few minutes later, 'gentleman says thanks for showing him Flat 7, but he's looking for something quite a bit bigger.'

Good. Good. Good.

* * *

Sidney Fleiss Memorial Home. Back in Room 6.

The bouquet is quite hopeless. There is no lizzianthus, rather four chrysanthemums in the most loathsome shade of tapioca. The white trumpet lilies are drooping. More like depressed tubas. Still, it is a bouquet.

Siklunli selects a vase which can only be a cremation urn, but I'm past caring.

'There is a note – would you like to read it?'

'No dear. I know what it says. Thank you. I said I *don't* need to read it. No – not in the bin. Put it in with the flowers.'

'They are very pretty,' says Siklunli.

'They are perfectly horrid, but they will help to do the trick. Now, you have reminded cook about lunch, haven't you? Yesterday's salmon, new pota...'

'Yes yes. Cook knows.'

Essie looks quite presentable this morning. Age in great amount has begun to improve her. Her twins really are the ugliest you ever saw. Quite remarkable – identically unlovely. The two husbands surprisingly pleasant to look at. Both girls married out. Poor Joe, far too liberal to voice a word of disapproval. I remember him saying at the Registry Office (I went alone, Gussu refusing), 'They do seem terribly happy though.' I thought it quite amazing they found anyone to marry them – though according to Essie, they inherited their father's singing voice.

41

Perhaps the husbands are musical and don't really see what we all see.

Both twins are in pillbox hats. Of course, it is unkind, but one would have thought someone would have taken them aside and re-dressed them. Joe was so dapper – almost a dandy. Mustard suede gloves, he wore. I've not seen them – Caroline and Linda, that is, not the gloves – since they were little girls. Their voices are all they took of Poor Joe. Their hair is pure Essie's – a crinkly black mass and goodness knows where they found the hats, but they're perched on top like sandcastles on a bed of seaweed.

* * *

Saturday occurs at 4.58am, 6.17, 6.19 and 11.11am.

I turn away from the blinking digits of the clock, doubling my pillow and pressing my face into it like a lover to a smoochie song. I have dreamt. I think it was that lifetime between 6.17 and 6.19. I was lying back on thick cream crushed-velvet cushions and Blue was photographing me and I could see myself, distorted in the lens of his camera – I was wearing jeans and a loose sweater, but when I looked in the lens, I was completely naked and the body I saw was much better than mine. The breasts were smaller and firmer – they reeked of pertness – and my hips seemed streamlined, the bare skin gleaming like oiled satin (What does oiled satin look like? Does one oil satin?). I asked myself these questions in my dream – and the asking of such things made me realise it was indeed a dream.

I expected that would in itself wake me, but it didn't. I wondered if I should tell Blue that he wasn't seeing the real me. That the me he saw was better. Then I thought 'why should I tell him – this is a dream'. Instead, I asked him why he was photographing me – and he grinned – he had bare shoulders, but I don't know if he was completely bare – fancy me not looking – and he said 'Because you're an endangered species and so you're special' and I ask 'Have you seen me on John Craven's *Newsround*' and he laughed and took my face in his beautiful hands and kissed my lips – not my mouth – just one lip, then the other and he tasted sweet like cinnamon.

'What would you do if I was put on a successful breeding programme like those ospreys – would you lose interest then?' And he smiled, I thought a little sadly, and he opened his mouth to answer and his telephone rang. And then rang again and I said, 'Aren't you going to answer it,' and then realised it was my telephone, the clock reading 11.11am, and as my subconscious world melts, I pick up the receiver and hear my mother's voice say 'Oh darling – I'm sorry. I wasn't trying to get you at all – I wanted your sister. I really am quite mad today – you'll be like this one day' and puts the 'phone down without another word.

Angry that the dream is no longer intact, and relieved it has been broken, I hold the receiver, feeling the earpiece warm against my ear, and dopily delight in the knowledge that my mother is telephoning my sister Suzi's number and is all the time still connected to me. I hear my mother's voice 'Ronnie? Ronnie! she's left the bloody phone off, how do you...' and then it clicks. Silence. I stay very still and think about seven o'clock tonight. I pick up the scrap with his address on it.

Flat 6L
demerara sugar £00.86
Mullerlight Assrt x 4 £02.41
Qukr prridge oats £00.97
Stanton Mount,
The Beeches,
West Dids.

I feel so excited, I think it might be nice to throw up. My fingertips trace around my body which is floating in a 100 per cent cotton womb right now, but I'm not going farther with this to you yet. You don't know me properly do you? Let's face it, you don't even know my name, so I'm sure now is not the time for a fingertip tour of the naked me.

Without moving an inch, or lifting my eyelids, I open my wardrobe door, and go through all my clothes, picturing myself in them standing at Blue's door tonight. My clothes are not tired. They are exhausted. I remind myself that if he's worth knowing, the only things he could possibly want me to wear are what I feel comfortable in. So says Belle Frithof's *You Are Yourself*, an ex-Wythenshawe Library 25p sell-off mother pretended she'd bought for herself 'but-thought-you-might-be-interested' after the last split up.

I further remind myself that Belle Frithof, a psychology lecturer from Berkley, California, had a third of a page obituary in *The Independent* after her suicide at 42. She is No Longer Herself. To be fair to the late Ms. Frithof, she's right, if I interpret feeling comfortable as comfortable in the knowledge that he'll be wowed. I've got all day to buy something gorgeous, but somehow I know I'm not going to abuse the next hours trawling round Manchester loathing my physical being in cubicles with vicious lights and hooks that don't take hangers.

Anyway, if I am the cookie that crumbles as I'm convincing myself Mr. Clegg expects, this is not the time for extravagance. I make a mug of coffee, press the remote control. Terrible, to turn this thing on during the day. But I do it. The box bursts to life as the opening credits roll for *Brief Encounter*. Bliss. An old movie. One I've somehow managed never to have seen before, but have always known of – something to do with Celia Johnson waving a hanky.

It's Saturday. Sky about to blubber grey tears of a Manchester March and three Thornton's chocolates left in my birthday box. Including the apricot parfait. Life is a blast indeed.

Eight

There will be one night's prayers here tonight for Joe Shabalan. Essie and the twins have returned, Essie apparently agitating for a telephone to call her husband in case no-one else has told him about prayers. Matthew (not quite champion wheelchair pusher) is delighting in telling Barry from maintenance that he (Barry) should 'just see this old duck in the car park'. 'Looks like Lady Penelope with this ferret thing round her neck and in a clapped out Maxi.' He's beside himself with pleasure. 'She's hit the wall about eight times and there's nothing else in the car park – you've gotta see it.'

He delivers all this above my head as I sit in the chair on my journey to lunch. We shall be having the salmon. It is quite as though he is pushing an empty chair. He clearly perceives me as deaf or dead.

'The ferret thing,' I say, looking up at Matthew who looks with surprise as I begin, 'is mink, and though I agree it is rather dated and more than a little disturbing with the mouth clasping its own tail, perhaps Lady Penelope as you call her would appreciate some guidance in with her car instead of mockery. She has tunnel vision.'

Lady Penelope, as a description, is quite perceptive really, but I'm determined not to share a joke at this moment. The concept of Lady Penelope with failing eyesight and swapping her pink Rolls Royce for a mustard coloured Austin Maxi causes uncontrollable mirth from Matthew, though Barry knows better. A stab of conscience makes me question whether Sylvia should indeed take Joe Shabalan's flat when Essie is moved into the nursing wing.

But I put myself first. I will regret this later, but without that foresight, my determination is admirable, to myself at least.

Sylvia is a Didsbury widow. Her home is off Spath Road, one of the most desirable parts, with the highest sleeping policemen marking it out as exclusive. Giant potholes are the calling cards of their private road chic. Sylvia once complained to our hard-of-hearing council that the policemen on Spath Road appeared to be sleeping standing up.

When Louis was alive, it was a really wonderful family house, with a crenellated tower on the western side overlooking lawns with a tennis

45

court and a spectacular oriel window depicting the banks of the Bosphorus which, when the lights were on on the main landing and the entrance hall, was quite wondrous, making the river appear to flow.

Gussu and I spent such a lot of time at Sylvia's. In the summer, we had dinner on the verandah of an old summer house in the garden. Sylvia had what we called an hour-glass figure and with her dark hair swept up in an almost black meringue, and her eyes like Whitby jet, she really did cut a most exotic figure. She also cooked with that sort of flair which makes one feel such jealousy, it's almost difficult to enjoy the food. Her spinach, fragrant with nutmeg and spices that were not quite identifiable tasted quite unlike the frugal-home-is-a-happy-home stuff I seemed to produce. She was a peacock, and I a sparrow, or perhaps a starling. She was passion cake – cloaked in cream cheese icing with scents of having hailed from places of eastern promise.

Of course, I know for a fact she actually hailed from Salford's Broughton Park, though if I ever make reference to her parents' perfectly pleasant home on Old Hall Road, she puts on a Sylvia look – a stare which is both piercing and strangely blank at the same time – which always reduces me to making a comment on the weather or about what we're eating.

'Oh Rhona!!' Sylvia is swirling towards me in the dining room right now. I am at the special table overlooking the Myrna Weinrich camelias. Sylvia's cape, bottle green dupion, somehow twists and unfurls as she sweeps towards me with that movement of grace and difficulty she has. The fearsome mink collar laps around her throat and her hair, which is a strange opaline blonde nowadays – sometimes vaguely green depending on how the dye has taken, is frothy. She really does look like bad weather at Whitby.

'How did it go dear? How was it? Foolish question. It was and now is not. Of course.'

Sylvia stares at me. A blackbird now. One cannot possibly tell if she is about to remonstrate or commiserate. It is not a look which suggests the joy of life, which I wish would happen sometimes as there really is no other point to life, is there?

'Oh Rhona,' she repeats quietly, and continues to look. So I look down. I can't bear it when she does this.

To start, we are served with vol-au-vents which makes me extremely cross. They are not rubbery, but that's not the point. I had been quite specific. The Chocolate Brownie and the Victoria Sponge are alone at their table making oft repeated observations (I can tell from their expressions), and I so want to enjoy the treat of real company. I am hoping in earnest Sylvia will soon tire of looking like a silent horror movie heroine. It is wasting perfectly good life – not to mention salmon which it seems has been perfectly poached, as I directed.

'Actually,' begins Sylvia with her breathily affected accent which Gussu used to call "Manchester Kensington", 'it was rather lovely.' She recounts the rabbi's words, and slowly, Sylvia and I begin proper sharing again. That is something I miss. People visiting not out of duty or because we were once close and there are always the memories, but someone who wants to talk to me now. With me, as someone who still has something to say worth hearing in reply.

She relates Rabbi Landau's words. Neither of us were ever concerned with religion. Neither of us during the past twenty years have attended synagogue more than twice a year (Rosh Hashana and Yom Kippur) – and then it largely centred around comparing hats. We would both retreat into reading the English, but somehow that made it all worse. Now, of course, I don't attend at all. But we retain great affection for our rabbi, the most charismatic charmer, who had escaped from Germany in '38, and who, as a Mahler-loving sophisticate, presided over a flock more interested in smoked salmon than Leviticus and rather better at bridge than Hebrew, but we were his flock all the same, and rather stood out as such.

Sylvia speaks very quietly, tilting her head northwest, then southeast and speaking while sighing – a technique I rather think she's created herself. It suits her stoical suffering to a tee. I am being unkind again. It's what I know best, horrid me. It's just that tunnel vision and alone-in-a-big-house aside, she can still do pretty well everything for herself and she never ever has to have dinner with anyone she doesn't want to.

'This salmon,' breathes Sylvia, 'is really quite wonderful!'

'Ah,' I say, with a smile of gratitude, 'we have a wonderful chef here you know.'

* * *

47

Still me. Sidney Fleiss Dining Hall.

'And how did Landau describe Joe?' I ask.

'Oh – it was all about his 'impeccable taste' – I think he called him Manchester's king of suave or chivalry or something.'

'And Essie?'

'Oh, she was his 'delicate, radiant queen', no less.'

'No! Oh how could he! Of all the things to accuse Essie of delicacy is surely not...'

'Actually, I've not told you about the twins,' Sylvia's eyes giggle endearingly and she collects herself like a schoolgirl about to recite a poem. 'Identical pearl drops from the ear lobes of a perfect union!'

'Good lord! Pearl drops! Joe would have laughed! Were there lots of people?'

'Actually, it was difficult to see.' Sylvia's ailments come back to her. 'The *ohel* seemed full, but I can't see a full picture without turning round and it was very dark in there. I think I trod on an old man, but he didn't seem to mind.' In little starts, between mouthfuls of very good food, she goes on 'Shirley and Jack were there. She's gone very fat – and Beattie Kreisner who didn't recognise me but then she never does – and Monty Rivkin – oh he's gone so *old* Rhona – I only recognised him because of that dolly daydream he took up with. She tried to stand with him. Can you imagine after all these years and she still doesn't know where the women stand ? How could he have left Sybil for that?'

The salmon is silky, the new potatoes waxy and white as the *yahrzeit* memorial candle already lit for Joe and sitting on the piano in the dining hall, and the wine is like very cold silk on the tongue. Sylvia's tunnel vision, as we eat, widens by the mouthful, as she recounts everyone standing in the little prayer house around the black velvet draped coffin containing poor, dear Joe who really is well out of it.

Lunch is going terribly well, and I am hardly aware of Hettie and Herta leaving until Hettie is wheeled right up to our table.

'Hello Rhona, hello Sylvia,' says Hettie, a deceptive picture of frail pleasantness in a beige Jaeger suit with a chiffon scarf around her thin throat. 'That looks much nicer than our meal,' she says. 'Mashed swede – more like mashed suede – I sent mine back. I meant to tell you,' she goes on blithely, 'my Joel took me out yesterday and we found this marvellous bakery – in Chorlton it is. Really very good. I mean, who'd have thought of a decent bakery there? They've got everything. Polish breads, bagels, strudel, cakes — I know you're not a great cake eater Rhona, are you? — anyway, you name it.' Mission accomplished, she smiles, her eyes twinkling through the bifocals. 'There's something I want to see on the telly so I must get back. Enjoy your lunch.'

* * *

I am like blotting paper, absorbing the people I come across and like.

By the time the film ends I am no longer slumped across the bed like an assassination victim in my thick towelling dressing gown. I am sitting instead in a black crêpe dress, straight backed, calves closed, one foot pointing elegantly at a painful angle at odds with its own ankle.

Well. Ok. I am still lying across the bed with my dressing gown on and a now empty box of Thornton's Continental, but inside myself, I am the glorious Ms. Johnson. I had no idea *Brief Encounter* was such a good film. My whole attitude to everything is, for now at least, tinted like brewing tea in the tones of the film.

Rather than padding into the kitchen to re-caffeinate my system, I tread on tip-toe, my bare feet raised by the heel of Celia's court shoes. Her clipped, reflective tones are the ones I hear in my head, but adapted to my own situation.

In *Brief Encounter*, she says 'Nothing lasts forever — not joy nor sadness. Not even life itself lasts very long.' She also seems prone to beginning much of what she says with 'It's silly really'. I find myself talking, very quietly, to myself as I make the coffee. They are Celia Johnson's manicured hands which take the milk from the 'fridge — and the 'fridge itself becomes a bow-fronted English Electric one as I let the decades blur in a colloidal of style.

'It's silly really,' I say to myself — and my accent is in black and white — I really shouldn't be visiting Blue at all. I'd be far better catching the 6.15 train home and stopping off perhaps for a cup of tea and a madeleine at the station waiting room.

It occurs to me as I breeze between my own life and the screen one which has affected me so today, that I should be much more relaxed about tonight's meeting with Blue.

'I suppose,' says Celia Johnson to my reflection in my bathroom mirror, 'That if it's meant to be, then I can have not the slightest effect on the outcome of events whatever I choose to wear or say tonight.' 'Perhaps,' Celia goes on, 'I will really fall in love with him and he will have to leave with his family for a post in Africa.'

Blue won't have seen *Brief Encounter*. It's hardly a boy film, and he's too young. It's impossible to impart to someone unfamiliar what I'm feeling after I've seen such a film. I'm the same with Woody Allen, wandering round in a Mia Farrow trance, stammering 'I...I...I...I mean if you, urm, look maybe I should just, urm, go', for up to an hour after it's over. I think I must be quite challenging company.

I am almost myself again as I set the alarm and close my front door and begin my walk to The Beeches in West Didsbury. Part of me is in a square shouldered coat, that bizarre sloping hat and Celia's shoes – but the part of me you could see, if you were walking past me instead of reading this, is an ankle length burnt orange silk skirt and a shocking pink sweater with a gathered waist. I put my grandmother's tiger's eye choker round my neck as a splash of dull. What am I? Brave. Vibrant, with Flair. Colour aware. Classical. Let's hope he thinks so.

Nine

We are back in my room, which is hot and cluttered with piles of correspondence which I don't seem to be getting done. No mention is made of the bouquet in its cremation urn on the escritoire. I wonder whether it is *so* ugly, Sylvia is tactfully ignoring its existence – or is her eyesight really so tunnelled now that its existence is ignoring her?

'It is so terribly hot isn't it – do open the window more Sylvia, and those poor flowers look as if they need smelling salts.' Still nothing. Living here, creating my own snatches of happiness, is like writing fiction, I suppose. I could never write fiction – I don't have the imagination – but I am able to interpret. I become quite convinced of what I say sometimes. I am almost anxious, for example, that my admirer should not visit and see the flowers wilted and consider me ungrateful for not slicing a bit off their stems or something.

'I'll put them nearer the window if you like,' says Sylvia, lifting her fullness from the chair and rather ostentatiously, I feel, gripping at everything as she makes her way towards the vase of hideous blooms.

'Oh – there's a note Rhona,' she adds, picking up the vase and holding it ahead of her as if it were a vomiting baby. 'Oh – I think it's slipped into the water.'

I can hardly ask her to fish it out. He probably won't come anyway.

'I thought lunch was beautiful,' she goes on, almost throwing herself back into her chair. 'Even the suede swedes – I think that description was lovely.'

'*You* don't have to sit opposite it every day,' I say, before realising I'd be fired as a publicist for the Home. 'But you're right – Hettie does say the funniest things sometimes.' I wrack my mind for a single one, but can only summon up irritating things which emit from her lips like bubbles. Hettie has the irksome habit of disagreeing for the sake of it. If I were a different person – one with more violent tendencies than I have, it would be rather fun to punch her from time to time. I am glad these are just my thoughts, and not apparently readable in my eyes.

'Anyway,' says Sylvia. 'before you do anything else to try and convince me – I'll save you the trouble.' I keep my head lowered, praying to what I am quite convinced is not there, that she will not say what I think she is about to say – that she is going to stay in her house or worse still, move to a flat in London to be near her daughter Irene who lives in something which sounds very dull and comfortable enough in Hendon or Finchley.

'I'm going to take a flat in here. Sell the house. I just can't manage it any more Rhona.' Sylvia's dark eyes glisten with coming tears. They come very easily, Sylvia's tears, like yawning does to others.

He who I know not to be there – He to whom we atone our sins on Yom Kippur in the hope he will spare us for another year of listening to mindless drivel around us. He to whom I occasionally turn despite a long term conviction that there is nothing to turn to – well, today, He is to be thanked, and thanked profusely. Even the chrysanthemums at this moment, look almost pretty.

* * *

Sidney Fleiss Memorial Home. Car Park.

Actually, you've got me. Sylvia. I know you're not expecting this – you're probably expecting to hear what happened when my beautiful granddaughter got to see her mystery man last night. She called me this morning, but hardly told me anything about him. She's obviously smitten, which is wonderful, really. It's a shame she can't find a boy from amongst 'us', but I suppose it's getting much harder.

When I was young we just didn't know anyone who wasn't our own. I'm not saying I wouldn't have chosen Louis anyway – because I would – but nowadays in South Manchester you've got to search a Jewish boy out – make a conscious decision – you don't just fall in love, you have to climb up to it, and it's a *shlep* not everyone makes. I'm more concerned she finds a soulmate. Someone she can really relate to. It's her mother who'll be on the 'phone to me asking where she went wrong.

Anyway. You'll hear all about the meeting with this young man, (don't let her know I've told you about the date) but I just have to interrupt for a moment or you'll think I'm as ridiculous as Rhona likes to paint me. Actually, she lies. Well – let's just say she can be parsimonious with the truth.

I'm just trying to find my car. You'd have thought it would be easy.

52

I've had this one – it's a Maxi – since it was new. 1974. I've got a very kind mechanic who comes and does things to it when it's being strange. Actually, it's not easy finding it now there are other cars here. I've got tunnel.... oh well, you know that from Rhona – but she thinks I make half of it up.

Did you see the look she gave me when I went to move those flowers for her? I mean, who would pretend they can only see a little penny sized circle if they can see everything. It's horrible, it really is. It's like constantly wearing binoculars but nothing's any bigger. The small disk of vision I do have is clear but a little dark – like looking in an unlit shop window after closing time.

I saw that note in the flowers, though. It's one of the ones she has written to herself. It's very sad really – I couldn't bring myself to say anything. Actually, I'm surprised she chose such awful flowers for it. If you must send yourself flowers – make them nice ones. Ah! – found it. I feel for the key. I know what you're thinking – how the hell can she drive the sodding thing if she can't see to get in it. I know. I know. And it can't go on much longer, but I can't quite give it up. I'll have to stop at the next eye test anyway.

It's been the same with the house. It's a beautiful house, but it's killing me. Kills me to leave it too. I'm so frightened that when it sells, there'll be less of me, somehow. At the moment, I live at Lynton, off Spath Road (if you listen to Rhona long enough, she'll tell you how non-U I am, putting inverted commas round the name of the house on my letter-heading. She's so 'U', Louis used to say she's in a category of her own. A 'W'.

I've brought up two daughters and made three weddings for them in that house. Found my husband dead in our bed in it. I've made love in that same bed, and in the hallway, and the kitchen. Actually, that was a terrible mistake. Ivory Formica is not a good backdrop to orgasm. I can't believe I've just said that. But, I can tell you – can't I?

When my parents died, twenty years ago, we sat *shiva* in the main living room, covering the mirrors with sheets and having a row with my sister and brother-in-law who said I was turning it into a party. We had hundreds of people come from out of town. I couldn't not offer them something to eat... anyway. It all happened at Lynton – quotation marks or not. When they were little, Irene's girls and Angela's two boys played in the gardens. I've shed a lot of tears there too. (I suppose

Rhona's told you I'm always crying, but it's not true). There's been enough to cry about over the years, I can tell you.

'Oh shut up you silly sod.' Some imbecile behind hooting me. I can't see the road ahead and the traffic lights without bobbing my head about. I know what they call me. 'Lady Penelope'. Actually, I think that's quite funny. I didn't know who they meant, till my granddaughter Suzie showed me a *Thunderbird* video she'd got for her own kids. I wouldn't mind Lady Penelope's figure though. I used to be hour-glass. More like half-a-day glass now.

* * *

Still me

This morning, I woke up and heard running water on the landing. At first I thought it was my tinnitus, but when I went to the bathroom, I saw water was streaming down the wall. Carpet was sodden. I just can't bear it any more. I sat in this mossy mess of wet Axminster and looked up at my lovely high ceilings with cracks in the plaster and the leaded windows which all need replacing and I thought of winter when it gets so cold I live in the kitchen all day and make love to my electric blanket from nine each evening. Louis used to say 'If you can't see your breath, you're not cold'. But I *am* cold. And I can't see the kettle, never mind my breath.

I had to get myself ready for Joe Shabalan's funeral, and while I was dressing, I decided to sell. I'd visited Joe only a couple of weeks ago. We'd sat in the video lounge at the Home. I didn't tell Rhona – I wanted to talk to Joe alone. Essie was having a manicure with that strange girl, Marie (Rhona's always talking about her with her creative writing and abortions).

It was just Joe and me and half a dozen poor old things who could have been on an outing to the moon.

Joe was very serene. After a while, I could only see him as he used to be. So kind, so lovely, though not beautiful to look at. Rhona doesn't know it, but Joe and I were actually very close back in the days when. We were very proper of course. Oh – I suppose I can tell you – we were lovers for a time. His family lived off Wilmslow Road. Funny place it was – had a minstrels' gallery and a chequered, square hall, which makes it sound very grand, but it was always pitch dark in there. A warren of funny shaped rooms. He had the sort of voice that made you want to lick inside his throat, and know it would taste of warm mead. Sod it. I've stalled again. Oh God. Where are you when I need you? It's supposed to have just had a service. Ah. Good. Thank you. I'm off. These sleeping policemen are just impossible.

Anyway. Where was I? Yes. Joe told me the other day in the video room that he felt he was ready to go. I didn't try and tell him he wasn't. Why should I know better? I felt very sad, but elated, too, that he knew, and seemed to be in control of it. He told me they'd have to move Essie into the nursing wing after he died. Something rather warming, hearing him talk to me as if I were his wife, the one to confide in. He said I should take his flat. It's one of the best in the block.

'Call them now and tell them you'll take the next one that becomes available,' he told me. We laughed then. 'I know what you're thinking – you could get lumbered with half a dozen flats between now and next week.' And he died exactly a week later.

It's not so surprising he spoke to me as though I were his wife. He once said that he'd never marry anyone if he couldn't marry me. It's true. He really wanted to marry me. My parents didn't think he was 'suitable' – God knows why not. Still, he didn't marry Essie Glick till I was married to Louis. Ah, we're home. I still think of 'we', though of course, it's just me. The Bosphorus is in full flow through the landing stained glass. Hopefully, the other Bosphorus down the bathroom wall has stopped. The man said it was the water tank again.

As I get out of the car in the drive (I can't negotiate it into the garage anymore), I look up at the past forty years and decide. Tomorrow, this is going on the market. The decision gives me my first lift of the week.

Ten

'Hello!'

'Hello.'

'You found it ok?'

'It wasn't hard.'

'No – s'ppose not. Come on in.'

Blue leads the way through his hallway, originally the landing of a consulate – Greek or Belgian or something, into his living room. There's a sweet pungency in the air. 'Are you roasting passion fruit?' I ask wildly. Somehow the word – passion fruit – sounds absurd. Pushy. A little obscene.

'Beetroot – fresh. I've got sour cream and pickled lemons to go with them.'

'Oh lovely. How delicious!' enthuses Celia Johnson. But the flat! Blue disappears to make 'tea'. He doesn't offer coffee. Every wall is covered with photographs – some of them huge, like murals. The pictures seem magical – a strange fusion of the very familiar with the sort of unfamiliar I recognise as being from the edges of my memory, daydreams. The bits only a rubber spatula could scrape from the walls of my subconscious. The pictures, some over six foot square are black and white, but bleed colour here and there. They are of houses- and somehow I know the houses. They are here, all around. Didsbury houses, but from strange angles – seen from the inside out. Views through old windows, but not the views that are really from those windows. Real views, but not from where they purport to be.

In one, the leaves of stained glass tulips are green. That's the only colour. The view through this window is framed by huge tree branches. I look at the photograph – far bigger than the real window must have been, and recognise the rhododendrons – all dark greys – and beyond is a bus stop, just visible. There are people at the bus stop. They are tiny – even on this picture, just a couple of inches tall. Beyond is a street of trees, and above the trees, on the far side of the road, is a house I do recognise – spire turrets peeping up above the foliage, and within the dark slate roof line, little windows. Blue walks back in with a tarnished pewter teapot smelling of fresh mint leaves.

'Recognise it?' he asks, nodding at the picture and grinning. And I do. The tiny attic windows, seen through the big windows with the whole street and gardens in between are also decorated with leaded tulips, and standing close up to the photograph, I can see that their leaves are green too.

'It's amazing – it's that house with the strange name by the bus stop.'

'Davrach – yeah,' says Blue, pouring the hot, fresh minty liquid into a glass and handing it to me.

'But where were you to get that view – I mean, you'd have to be somewhere pretty high up to get that view, and I didn't think there was any...'

'I'm standing in the attics of Davrach – see the tulip leaves, the big ones, up close.'

It's quite brilliant. Not just clever techniques he must have used. I'm so useless on things of technical complexity, I could believe anything was possible. It's what's captured. A scene that's lost. Of course, any demolished building is a scene that's gone, but this is different – and other pictures around the room too – they're pictured with a passion, an excitement of the subject – a subject that's gone. Forever. I want to walk into the picture. I want to push back the frame and see beyond. I want to kiss its creator.

'So, this is what I do,' he says.

'They're brilliant,' I say. I'm feeling strangely flat about myself. How can I compete with this? How can I compete with Davrach or any of these gloriously off kilter views of Didsbury – doorways I feel I know, but in streets I don't recognise? Local streets with houses from elsewhere behind trees which really do grow there. Davrach is demolished. A dead lover. No competition.

All I can think of doing is to appear a bit mysterious – but what can I say? I try and think what I'm doing with my life. I think of Mr. Moyne selling his house to Mrs. Webster, and offering to leave the garden furniture. It doesn't begin to compare. I try and think of something to make up that would sound intriguing. In a mad moment, I wonder about inventing a ghost in a house we're selling. God, doing an overtime shift on my behalf, lets me stay silent instead. That was a close one.

Blue would loathe talk of a ghost. He has no need of a ghost. He's just plain boiled inspired.

'Do you want to watch me dish up?' he asks, before I have chance to be fascinating. I follow him into his kitchen, and passing the biggest picture, the one of Davrach, I see something familiar. Very familiar.

* * *

Sidney Fleiss Memorial Home. Room 6.

Rebwar arrives at 2pm, and I am ready in my room. I was in my bathroom when the telephone went. It takes me so long to negotiate myself out, even with the endless ringing, whoever it was had rung off by the time I reached it. Perhaps it was Howard. It's certainly possible. Wouldn't it be so lovely to hear from him! I am about to dial 1.4.7.1 to check, but I stop myself. I will not say so to myself, but I will admit to you – this once and never again that I do not want to know that the number which dialled was not a Hertfordshire number. There. I shan't say it again. Promise.

The Victoria Sponge is thankfully nowhere to be seen as Rebwar wheels me to the entrance. Doubtless on the telephone to one of the brood. Really on the telephone and really to one of the very real brood. The Chocolate Brownie is being taken by 'her Joel' to the Cheshire Flower Show. She is sitting in a red silk suit from Stella Bagnall's, the dress shop in the parade. It's not called that now – hasn't been for years, but we still all call it that.

'That suits you perfectly Hettie,' I say. And it does. And then I go on. I don't know why. I am not trying to upset anyone at all. I am really very content – Rebwar taking me out for tea with Max's sister (Max was an only child, but I feel I have to spread the load a little), and Sylvia coming to live in Joe and Essie's flat as soon as she can get her house sold. But it comes out anyway.

'I heard the most extraordinary thing Hettie,' I hear myself say. 'Matthew told me that Stella Bagnall's is quite a haunt of the transvestite community. Isn't that strange? Apparently they like what she has in the right-hand window, and everyone else buys the more, well, discreet outfits from the left-hand display.'

I hate myself straight away and when Hettie says 'Does he really say that? What a funny thing,' and looks crestfallen, I want her to reach out and slap me. Hettie is a little jowly, and it occurs to me that with her rather showy jewellery, she might know she could pass as drag herself.

As Rebwar lifts me deftly into his Nissan Bluebird, I tell him we will no longer be able to go to the Polish bakery in Chorlton. 'Mrs Fox has discovered it!' I say.

'Ah!' he says, and smiles. We sit in the car for a few moments, and I admire his long-fingered hands and his simple gold wedding band, flat against the steering wheel.

'You were, I think, very unkind to Mrs. Chocolate Brownie,' he says after a few moments. He says this softly, as a statement of fact, and he looks straight ahead as he does so.

'Yes. I was,' I say. And I feel utterly chastised. He faces me then. 'I have an idea. May I take you on a mystery trip?' he asks, looking at me now and smiling again. Remonstration over. It is as though the child has been slapped and is now hugged once more to reassure it.

'That sounds splendid,' I say, and we slide into first gear, past the building site which, for so long, was Davrach.

* * *

I look at Blue properly in his kitchen. Loose, linen pants, a grey t-shirt and bare feet. I do not believe he and I have been through similar agonies today, though I may be wrong. Maybe he will speak to you and tell you. Or maybe not.

His feet are like his hands. Tanned and intelligent. A pianist's feet, I think oddly. The kitchen is wooden, built into the eaves and painted the gloss colours of a toucan's beak. He slices fennel on a purple table and I glance at the cookery books on a canary yellow shelf. Pulses seem to play a big part. There's something a bit self-righteous in the collection. Some extol virtues of a particular foodstuff. *Beanz Meanz Friendz, A hundred things to do with Celeriac* – I can only imagine some of them aren't culinary. The rest are finger-waggers. *Meatless Meals, No Need To Kill*, and wedged in between is *The Higher Taste*, which I recognise as a Hare Krishna handout. The liquorice scent of the raw fennel has taken over from the beetroots which are cooling in a colander.

'So how did you get yourself invited inside Davrach – I always wondered what it was like inside,' I say, as he grates a small block of creamed coconut over the fennel which is laid out on a baking tray. The coconut falls like soapflakes in a light snow.

'Not exactly an invitation – well, a sign saying *Keep Out: Demolition Site*, I guess that was my invitation.'

He flattens some already shredded celeriac onto another baking sheet and chops a little fresh ginger over it. Only ninety nine possible variations left.

'I knew if I didn't see inside the house soon, it wouldn't exist ever again, so I had to break in.' The ginger and liquorice have blended in the air as he trickles maple syrup over shredded carrot.

'There was a cellar door open at the back. Well, it had been boarded up, but kicked in. I just felt my way over the junk and found stairs up to the ground floor. Amazing place. There was this massive room with an incredible ceiling – all plaster birds and ivy leaves – there's a close up of it in the loo.'

Olive oil is drizzled. I've never known how to drizzle. With me, great globules fall over and drown some vegetables while others never get a look in. There's an ease to his actions which makes him seem so co-ordinated. Balanced. It's a pleasure and a pain to watch. Throws me off my already poor balance. And then there's a sudden rush of heat as his old oven door opens and the trays of mingling scents disappear. At the same moment, the unmistakable savoury sensation of cooking animal flesh bursts out of the same black hole.

'Meat!' I exclaim like someone who's not quite all there.

'Yeah – oh shit – are you veggie?'

'No – not at all – but I assumed you were. All the "My-best-friend's-a-lettuce" books on the shelf.' He laughs richly at this, and I feel a little gush of confidence seep into me. I can make him laugh. That's what I can do.

'Oh, those are mostly my ex's. I'm more your *Killing For One Can Be Fun*.' Then I laugh too, and he goes on laughing, and I picture him in West Didsbury's wine bar "The Nose" on a Sunday morning wearing a Norwegian wool sweater and holding our baby in his arms. Well, only for a moment.

Eleven

The little boy from the estate agents arrived about quarter of an hour ago. I'm sitting opposite him at the kitchen table. He's drinking a mug of tea. He can't be more than eighteen, and he's called Guy, and he knows nothing. I mean he really knows nothing. I wouldn't, actually, have picked this firm, "Something Holland and Something", but having a granddaughter working there instead of using her degree – I thought it might be brownie points for her – you know, bringing in a big house like this. When I called, this smarmy little man said that he would deal with me personally. He's called Mr. Dreg or something. He looks after 'distinctive homes' apparently, which makes this child's appearance a bit mystifying. I mean, Lynton may be sodding cold for nine months of the year and falling apart at the seams, but no-one could accuse it of not being distinctive.

'It's a nice house this,' he tells me through slurps. 'A superior thirties detached.' I suppose to Guy, the 1930s must seem somewhere between second Ice Age and Jacobean.

'It's 1882 actually,' I say. It comes out as a sigh. Rhona's always saying I speak in sighs.

'Well I'd say,' he says, actually pressing buttons on a calculator, 'that considering the current market situation, and taking into consideration the condition of the property, together with such other, urm, considerations from a marketing perspective, you should be looking at...' He presses digits. I wish I could see if his toy is actually turned on. 'Yes. You're looking at making quite a lot on this. Very popular, these big houses here.'

'Do you think for so much consideration, we might be even more specific than quite-a-lot?' It seems this will involve another visit from a grown up. He's rather sweet really, but quite clueless. He leaves Lynton slightly less clueless than when he arrived. He leaves it aware that the fourth piece in the four piece bathroom suite is called a bidet. And he leaves it knowing what it's used for.

* * *

I don't know why people are forever wanting to mix food and sex. While we eat Blue's food, I feel perfectly consumed myself. It is sensual pleasure enough. Food and sex work just fine together as analogies – you know – you can spend hours preparing for them both in the hope the subtlety will be appreciated – and it sometimes is, and just as often not. They're both hungers, satiated with a quick, lonesome fantasy or a Mars bar, when you need either it's impossible to believe the need will ever be satisfied, but it always is, for a time at least – and there are those moments of regret which dance and skip among the warm, happy feelings. Should I have indulged? What's the punishment? Now. Later.

And I'm thinking about this – and why no-one ever complains there's too much sex and food on t.v. nowadays, while Blue pours something into Denby coffee mugs and sets them on the little table.

'There's the porn as well – and nylon sleeping bags and always one woman's shoe – a cork wedge or a navy slingback,' he says, and I feel caught out in class – suddenly asked to interpret a meaningless poem I've not heard in the first place. I haven't the slightest notion what Blue's saying. I should just say so, but instead I repeat his words.

'Woman's shoe,' I say in a spellbound tone – like a mantra.

'You sound like Wendy Craig in front of the children,' says Blue grinning. 'You're miles away – are you still in Manchester?'

'Sorry,' I can't tell him what I was really thinking.

'What were you just thinking?'

'Nothing really.'

'Nobody thinks nothing. At least, they do – but you weren't.'

This is my chance to be faintly suggestive and spiked with interestingness.

'No. You're right. But I'm choosing not to say.' We both seem pleased with this.

'I,' says Blue, turning his kitchen chair around so he can straddle the back and give me a fine vista of opened thighs, 'was saying what I found in Davrach when I broke in before they pulled it down – I'm doing a series of pictures called 'Final Days' – these houses, when they've been converted into flats and then everyone's left and the whole place is about to come down – they share a sort of lament – it's so potent. A tramp or two finds an opening. Someone's always left some porn. Softish stuff – you know – tits and endless legs in strappy heels.

And then there's always a single shoe, lying about in the mess. I like to picture it in these last days.'

He shows me a series of photographs – all black and white, from a pile wedged inside the bowl of a '50s Kenwood mixer. Ragged pages of said tits on a mosaic floor – 'the front hall' he explains. An old windjammer with a furry edged hood over a carved mahogany newel post, the bannisters all hanging away from their moorings like a half opened fan.

And suddenly, I feel a huge sadness followed straight away by the intense pleasure of common interest – except it is for me a most rare and uncommon pleasure to feel it. I can feel the sense of slipping into non-existence that Blue is trying to capture – as if his clever fingers are grabbing the bricks as they slide beneath the bulldozer.

'I know just where you're at,' I say, looking at him.

'Yes. Yes. I know you do,' he says, and we both sip the sweet, nutty hotness of amaretto coffee.

When the mugs are drained, he doesn't offer me another one, but says, 'I've something to show you – in the bedroom.' I can't stop myself smiling as he leads the way into a vast room with a wide bay overlooking the back of the house and its half-lost gardens. The floor boards were painted mauve some time ago in here, and the bed is on the floor – a huge futon on palettes. I'd have expected an Indian mirrored throw over it, but instead it's a sky grey duvet and charcoal pillows which I want to touch.

On one wall is a close-up of the huge strange picture on the living room wall – it's the view from Davrach onto Davrach, but the focus is on the little group standing at the bus stop on the road in between. There's a fat old woman in a raincoat and a thin, tall, black man. I know the black man. He asked me for a light once. The old woman looks familiar too, but not as familiar as the figure between them. Me.

'I'm really glad you came over,' says Blue as I stand, hovering in the hallway and thinking what will be will not, it seems, be tonight.

'Yeah. So am I.' I am a bit blown by being in the picture. I don't ask any questions though.

'I'll come in to see about that house then,' says Blue, and I tell him I'll expect him then.

As I trample past an old Ford Zodiac hearse that's been converted into an intentionally frightening motor-home by another tenant somewhere in this old, rambling house, I wonder what Blue is really thinking now. Should I walk slowly, giving him time to open the door and call me back. I do slow my pace, but at the gatepost, the door hasn't opened again.

* * *

Further And Further From Sidney Fleiss Memorial Home, Room 6.

It is tremendous fun to be in Rebwar's Nissan Bluebird motorcar and not knowing where we are going. I do not mind that we do not appear to be heading towards the Marie Louise Gardens at all. Neither are we off to the Polish bakery in Chorlton.

'I suppose it is a good thing that Didsbury is sprouting so many new homes,' I say as we look at the huge billboard, suggesting that the luxury two bedroom apartments are to be built 'within a mature, park land setting yet so close to the village centre with its cafes and amenities.'

'Why do you suppose this?' asks Rebwar. 'It is very strange, I think, to describe these flats to be built in a park setting, when by building them, the park setting will be destroyed.' He is so clear-sighted. I feel such a fool. I have sold him short, saying that the new flats are a good thing. Of course I believe nothing of the sort, but I would have imagined that that is what a young immigrant man would think, and I wanted to please him. And now I have made rather a mess of it.

'Why do you think the development has been allowed?' I ask. A question, put neutrally, cannot be foolish. Rebwar rubs his fingers together.

'Someone is scratching a scratchable back,' he says.

'Oh – do you think so?' I ask.

'Well,' he replies, 'when my neighbour, a lady of perhaps your age, wanted to build a downstairs toilet, she was told it was not in keeping with the area.'

'Perhaps her fingers were too arthritic to do any back-scratching,' I say. Rebwar laughs. He has a gold crown which glints like marmalade in a cut-glass bowl.

'You are understanding exactly, Mrs. Laski.'

We are driving past houses I have known so well – now homes to rather more people than they were built for. Windows from which I have gazed. Doors before which I have stood, bearing small gifts, about to swap them in return for lunch or coffee or supper. These facades are like human faces to me. I have associated these villas with smiles, some with frowns, still others with winks – winks of acknowledgement, and winks across a room from friends saying, 'We'll talk about all this on the 'phone tomorrow.'

Rebwar is listening to something rather dreadful on the radio. I can't imagine how he bears it – a bland song, and then endless prattle. It's really worse than Hettie and Herta together. At least they're unpleasant – there is some spark of stimulation in that. It occurs to me that the houses we're passing, and my friends, are all going the same way.

Some houses have been pulled down altogether, while the friends lie as if in single white beds at Southern Cemetery. Dear Joe's just put his eternal electric blanket on and crawled in. And there... there are the houses which have rather gone to ruin, just like the friends – tudoring falling off, hair falling out, paint blistered and flaking off, laughter lines and lines not at all born of laughter – damp browning attic ceilings and liver spots on wrists. Ugly obvious replacement windows and ugly obvious facelifts.

Where can Rebwar be taking me? I won't ask. I am suddenly very wise. I can prophesy, with my limp, unuseful hands in my lap. He will kill me. He looks kind, but he will cause me to be dead. It will happen within the next hour. Perhaps the next few minutes. It will be very simple. He will turn off the engine of his Nissan Bluebird and turn to me, and his smile will be different – his dark eyes glinting, not with concern but with relish – that his beautiful, long-fingered hands have the power to end a life. My life.

He will drive me, I can see, to the oldest part of the village. We will wait a few moments as he indicates right and cars pass in front of the two old pubs which have been coaching inns, and I will raise my head and see between these old, white stuccoed watering holes, the city's oldest gateway, brought from Hanging Ditch by Didsbury's best-loved son, Fletcher Moss. The old arch with its sandstone curlicews and the gargoyles which are a brighter butterscotch yellow than the rest of the arch as the original leching mouths and bulging eyes were stolen.

I am not unhappy. How strange to worry, as I have done through my life, about walking under buses and of cancer – and now that I am about to be put an end to, I feel quite calm. My will is written and lodged with Merton, my solicitor. Howard will not miss not telephoning me. I will certainly not miss not being telephoned by Elaine. Elaine who is pretty in her own way, but quite without a hint of charm. Elaine, in her pinks and reds and her lack of love — a baked Alaska who children love because they cannot see through to the ice cream beneath. And my grandson. Well, he can hardly miss me. He hasn't seen me in so long. I wouldn't recognise him in the street. I don't even know where he lives now.

Rebwar will lead me past the great gates, past the old parsonage with the huge Cedar of Lebanon, and past the ancient church, so squat and dirty pink which appeared in Domesday and then again in Coronation Street, and as the Nissan Bluebird glides so comfortably past the 18th century cottages opposite the park and Alpine gardens, it will become darker with the overhanging trees, and as we approach close to where the Mersey flows slow and wide, he will turn off the engine. He will turn to me, and though I can't be sure, I believe he will stroke my hand, lifting my fingers, the nails of which Marie has done in toasted coconut by Rimmel, and he will smile gently, because he really does like me. He does not bear me ill thoughts. And then the darkness of the overhanging foliage will become darker still, and quite what he does with me before he returns to SupaKars, his heart beating faster than usual, I cannot know. But it will not be a problem any more. No more problems. No more pills brought in by Penny. I feel quite, quite happy.

And yes! we are indeed driving towards the two ancient pubs right now. In a moment, Rebwar's left hand, the one with the gold wedding band, will push the indicator and we will turn. Will anyone think to tell Sylvia so she can come to the funeral? She will want to be at my funeral. She will be sad I have gone, but she will also be a little pleased that she has outlived me. And now, faced with the biggest thing, I can be pleased for her.

Twelve

Wait a minute. Don't go. Don't go. It's me. Sylvia. I've just tripped over some bloody – oh, it's my bag. I can't tell you how pleased I am you're reading this. I've just had the most bloody awful day. Actually, I think I'm going to change estate agents.

Last night I was on my wheel in the studio – I make pots. Actually, I'm rather good. I'm just too avant-garde for Manchester – all the galleries here know what they like and like what they've known for a hundred years, and prefer you to be dead before they give you space. Anyway, apart from a few exceptions, the Jewish crowd are much more violin concertos than cobalt glaze. Anyway – I'm digressing as much as Rhona, and if I turn into her in the Sidney Fleiss, I might as well throw myself in front of a bus now.

Bloody Edward Marcatta. Little rat-like thing – grew up in a huge old Gothic nonsense named after his parents. Mummy Rat and Daddy Rat. She was called Rachel – had a bust like a shoebox strapped on sideways. Anyway. I saw they've pulled it down. Actually, I'm glad to see it go. Great looming thing. I was going to look at getting one of the new flats they're putting up instead, but they're so bloody expensive and the rooms are like doll's house ones, and anyway, I don't think I could live on the land of a house where little Edward Mar-Rat-ta – that's what I've always called him – lived.

So last night, I was at my wheel, and I had the window open. It's upstairs, and my fingers are just beginning to really understand the clay – to be at one with it – really feel its soul, and I've got *Classic FM* on, and I don't know what it was, because I'm actually one of the exceptions who doesn't know Bach from the Beatles – and there's this wonderful atmosphere in the room – and it feels as if it's been forever since the last bloody interruption to tell you to 'relax with *Classic FM*'.

I've got candles all round, those little tea candle things in tin boxes, and my palms are singing into the clay, and I'm creating and it's all lovely and the clay rises – actually it's quite magical, and the music comes to a sort of crescendo – and as I'm just about to bring my fingers away, I hear my name, like a siren – and I listen, because it sounds like a ghost.

'Sy-l-vee-ah.' And I turn the music down and walk over to the window and look out. And on the gravel outside, looking up at me, it's the little Edward Rat. And it's difficult to see him properly because of my tunnel vision, but I can see this horrible little man and he's put his little car across the front of the drive because he can't see any better than me. And he's got flowers in his hand. Yellow ones. And he calls up to me and says, 'Ah ! See-l-vee-ah – I hear you will be joining us at the See-d-neey-Flee-se – I want you to know how happy I weel be. You and me-ee together again.'

I don't know exactly what happened next – only I remember looking back, and seeing that my magical rising phoenix had collapsed in a bloody mess, and there was wet clay all over the floor, and when I looked back, I could just see the Little Rat's teeth – I think it was smiling, and those bloody flowers, and I'm not sure how it came about – I must have lifted up my water jar where I keep my clay pieces moist, because the next thing I heard was a sort of scream and a little splash and a tinkling of glass on gravel, and I felt thirty years younger.

And then the following morning, this morning, there's a letter from the estate agents. Full of mistakes, and for some reason advising me it would be best not to have a "For Sale" board outside. I always thought it was supposed to be women on their own like me who'd argue that, but the agent seems to think it best. Oh God the doorbell, and I'm still in my dressing gown, and it's gone noon.

* * *

Mr. Clegg has gone to The Royal Oak for a meeting with that man who came looking at big houses. Trish and Pam are out picking a christening gift for yet another niece for Pam, and the 'phone is pleading with me to make a long, expensive personal call on it.

I've just called Grandma Yess!?! That's what Suzie and I always call Grandma Sylvia, because whenever anyone calls, she picks up the receiver and hisses 'Yes?!?' down the line as if she's had it up to here with answering the 'phone, despite constant moaning that no-one ever calls her. I love the melting effect I seem to have on her – getting the frozen citrus 'Yes!?!' and then the tragic sigh that always follows, followed by her telling me how wonderful it is to hear me – she turns into warm, soft-set jam for this.

She's just told me some garbled tale which seems to suggest she poured a bucket of mud over poor old Mr. Marcatta who lives in the Old Home. Apparently, he made her spoil one of her terrible pots. I've got one as a toothbrush mug, and another as a doorstop. They're hideous really, all lop-sided with great cancerous lumps of too much glaze on some bits and no glaze at all on the rest – but they're absurdly resilient. I'm always placing them near the edge of things in the hope they'll fall, but they never do, and if they do, they just won't break.

They're just like Grandma Yess!?! really – colourful, looks as if they're falling to pieces but somehow don't, always close to but never quite useful and without question strange. Hard-glazed, but all billowing curves, and somehow, impossible not to be fond of, though you can't always have them out in front of visitors.

Mr. Marcatta, who must be ninety-something, apparently came round trying to light Grandma Yes!?!'s fire again – this is something he's been attempting on and off since the outbreak of World War Two, despite his sixty year marriage to Valda, or whatever she's called. Grandma's taken against him – I think he told her she was pleasantly plump or something in the early '60s – anyway, he's been *persona non grata* ever since. It's a shame really. Grandma Yes!?! always pushes people away, but behind it all, she wants more than anything to hold and be held. I've told her about Blue. It's easier than telling mum. She'd say I was mad to go to his flat without a police escort. Grandma Yess !?! loves the idea of me having fun. I think she enjoys it more than me.

The fact that Blue's not Jewish goes against the grain for her a bit, but she wouldn't admit it.

'Never mind what your mother says,' she told me. 'If you keep a bit mysterious, you'll keep him. The way to a man's heart-attack is through his stomach – it's other parts you need to concentrate on if you want him to stay.'

And I said, 'You must have concentrated pretty hard on Mr. Marcatta's other parts to have him still turning up for midnight mud baths after all these years,' and she laughed and said I keep her young and beautiful and then the phone went dead. She never bothers to say goodbye. I know where Mum gets it from.

It's 12.41pm. I don't want to go out for lunch in case Blue comes in. He hasn't called yet. A young couple are looking through the details on August Cottage, and I can hear them debating how to strip it of its patina. I'd like to suggest they pick something with no character to start with instead of buggering up one of the villages best examples of late eighteenth century vernacular, but instead, I press the tip of my biro into the black ash desktop and try and remember if I said or did (or didn't say or do) anything which might mean Blue doesn't come in again.

Professionals don't make notes directly onto their desks, so I doodle in the desk diary – eyes with long, Mary Quant lashes, mostly. It occurs to me that professionals occasionally check in their diaries – and I flick idly through. Pam's handwriting reminds me of playdoh. Her "I"s are little circles and she loops her "y"s as if she's just learnt how to do them. She has scribbled that a Prof. & Mrs. Carr would like to view Maplehurst on Tuesday morning. Diagonally through this an older, more petulant hand (ok. I'm guessing here) has scrawled 'cancelled'.

I remember the Carrs coming in about a week ago. South Africans, middle-aged, she with a severe grey fringed bob and choking on ebony beads, and he with the smiling, sensible eyes of a gynaecologist. I think it was a Cape Town accent. She said she loved Maplehurst's 'blick end whart' gables and the square hall with its 'blick end whart' tiles and its minstrels gallery, and that the house was 'ah-deel' for them, as her husband had a new post at Manchester University, and they had two adult children who seemed to be making no moves to leave home, and another who had left, married, given birth, divorced and was back. Ah well, they must have found somewhere even more ah-deel. Maplehurst is one of the houses I'd like to show Blue. So where is he? It's almost two o'clock. Should I have thrown myself at him more?

Thirteen

If Rebwar is going to end my life by strangling me with his rather beautiful hands, it seems he is going to do it outside an Indian restaurant on the Burnage borders which boasts that easy parking is an added pleasure. I feel deeply foolish.

He turns off the ignition, and faces me with the smile I knew was coming, and says 'Well, Mrs. Laski. We have arrived at your surprise destination. Let me help you.' And he lifts me out of the car and into my chair, and trundles me right through the added pleasure of the easy parking area, through a rather unlovely ginnel where wheelie bins are whispering in conspiracy, through to a rather battered door. Pushing it open with his hip, he carries me, in my chair, through to a room which after the bright sunlight of outside, seems draped in a mustard gauze.

There is lots of chocolate-brown big soft furniture and the carpet is all autumnal sycamore leaves. And on one of the dark, velour cushions is the most beautiful boy. He is perhaps two years old and looking at him, with his darkly glittering eyes and his clever little fingers, I have a vision of Rebwar, naked and sweating, rhythmically pounding into a faceless, panting woman and all his features – his own clever fingered hands which I watch playing the steering wheel of the Nissan Bluebird are stroking her hair, and the eyes which look with such concern at me look with such energised desire into hers, and the seed which will make this little boy rises joyfully within him. And I am so grateful that my thoughts are not betrayed at all in my face, which smiles in my most practised way as the door opens from what must be a grim little kitchen, and a young woman with an auburn bob and the prettiest face comes out.

I say, 'Ah – you must be Lesley, you are from Todmorden? – an S.R.N.? – and you were a nanny for a family in Aix-En-Provence for a year before you met Rebwar when he was driving you to your cousin's wedding in Glossop?'

Lesley makes tea, and Rebwar plays with the child and I feel utterly at home in the messy, tattered comfort of their two room flat behind the restaurant which has, it seems, nothing to do with them at all.

'We must go soon, or it will be too cold for your visit to the Gardens,' says Rebwar, and I want to say that I would be perfectly happy not to visit the gardens today, but he disappears and returns with a scrunched up piece of tinfoil. He opens it up, and I instinctively close my eyes and breathe in a glorious mix of orange flowerwater and honey and almonds. Then I look, and see a large slice of cake, as soaked in aromatic syrup as a sponge in water. 'I do not think Mrs. Fox will find our kitchen,' says Rebwar grinning, and Lesley grins too, and we are all, for a moment, old friends and they are quite as wonderful to be with as Max and Trudi, and they are real which makes them better still.

Lesley kisses me as her husband helps me into my chair, and I think to myself that £5000 would replace their suite and perhaps help them move somewhere brighter. Howard, after all, doesn't need the money.

* * *

'Lynton', off Spath Road, Didsbury, M20.

There are two of whatever they are in the porch. One's got a green face and the other one's sort of purple and wearing a hat. I love the way the stained glass does that. I just hope it's not that woman from the house opposite again. Peculiar creature ringing the bell at eight in the morning – maybe earlier. Anyway. It was the middle of the night as far as I'm concerned. She's lived opposite for thirty years and likes to do good. She'd like to do better and actually get inside the house for a good look round, but she never managed it when Louis was alive, and she won't now.

'I'm terribly sorry to trouble you, but did you know there's a bouquet for you?' she asked. It was so early, I didn't even have tunnel vision. I think I answered the door with my eyes still closed. I could hear her hello-ing through the letterbox, so I kept them closed.

'What?' I asked her. Just because she doesn't know how to sleep through 'til ten, she has to inflict herself on anyone who does.

'A bouquet – beautiful blooms. Yellow chrysanthemums. They seemed to be, urm, in the hedge. There's a sort of vase too. Only, urm, it's, well, I'm afraid I think it's broken.'

I must have managed to open an eye by then. I do find it easier to open one at a time for the first few minutes of the day. In one hand she's brandishing those bloody awful flowers the Rat had scampered along with last night, and in the other is a clay-moistening jug in pieces. Both eyes are open now. Actually, I think she was trying to be kind, and I reached forward to take the flowers and the pot and I thought I might almost run to a hug at the same time. Only she's not like us, and anyway, I must have missed the step down which I can't see and although you'd have thought I'd have known it was there after forty five years, I'd forgotten about it, and she leapt backwards. I think I frightened her. Anyway. She was gone before I could offer her coffee or something.

It's not her standing at the door now. There are two of them. I suppose I should put the chain on, but it's still light and if they're going to rape and beat me up, there's no-one to hear them and I doubt the chain'll make much difference. I open the front door.

* * *

Blue never called into the office again. Well, hasn't done so far, and he said he would.

'I'll come in and see about that house then,' he had said. They were his last words to me. That was four days ago. I've been determined not to be a sad old cow sitting by the 'phone doing my Connie Francis impression, 'Let it please be him, Oh dear God it MUST be him, but it's not him, and so, I die.' But there's so little else to do and I want him to come in so much.

I was supposed to be doing an accompanied viewing round Maplehurst, but Mr. Clegg said whoever it was had called in to cry off. Seems a bit strange really. Most people lose interest after seeing a house, not before. Grandma Yes!?! called to ask when she could expect all the hordes of people she was told would be tripping each other up on their way to make offers on her house. She insists on calling the boss 'that Dreggs man'. I said I'd go round there this evening. I'm going to call Caroline, who has been my best friend since that day in October 1974 when the captains of the school rounders teams fought a bitter and offensive battle to ensure each of us was on the other's team. That day we learnt the meaning of humiliation and comradeship in the same moment. As Caroline, who has always had a thing about inverting her sentences, would say; 'The chosen people, we were not.'

Our aversion to physical exercise, our non-aversion to Beeches Continental misshapes and a shared ethnicity which we both recognised as responsible for the aforesaid aversion and distinct non-aversion respectively, were the foundation of a friendship to which quarter of a century has added a deep and lovely lustre.

That's not to say she's not, on occasion, the touchiest and most unforgiving of souls, but if I want to have a real moan – the kind where I can admit to loathing people everyone else finds nice, to terror of menopause before achieving even the first step towards reproduction, or big bad jealousy every time I've had to exclaim unabridged joy at hearing of an engagement or a birth – then it's Caroline to whom I can turn.

'Hello Caz? It's me. Listen. Is there the slightest possibility you could make it out for an hour. I just need to ask your advice about something. Somewhere, like, not at yours. Lovely as yours is.' Caroline is a mother and unlike me, is not able to put her darlings back in the box when she's finished cooing at them. Selfish and inconsiderate of me, I know, but there is something maddening about asking a real question of a close friend, watching while she looks you straight in the eye, nodding sagely as you speak, clearly formulating a considered and uplifting response, and then instead of answering, turning to her young who has been clawing ceaselessly at her arm like a woodpecker with Alzheimer's, and answering its inane, purposeless question instead before looking back, and saying, 'Sorry. Could you run all that by me again?'

This is, perhaps, why Caroline is a mother and I am not. She does not, it seems, mind her train of thought being torn to confetti, all day and every day. As I point out to her as if she has forgotten, the whole point of big, pink Maija-Lisa from Finland with her huge forearms, on one of which she carries both little boys while the other makes her famous blueberry tarts, is that Caroline can escape when she wants.

I tell her to come to the office. She is interested in viewing, say, the £300,000 penthouse apartment at the top of a "sympathetic development of five exquisite living spaces in one of Didsbury's most magnificent settings." Well, the setting had been magnificent before the development, and it was really only sympathetic to the developer's overdraft, but it gets me out of the office for an hour, and Caroline is someone who will look to whichever of Pam, Trish and Mr. Clegg are loitering in the office when she arrives, as if she might be a real purchaser.

* * *

'Lynton', off Spath Road, Didsbury, M20.

Do I know I'm not alone? This is what they ask me, these two people standing at my front door. I'm not certain whether this is a threat or they wonder if I'm mad or blind. Actually, I can feel my hiatus hernia starting up again.

I suppose I am a bit mad and more than a bit blind. I can see their faces, and their tone isn't threatening, but then people making threats often don't sound threatening, do they? Oh God. I reach behind me to the radiator ledge. I can feel my hand on the jagged top of my paint-brush pot, and feel a rush of relief that Mrs. Woman from across the road did come over this morning.

I'm just contemplating screaming, when the voice who asked if I know I'm not alone – a voice belonging to a thin-faced, smiling man with a hairless wart like a strawberry jelly-bean above his upper lip, says, 'You're being watched all the time.'

I feel like vomiting, and wonder if I can fill my lungs and shriek so loud they'll disappear. There's a pain running up through my body, and I think how I could have avoided this if I'd moved into the Sidney Fleiss with only that little rodent Mar-Ratt-a to contend with. I hate the idea that this is it. That it's possible to take the front door chain off to death. But all the time, I'm thinking that life is supposed to be passing before me in quick shots. My parents and my childhood home in Old Hall Road in North Manchester, Louis, the girls, my granddaughters. But I don't. I see all sorts of images I don't understand.

How bloody typical of me for someone else's life to pass before my eyes before my own death. In a strange way, whoever's life it is, being not mine, it makes me feel strong. Bullet-proofed.

'Look. You're disturbing the many people who live here. We're doing – meditation – thirty of us – upstairs. We're a commune. Now what do you want?' And I stand in my hall, wondering briefly if thirty people could really stay so silent for so long. The jagged paintbrush pot is in one hand, and without thinking I've twisted my engagement ring round to face inwards. 'Well?' The other person, a woman, is wearing specs, and I can see myself, an inch tall, reflected in the glass of them. I think I can see one eyebrow raised as I stare them out.

It is then that the woman, whose voice is soft and earnest, reveals that the one who is watching me all the time – the one watching me trying to back the Maxi out of the long drive, the one watching me staring at my coffee mug, not knowing whether the second hermaseta actually went in or not – the one watching me burn my fingertips on the cooker pilot light when I can't see any flame and can picture a huge explosion – that this one is none other than Jesus.

I never thought it would be a relief to hear that. I begin to recover. Feel a bit giggly. 'I don't suppose Jesus knows anything about washer-dryers, does he? Only my Bendix man's on holiday again and the cycle's going on forever.' The man and the woman smile. It occurs to me there's something they might even find symbolic in the seamless revolutions of the washing machine spinning on forever. Actually, I think they hate me for making light, but I didn't ask them to come.

'Actually I'm Jewish and if I needed a transfusion I'd have one,' I say resolutely. They begin to quote something, telling me it's Old Testament.

'Listen,' I say, plonking the broken paint-brush jar back on the radiator shelf as it doesn't seem very friendly to brandish it in their faces any more. 'I don't know whether God is looking down on me. Perhaps it'd be a better use of his time to stare at someone else.

Being Jewish has nothing to do with religion for me. It's something else. It's the essence in my blood which makes me able to laugh when I do and cry when I do. It's five thousand years of preferring food to drink and it's that very strange feeling of unity with someone you meet, anywhere in the world, whatever they look like, whose ancestors shared the same fears and ate too much as well.

It's a bonding which we'd like to break when it's thrust down our throats and we're surrounded by it, and it's a bonding which we want to wrap ourselves in ever tighter whenever we feel it's threatened when we're away from the others. It's about how a shrug can paint a thousand words. It's about always being the exception and always being part of a family. It's about sharing certain rules, and sharing the way we feel when we break them.'

They stood, staring and smiling at me. I don't think Jesus can have told them what his people are really like. Anyway, I've put the chain on now. They've gone. Actually, I've done them a favour. They know what it's like to open the door to themselves now.

Fourteen

Ah! Marie-Therese! Thirty one? Aversion to spiders? Hailing from Higher Openshaw? Share your life with Pauline who reads tarot? Vegetarian but on occasion succumbs to bacon if you don't need to actually cook it?'

Marie-Therese insists on standing behind my chair when she comes in with my coffee and those dreadful biscuits Howard used to like. Jammy Dodgers. I imagine they're called that because the bullet-proof centre dodges all definition of jam. Marie-Therese is new. They can't get them to stay here long at the moment. Marie-Therese doesn't even acknowledge I am speaking. She neither denies nor affirms my memories of our last meeting. It all rather needed dragging out of her when she came in to dress me and change my bandages on her first day, and I rather think she regrets giving away that much.

I am tempted, as she stands behind my chair, to add "twisted down mouth? mean lips? slovenly appearance? graceless gait? over made-up pock-marked face?" all of which I remember quite as clearly as the little curriculum vitae I try and retain for everyone I see. It is so important to keep a grip on these pointless little facts, you see. I know I repeat myself, but it is all in the name of retained sanity.

When I look up and need the name tag to recognise these girls, I will start turning into Essie Shabalan, and that really is the worst. Only the completely stupid like to say, 'Ah well, at least so-and-so is happy. After all. She doesn't know she doesn't know anything.' But it doesn't work like that. I've seen Essie's face, ugly and familiar and warm, looking up from the table where now she sits alone, poking her finger at the scoops of chopped liver wondering if it's food – and when she looks up and doesn't recognise anyone, it isn't a happy face that doesn't mind being made. It's a blind face at an art gallery, or a deaf face at a concert.

I shoud like to bash Essie Glick very hard on the head, and then she need never look so lost again. But then the hideous twins would not have her big, warm hand to hold when they visit and natter to themselves for hours on end. Besides. My hands don't work.

It was *Kol Nidre* night last night. The most solemn night of the year.

And today is *Yom Kippur*. It is a strange thing, but even with no feeling of religious commitment at all, there is something enormous, something stripped quite bare and beautiful about *Yom Kippur*. It is a day when Jews the world over fast from sun down for twenty five hours. Not a drop of water passing their lips. I shall use my time in the Marie Louise Gardens today to reflect on *Yom Kippur*. Rebwar will come and pick me up soon in his Nissan Bluebird. It is one day of the year I am not under any pressure to return brandishing cakes from ever more remote bakeries.

I have never fasted since I was a girl. Gussu and I always refrained from eating anything in front of Howard when he was growing up as Gussu believed it was important for the boy to know by example the rules of the faith. It was rather silly really. Howard could eat because as a child he was not required to fast – but in the state of natural rebellion which affected him well before puberty, he insisted on devouring nothing until the official break of the fast. I, on the other hand, found that while on any other day I could quite easily have managed without breakfast or even lunch, on *Yom Kippur* I felt an unnaturally strong desire to munch on anything, from the moment I woke.

Later, when Howard married Elaine, they seemed to delight in being on holiday during *Yom Kippur*, though I learnt years later that whatever he was doing – water-skiing, mountain-climbing, or, of course, visiting ancient churches – Elaine once wrote a book on fonts in disused churches – I think she had a natural affinity with cold, stone redundant things in empty places – he always did so without eating anything during that day. Then my grandson was born. I remember driving down to their little house in Hemel Hempstead when the baby was one or two or so. It was a terraced house, pebble-dashed with flint, like bits of Thornton's toffee sunk in the plaster.

And Elaine greeted me on the steep front steps. She wore long, maxi skirts then which disguised her rather broad beam beautifully, and she kissed me on the cheek. I've always rather loathed being kissed, especially when there's what Gussu used to call "an A.T. in the affection". You know. AffectATion. Anyway. Inside she was making a casserole. I could smell sweet, roasted garlic and the pungent herbiness of basil. And poor Howard was sitting on the corduroy sofa pretending not to notice, and I asked if they were having lunch and he said,

'It's *Yom Kippur*, Mother. I'm not eating. Elaine's making it for the freezer.' That must have been thirty years ago. I can picture Elaine now, a smile on her pale face that would last, well-wrapped for months and months in the freezer. Cooking on *Yom Kippur*, dousing the air with all that sweet and savoury fragrance, making the fast so impossible for Howard, yet doing nothing one could pinpoint as wrong. Cooking to freeze. She wasn't Jewish, after all. Nothing to stop her. For one of the only times in my life, I felt the strongest identification with the ancient laws. Just for a moment, I thought I should like to fast for a week. I did not admit to myself then, and am only just about do so now, that what annoyed me so intently about Elaine back then, was that she made me stand up for what was mine by right, and mine to disown by right too. She forced pride where it wasn't wanted, and I resented her terribly.

Elaine was still smiling, that serene smirk which I had assumed to be more to do with her being stoned than anything else, but later discovered was worn like her Revlon foundation – smeared on in the bathroom mirror when she heard me arrive.

She did not offer me coffee. She knew the battle rules.

'Ah!' I declared, and marched into the kitchen. Elaine followed, wooden spoon in hand.

'What is it ma?' she asked. She always called me Ma. A pretend attempt at 'mother' on birthday cards and Jewish New Year cards (I never sent those, but I always sent her one for Christmas). But spoken, it sounded simply like marr. A blot on the landscape. She would perhaps have liked my little grandson to call me Grand-Marr. The Great Blemish. I remember walking straight over to the huge orange Pyrex cauldron I had given them as part of a set. Their little galley kitchen with its silver and purple wallpaper and those absurd pine louvred saloon doors, was full of steam. Sweet, tasty vapour. I took a deep stainless steel ladle from the rack, filled it with the bubbling liquid and swung round towards Elaine. I saw her wince, and fall back, her eyes seeing the hot luring nourishment about to come hurtling through the air and smashing her straight on her smile.

I smiled myself as I turned, and brought the soupy stuff up to my own lips and slurped it back. It burnt on my tongue and down my throat straight away, but I grinned, and opened my watering eyes wide.

'Oh Elaine, it's delicious! Quite splendid! You must, must, must give me the recipe! What a clever girl you are, Elaine dear!' And that afternoon, Elaine did type out the recipe, bashing at the letter "o" so hard it made a polo mint. And I was never invited to the house again.

Penny is here now, ready to take me to the main entrance to await Rebwar.

'You off to the synagogue Mrs. L.?', she asks cheerfully, gently lifting my little stick legs which look like water towers in their bandages, into the wheelchair.

'Ah no. Penny. No. I shall repent alone dear. This is God's busiest surgery of the year and I have never found the need to go private with him. I don't think he'll have the time to listen to me today.'

'Will 'e not,' says Penny. She is not really listening. No one really listens. Perhaps because sitting here, achieving nothing all day, every day, we really don't have anything to say worth listening to. It's true!

There are only so many times Penny and Siklunli and the slightly effeminate and rather dim Matthew can be expected to hear my memories of yester-decade. They suggest, in between those charming stifled yawns when their mouths stay closed and their eyes water, that I should write a book, comfortable in the knowledge that my hands can't write. They are good souls, Penny and Siklunli. If I were their only charge, I'm quite sure Siklunli would let me dictate to her or speak into one of those tape recorders she's always saying she will bring in for me. But there are so many of us. All with a tale to tell, and most of us with the same tale to tell many times. I did put up an advertisement on the noticeboard for an amanuensis, but nobody responded.

Herta Fox thought it was a houseplant and said she was given one by one of her many offspring, which didn't flower for three years, and then one year came out in the most wonderful magenta petals.

Hettie Oppenheim said, 'that was a cyclamen dear', and then said to me, 'What *does* it mean?', as we waited for our chopped herring on water biscuits and I said, 'It means someone to help me with my writing. A literary assistant,' and she said, 'Well why not put that then?', and I told her she had a bit of chopped egg on her moustache.

They are out in the hallway now, Hettie Oppenheim and Herta Fox. The Chocolate Brownie and the Victoria Sponge. The Brownie is sitting in an amorphous sea of navy Jaeger with little brass lifebuoy buttons. She is waiting for one of her sons, and is holding a very pretty embossed prayerbook upside down in her navy kid-gloved hands. And there is The Victoria Sponge, iced in tennis-cake green, and like a buddha amid her offspring's offspring. I tense what I can feel of my fingers, and as if I am pressing a nozzle of pleasantness from the inside of myself, I spray on a smile from within.

The Victoria Sponge grins when I appear, as if the sight of me is something she finds most pleasant.

'Ah Rhona, come and meet my great granddaughter Shona. How old are you Shona dolly? Three? You're not three sweetheart, you're nearly seven. Yes! And This is Shona's brother Jonathan who's nearly two and this is their mummy. You've met Melanie haven't you. Melanie, this is Rhona Laski. I've told you about Mrs. Laski.'

And Melanie, who has inherited the prettiness her grandmother is always telling us was her own, looks at me and says 'hiya', and I can just imagine what she has been told.

'And my son Lionel, and his eldest Martin, who lives in Israel.' She pronounces the land of our forefathers 'Isrul.' And an intense looking young man wearing a *yarmulke* and sporting a beard nods to me, and I wonder if he doesn't shake my hand because he can see it is not really shakeable, or because he doesn't touch women.

I know this to be the grandson who has become strictly orthodox (Herta describes him at table as *meshugah frum*, but what can you do? He's very happy and they've got six kids so there's no complaints). These are all pointed out for me. Their names all seem more vowels than consonants, and though I have not yet seen their mother, who I assume is in the lavatories, or perhaps giving birth again, I feel certain she has red hair and buck teeth.

'Well, I think you all look extremely smart for this special day,' I say, and then I point to each child, and state its name. Herta looks at me with awe and distaste. For her, the names are like unfortunate scrabble letters. Martin is clearly impressed. Herta coughs into the back of her hand.

'And what day is it today?', I ask one of the ginger tots who looks about four. I am hoping, I suppose, it will say 'Thursday', and let the side down. But it looks at me quizzically, as if trying to assess if I have lost it completely, and says '*Yom Kippur* of course', and I wonder how old Howard was before he grasped the occasion. I remember my embarrassment when my own mother asked Howard one Friday night 'And what do we say when the candles are lit, sweetheart?' And Howard beamed with pride and shouted 'Happy Birthday!'

'Well, if we don't make a move, we won't make it for the sermon,' says Herta, twisting her face up to stare pointedly at Lionel. He looks at me, and we both think that this is a perfect reason for not moving. Martin and his brood will be walking to synagogue through the rain, but Lionel and his wife Joy (a misnomer if ever there was one) will be driving Herta. Herta looks cross. But she has nothing to be cross about. Not with the steady flow of births which keep perpetuating her name. There is now a veritable lair of them. Howard is not here, leading me to his car, and driving me to the synagogue. It is Rebwar from SupaKars, not Howard, who is coming to pick me up, and I will not be listening to any sermons or trying to remember any great grandchildren's names today. But that is not me at all. I am perfectly happy – more than perfectly happy – to spend the day peacefully in contemplation of nature in our charming local park. I have no need to be fussed over.

I feel Penny press the brake off the chair and move towards the door. Hettie looks up and says, 'I can't see! Whether I'm reading or trying to go down the stairs – it's always a blur.'

'You've got them bi-focals on upside down Mrs.O.,' says Penny helpfully, and after a moment or so of fumbling, the senility chain getting caught in Hettie's hair which has been laquered into silvery submission, Hettie's world is once again a clear one. She laughs with relief, and I feel real pleasure for her. How lovely for something to get better for once. Apart from the odd cataract operation, that almost never happens and even then it's not always to the good. I had my Mrs. Norcroft for twenty years coming in to clean twice a week. Then she had her cataracts done, came in once more and was so horrified at the dirt she'd never seen and I'd never really noticed, she never came back.

'You're not fasting are you?' says Hettie to me, and I know she is not being accusing. 'I'm not this year,' she goes on, jabbing her kid-gloved fingers into the Jaeger wadding at some unidentifiable area of her body and wearing a pained look on her heavily made-up face. 'My Barry's supposed to be here. I don't know where he's got to,' she says. 'I see your young man's arrived.' And I look, and see Rebwar, so handsome and tall, striding towards the sliding doors. He is indeed my young man. Neither a son nor a lover, a husband nor a mentor. I have none of these things. But he is my friend.

* * *

'Hello, I'd like to see the £300,000 apartment please.' Caroline is standing in the office and has come face to face with Trish who has just been to-be-honesting herself into a frenzy with a man who had come in wanting to make an offer on a deceptively small eighteenth century cottage in Ladybarn.

Mr. Clegg had it down as Didsbury and Trish had made the mistake of wittering, 'To be honest, I think Ladybarn's really nice and up and coming,' as her long talons flicked through the 'particulars' drawer in the filing cabinet. The man, who did not know Manchester, suggested that the cottage was in Didsbury, to which Trish had replied, 'Oh it is. I'm just saying – Ladybarn is very nice.' Silly bitch isn't bright enough to lie properly, and in her panic when she couldn't find the right papers straight away, went into super-witter mode and told the man that, to be absolutely honest, the whole crime wave thing you keep hearing about is just made up to sell the local papers.

I could see the thrill of Apple Blossom Cottage, with its original inglenook fireplace and stone flagged kitchen leading to paved south facing rear courtyard with mature shrubs, fade on the man's face.

He was clearly picturing balaclava-clad hooligans lurching over the eighteenth century cottage garden walls and bashing down the charming pannelled front door leading onto reception vestibule, where they would doubtless crack his wife's head open all over the nine foot by four foot six hallway boasting a fine leaded casement side window, before making off with whatever objet d'art was on the delightful recessed shelving, all warmed by comprehensive gas central heating.

And now here was Caroline, who had expected to get me, and could hardly remember a thing about the flat she was supposed to want.

'And what is the address of the apartment you're interested in,' says Trish, still reeling from her blunders.

'Urm. Didsbury,' says Caroline. 'Urm. It was my husband who saw it. Yes. He thought it looked very nice. Just right for us. And I'd like to view it.' Trish looks sceptical. She's had these types in before. She can never believe that someone is seriously going to buy an apartment for the same price as the entire mansion which was carved up to create it. You'd have to be stupid, and anyone that stupid wouldn't have made the sort of money needed to buy it. A sort of reassuring, non-vicious circle.

Caroline smiles at me. 'Can this lady help me?' she says. 'She was very helpful last time I came in,' she adds with that soothing, level tone which makes workmen happy to pull down walls they've put up in the wrong place and start again. There is something both funny and alarming about what Caroline says and how she says it.

We are the same age, went to school together, and her grandmother used to play bridge with mine, before hers went into the Sidney Fleiss and mine decided life was too short to waste on cards, and started making terrible pots instead. But we could be from different worlds now. She seems to have woven herself into a wysteria blue jersey suit, its skirt hem just above the sheer knee, a belted cashmere camel coat, which ought to look much frumpier than it does on her, and wysteria suede court shoes with remarkable sloping heels shaped like the back window of a Ford Anglia.

The morning is bright and blustery and it is the day before Yom Kippur which means I've got to think what I'm wearing tomorrow. I can always picture myself arriving at synagogue and I have a vision of myself leaving it again. The middle bit – those eight hours of standing up and sitting down in between – somehow never wedge themselves in my memory from one year to the next. I suppose it's like childbirth. God must know if we remembered, we'd never do it again. Well, it's not just tedium, of course. It's the day God decides who of us shall live and who shall die in the next year. Caroline and I were brought up to believe that if we prayed hard enough on this day, God would think 'Oh, go on then, you two – I'll put you in for another year.'

We head off now for "The Nose", in West Didsbury. It was one of those one-off caffe latté joints opened by a charming psychologist from Tashkent called Yusupoff and was where everyone came for buttery cinnamon toast and wonderful hummous and leaning back against dark walls covered in paintings by Mr. Yusupoff's mother-in-law. It would have been quicker to go with Caroline to one of the chains in the village – a Café Rouge sort of place, but we have our reputation for individuality to think about.

Caroline is, for me, summed up by the click of her Jane Shilton shoulder bag, the absence of any jewellery except that pear-shaped solitaire on a finger as long and smooth as first-of-the-season asparagus. It's the way she organises everything so her definition of last-minute refers to a month back despite her sparkling dinner party fiction that life is a series of catastrophes, humiliations and disasters avoided by the skin of her beautifully capped teeth and luck alone.

In our twenties, she dated ferociously, weeding out and discarding the too physically attractive, the too original in their approach to life and those who thought that camping under the stars might be fun – unless they were referring to five stars of course. It was not that she was acquisitive. She liked plain and simple. But she liked her plain, plain good and her simple, simply the best.

Now we are cocooned in the purring, leather-scented smoothness of her charcoal grey Saab coupe on our way to "The Nose", because my own reputation is for not adhering to any of the rules by which Caroline lives. I do not drink my coffees in overpriced café chains (well, I do, but not in front of her).

Invitations arrive for me 'and friend'. I am not the 'and Mrs'. I suppose I feel a certain pressure to show the advantages of my lifestyle, and the only one which I really feel at the moment is that where I live, the autumn leaves fall around such an intoxicating blend of poor and rich, foreign and local, shabby and chic, cultured and crass, while Caroline's smooth Saab will head back this afternoon to the sculpted lawns of new-moneyed, electric-gated Cheshire where firms from east Manchester remove the leaves professionally and flypost the resident victims with offers of repaving their drives with natural York stone or building them faux-Edwardian conservatories from the best endangered hardwoods.

I am sounding radical, which I'm not. But an awful lot of money goes into creating a lifestyle I really don't want – and the grapes are not sour at all. It's just that right now, Caroline at least knows where her husband is, while Blue could be anywhere and can hardly be described as mine.

'If he said he would call and he hasn't, I wouldn't waste more time on him,' she says, carefully picking off anything interesting from the garnish on the house salad. 'I mean you can't very well ring him, can you?' Caroline is the voice of my mother at times, but at least she does listen in the first place.

'Is there really any reason why not?' I ask. Caroline played by rules about which her dates rarely had much idea, which brought potential flingettes as she called them, to come to abruptly premature ends because the man in question suggested theatre when dinner would have been the correct answer, or suggested coffee on date two instead of three, or something more than coffee on date three when coffee and nothing but the coffee was called for. One, an over-confident Australian linguist who Caroline dismissed as 'well versed in the art of cultural bullshit' kept taking her for splendid dinners at Manchester's best restaurants and then failing to ask if he could come up for coffee well after it had become indecent not to. You're probably asking why I'd want advice from her in the first place, but she's so spendidly wrong on these issues, her advice is always valuable as the perfect opposite of what I should do.

'Where does he get a name like Blue?' asks Caroline.

'I don't know. It's not after a great uncle Baruch if that's what you're wondering. I really don't know anything about his background. It's just there's something there. He's gorgeous and he's just...'

'So not interested,' says Caroline. 'That's what's sparking you. If he'd been all over you, you'd be saying you weren't sure what you thought of him. Maybe you should try and lose interest in him, and he'll come running. Or maybe he's gay. The really pretty ones always are.'

'I don't think he's the come-running type. Besides, I shouldn't imagine he's got the slightest idea what I think of him.' I don't make any comment on the thought that he might be gay. It had occurred to me before, and he wouldn't be the first I'd found.

One of life's most sweet and sour ironies has to be that the only men who really understand, who actually listen and have the slightest idea if they've seen something I'm wearing before, always crave the same selfish sods as me. I remember Marcus. Mum adored him. Dad thought he was funny ha ha, but was always surprised when he bounced up and offered to make coffee when the theme tune to *Match of the Day* started. Grandma Yes?!? said that Cheadle wasn't ready for him and one day I'd know what she meant. Then she said she was being silly.

I thought he was great. Good-looking, bright, not so sensitive you'd worry, but more at home with *Wood & Walters* than *Question of Sport*. I suppose I should have seen it coming. Cheadle didn't hold him in the end, and he lives with the ex-husband of Caroline's bridesmaid in Homerton now. His mother still describes him as 'not married yet', and mine looks witheringly at me and says 'if *he* can find a lovely Jewish boy, why the hell can't you?'

Anyway. Blue's not like that. I can't say what it is, but he just isn't. 'Well, maybe you should ring him up and tell him. Go on, call him right now,' says Caroline and snaps open her bag to reveal a tortoiseshell mobile. 'I'll go to the loo and shore up any signs of subsidence. Elliot's taking me out to dinner tonight. It's a surprise.'

'For Elliot?'

'For me. Elliot's going to suggest taking me to that Raymond Blanc restaurant we haven't been to yet. It's going to be a spur of the moment idea, when he gets in from work, and I'm going to be duly delighted and taken aback.' Caroline slithers between the tables. 'Well Elliot can't be expected to book tables at somewhere we'd actually want to go, so it makes much more sense. It means I can honestly enjoy my surprises instead of wanting to cry. The last surprise he organised off his own bat was to the races. Did we enjoy ourselves dressed in rags and so bitterly cold the tears of boredom froze on our cheeks? We did not. I'll be back in a minute. You ring your man.'

She has made it difficult. She has suggested ringing him now, which means it's probably not the right thing to do. But I want to. But I can't. Not now. Not with the pressure of Caroline coming back in a minute. And what would I say?

'Well? Does he want to make you Mrs. Blue?'

'I've not called. Anyway. I don't want to be Mrs. Blue. Why can't he be Mr. Me? ...I don't mean that. I'm not looking for marriage.' Caroline looks at me as a mother looks at a little boy, with chocolate smeared around his mouth, swearing he hasn't raided the sweet tin. It is a have-it-your-own-way smile. Caroline must go. She grabs the unused mobile and calls home to what Elliot calls the Big Pink Finn.

'Maija-Lisa? It's me. Is everything alright? Yeah Yeah A-ha. Oh my God! No! Right under? Oh my God, I knew I shouldn't... Just stay where you are. Don't... No. Just listen...'

Caroline takes control of a situation which will have been under control anyway. I glean that one darling has attempted to drown the other darling by holding his head under the water for a period which, in reality, will have approached one second. Maija-Lisa didn't, it seems, pull the more guilty darling off for another fraction of a second, and then was foolish enough to actually admit her actions to Caroline when she calls.

It wouldn't surprise me if that is the end of the Big Pink Finn. A shame, really, as she's a lovely, efficient and well-meaning girl whose upbringing among the silver birches and peaceful lakes of eastern

Finland where her naked siblings were happy to jump from wood saunas into icy waters and beat each other with birch twigs left her woefully unprepared for the smile-veiled neuroticisms of a Jewish mum from Hale. Caroline asks if I'd mind terribly walking back to the office as she must make haste to her home of juveniles of murderous intent. I do not mind. The walk will be enjoyable, and Caroline has quite forgotten her demand that I telephone the elusive Blue.

'So the flat isn't for you then?' I say as Caroline scribbles her signature on her Barclaycard which is a different colour from mine.

'The what?'

'The flat. The one I've been showing you.'

'Oh. Sorry. Whatever you like,' she says, and within a minute, she is gliding away from "The Nose" oblivious to the red light through which she is driving.

I walk back to the office slowly. The sun on this late autumn afternoon falls in spotlight pools turning old roof tiles paprika red, the penny-shaped leaves of an immature eucalyptus bruised blue, and Velux windows in heavy, slate roofs like young eyes in an old face. And now I pass the diamante shards of a bus shelter kicked in by retreating drunks from last night, glinting with opalescent beauty. This is the bus stop at which I've spent so much time standing, immortalised on Blue's wall in that amazing photograph taken from the attics of Davrach.

The old gateway, flanked by what Blue had called 'those grand old hard-on dicks' is sealed off now with hoarding painted a vicious blue, and through the drooping foliage of rhododendrons I can see the brightly bland ground floor of what will, in a few months, be Windsor Court. The bricks are sharp, ugly red and workmen are laying a band of margarine yellow ones just above the first floor level, no doubt in the name of 'individual character'.

There's a large hoarding with HouseBryte Homes inscribed in a flourish of gold and green with "coming soon, contemporary luxury apartments and townhouses". I'm so glad Blue took those precious photographs. I can feel all the fury he must feel at this mindless rape – all given the thumbs up by our myopic and, I can only imagine, vindictive council.

I pop into the health food shop on my way back, and it is thus with a mouth clogged full of organic chocolate almond cake made with humanely ground flour that I swing open the door to Anthony Holland & Clegg and come face to stuffed face with the delectable Blue.

'Hello,' he says grinning warmly as Pam, sitting behind her desk, tries to de-glisten her eyes and look uninterested. 'You said there's a house I'd be interested in.' Frantically attempting to swallow the cloying wedge of sweetness in one gulp, I discover to my horror that some of the topping has secured itself to the roof of my mouth, and now is not the moment to try and scrape it away. It is with me affecting an apparent impersonation of Janet Street Porter that we arrange to view "Maplehurst" the day after tomorrow. The moment Blue has gone, the chocolate rooftile dislodges itself and I return to sounding normal.

Fifteen

'Lynton', off Spath Road, Didsbury, M20.

I'm shattered. It's ten in the morning and I've not slept all night. Not since that banging started. Oh, it was horrible. It was about one in the morning, and I'd just found a position I was comfortable in when I heard a knocking at the front door. I must have been just about asleep, because I thought it was those Jehovah's witnesses come back for another dose. But then I thought surely they don't want to spread the word at one o'clock in the bloody morning. Then I heard glass breaking.

I struggled out of bed and into my dressing gown. Actually, I've always loved sexy nightclothes and my nightie is a rather wonderful black satin with lace and silk bows, but whoever it was breaking in, I don't suppose it would be fair for them to be faced with the vision of my uncovered loveliness from the Lady Penelope range. My granddaughter bought it for me for my last birthday and I love it. When I'm lying in bed and can feel the smoothness over myself, I could be any age or shape at all.

I didn't go to synagogue last night, *Kol Nidre* night. Too much standing up and sitting down. There'll be enough of that today if I can face going. I went to stand on the landing, and listened. There was such pain running up through me. Banging stopped. Silence. I didn't want to put any lights on. In the dark, I can feel my way round this house better than people with better vision can see when it's light. Everything looked very still. Too still. I could see the front door, and the stained glass panels lit by a moon like tiny dabs of white paint. I could picture people crouching beneath it. Waiting for me to go back to bed. I thought of Cynthia Rubin and that tape recording she kept by the front door of alsatians barking. Maybe I should have had something like that in this big old house on my own. But then I remembered that the one time she needed it, the batteries had run down and the dogs sounded like Louis Armstrong and not at all convincing.

I made my way downstairs and into the morning room. Nothing. Still and dark. I looked through to the kitchen. Just the tiny pilot light flames and the blinking green of the microwave clock. I was thinking of the crashing glass sound. It had sounded so close. I thought of the silver in the dining room I hardly ever use. The battered leather boxes of mother-of-pearl handled fish knives and forks in their old satin linings. Gussu's mother's silver table centrepiece, permanently wrapped in plastic bags and stuffed in the back of the chiffonier. The *shabbos* candlesticks. My grandmother, who we all believed to be Viennese despite her coming from some little east Prussian *shtetl* in the 1870s, left them to me.

My hand trembles at the door as I imagine them gone. In the same family for two hundred years maybe, and some little bastard snatches them now. For a moment, I can't bear to look. I think about just going back to bed and pulling the covers over my head. But I can't do that. Maybe there's a man still in the house. Actually, the pain's intense now. I fling open the dining room door and stare violently and coldly at whoever is standing there.

'Yes?!?' I shout, and my panic seems to make my vision tunnel all the more. The room is cold. And empty of people. There is no-one here. I don't see it at first, but as I move into the room I can feel the cold from an alcove window. One of the leaded window panes is smashed. There are shards on the sill, and the window has been opened slightly. Swallowing, I turn, and want to cry.

My grandmother's candlesticks, carried God knows how from God knows where to Manchester, and polished for decades and decades, lit by my mother every Friday night when I was a girl, and by me for the first twenty years of my own marriage, and then every so often. Those lovely sticks with their Corinthian tops and the bash in the side of one of them where it fell on the quarry tile kitchen floor years ago while being cleaned. They're still there! The cutlery in the top drawer, when I pull at the cold mahogany handle, is all still there too. So's the centre piece, in its Marks and Sparks bag to prevent it going the same vinegar brown as everything left out.

I can't quite believe it. Maybe they realised the fish knives are only plate. But what thieves in their right mind would check? Anyway, the candlesticks are solid. I spent the next hour trying to get someone to come and board up the window. My *Yellow Pages* is two years out of date, which is long enough it seems for everyone in them to be out of business. Then I find one, but because I haven't got a touch-tone phone, I have to listen to *Total Eclipse of the Heart* four times before a Scottish accent answers and by the time a fellow arrives I'm crying again. I know. It's just what Rhona says I do all the time. But it's so frightening. I feel so vulnerable like this.

I took the candlesticks upstairs, and then I don't know what came over me, but I started to imagine that nothing was safe downstairs, and I started dragging everything up; the whole Minton dinner service, two plates at a time, all the family photographs in those curly frames engrained with bits of pink where the silver cleaner got stuck, all the bits and pieces which we were given for our wedding, or my parents were given for theirs. By four o'clock in the morning my bedroom looked like Steptoe's and it occurred to me that as *I* had managed to *shlep* it all up, only a particularly disabled thief wouldn't be able to take it all back down in two seconds flat. I've got to get out of here. I'm going to call that Dreggs man tomorrow, *Yom Kippur* or not.

* * *

'Ah Rebwar,' I say, after he has lifted me so gently into the passenger seat and adjusted all the cushions so I can see over the top of the dashboard. 'I'm not at all sure I really want to go to the Marie Louise Gardens today.' And he answers,

'There are no rules, Mrs. Laski. I will take you wherever you like.'

'Wherever I like. Ah. What about you choosing?'

'But today is your holy day. Your *Yom Kippur*. You would not like to attend your service?'

'How do you know about *Yom Kippur*?' I ask.

'I have already brought Mrs. Solomons to the synagogue this morning at half past nine.'

'Well! She is a glutton for punishment.' And I recognise the taste in my mouth as jealousy. Gracious. I am jealous that Mrs. Solomons, who is ninety four and is not always as others are, has been seeing Rebwar too. I am most ridiculous today.

'Yes,' continues Rebwar, quite oblivious to the feelings I am discovering, 'she said she would not travel in the same car as her daughter-in-law. These family feuds are very good for business,' he adds, grinning.

I know just how Mrs. Solomons feels. I am thinking again of Elaine, although there has never been the slightest suggestion of my sharing a car with her to a synagogue or anywhere else. Mrs. Solomons has the room next to mine, and I can hear her moaning drone – or is it a droning moan? – every time her son visits, which I imagine is twice a week more often than his wife would like. Earlier this morning, as I sat waiting to turn on the television for the news, I could hear her voice sawing away.

'I hate it here Philip. I want to come home.'

'Mum. This *is* your home. You live here.'

'I do not live here Philip.'

'You do.'

'And I can't put my shoe on that foot. It's still painful Philip.'

'I thought you said the corn was better? I rang the doctor again and he said you'd cancelled your appointment. I've done what I can mum. More than that I cannot do.'

'Well, it isn't better. If you cared, you'd have asked that feller.'

'What feller mum?'

'That *schvartsi* doctor, who else? The one who said it was alright for me to wear those shoes. Only I can't wear them. I don't know how I'm going to get to your house tonight to break the fast.'

'But you're not coming to our house tonight. You're coming on Friday. Rena's taking you to hers tonight.'

'What do you mean I'm not coming to your house tonight? Why've I got all dressed up if I'm not coming?'

'But you're not all dressed up mum. You're in your dressing gown.'

'Well you just said I wasn't coming. That's why I'm in a dressing gown. Make your mind up Philip. You're sixty-three, you should know what you mean by now.'

There was a pause then.

'I suppose that woman'll be there tonight.'

'That's my wife, mum. Sheila. She's been my wife for thirty eight years.'

'She put you up to not having me, didn't she?'

'No mum, she didn't.'

'So you're telling me it's you that doesn't want me. That's what *she's* done to you.'

'No, of course not.'

'So you admit she doesn't?'

'It's got nothing to do with Sheila mum. You're coming to us on Friday.'

'Right then. Well if I'm not wanted at yours tonight, I'll not waste any more of your time. You go to *shool* and start repenting. You won't have time to get it all done if you don't leave soon.'

And Philip makes his way out of the room, after kissing his mother's forehead as he always does. He smiles at me as he passes. He thinks he'd rather have me as his mother. I believe many of them fantasise about having someone else's mother until they're staring at the coffin.

'Could we have lunch together, Rebwar. My treat?' He looks at me, and I think how dreadful I am to put him in such a position. Of course he doesn't want lunch with an old trout like me. But he looks quizzical and says, 'It is not your fast day?' And I look up at him as I used to look up at Gussu when we first met in a way he said he liked. I say nothing, and Rebwar says, 'OK then. Yes. That would be very nice. Perhaps somewhere you normally go with your friends Max and Trudi?'

We both laugh.

Max and Trudi would not go, for example, to "Bumbles", a splendid antidote to the new Didsbury of focaccia with goat's cheese and red onion marmalade served very slowly, if at all, by pleasantly vacant staff in black who never have a clue what soup is the day's special. They would not go, I reflect as Rebwar pulls away from the Sidney Fleiss, only because they have been dead for half a century.

I have not been myself in a very long time. Howard took me last time. The place is in a little cobbled alleyway next to a very good antiquarian booksellers, and I remember finishing a whole piece of exceptional walnut and lime cake before Howard could tear himself away from the wonderful old tomes next door. I can't remember exactly when it was I came with Howard, only it must have been a long time ago, because I was quite able to walk and was still living at home. How strange. Living at home. It makes me sound like a teenager. Well, I suppose after second childhood comes second adolescence and second teenagehood. And, sadly, we are all dead before we reach second adulthood.

'What a perfectly dreadful thing is bursting out of the earth at poor old Davrach,' I comment as we go past what was little Edward Marcatta's lovely old house. I hope Edward hasn't seen it. I expect he has. He's still driving, though from the dints and scrapes all over his car, I doubt he's got spare vision to look sideways at his old home. Sylvia tells me he was round the other night, and she by all accounts was doing her Rapunzel impression. I don't believe for a moment she was that horrified when he came bearing flowers. She just wants me to know that she gets flowers from gentleman admirers too.

Well, Rebwar and I are installed in this very cosy, old Didsbury tea rooms. The rather cold sun is shining brightly onto the beautifully unfashionable carpet, and Rebwar is reading from the blackboard menu all the homemade desserts which all sound perfectly lovely. Mr.Armitage, who at eighty-six cycles everywhere with an elderly Yorkshire terrier in the wicker basket on the front of his bicycle, is devouring a baked potato and is quite alone. I smile at him, and he greets me.

In the darkest recess of the tearoom, part hidden by a spray of dried flowers, a middle-aged man is seemingly engrossed in the menu despite his clearly having finished a hearty meal which, from his plate, involved fat, golden chips dipped in tomato ketchup. He has the menu quite pressed to his face, and is facing the wall. The pretty, pleasant woman who runs Bumbles returns to his table with change and seeing him almost licking the plastic coated menu, asks if he wants anything else after all. It seems he does not. What he wants is to be out of the little tearooms *poste haste*.

It is rather difficult for me to pick up my own menu, and I have decided on two desserts instead of a main course anyway. Raspberry crumble to start, followed by steamed syrup pudding. Watching me as I stare down at my useless hands, Herta's son Lionel Fox decides this is the moment to make his escape, and lurches towards the door. He is unsure whether, at half past one on *Yom Kippur* day, he has been seen in the one place he expected not to encounter any Jews, and will doubtless wonder what mischief I will make of it next time Herta irritates me beyond endurance. She is always telling me how rich she is. 'Not in money maybe, but that isn't wealth anyway. After all, a shroud has no pockets,' she likes to chortle, partly for Hettie's benefit as Hettie, it seems, has asked her Spanish dressmaker woman to put a couple of pockets in hers.

'My wealth is my family.' Had she the faculty to think, she would perhaps have stayed silent. She smiles her plump, content smile. She is an insensitive bitch.

I am still staring at my hands when Rebwar gives our order.

'A new colour, Mrs. Laski?' he says, looking at my nails. They are indeed! I feel myself flushing that Rebwar has noticed such a thing.

'Yes. Marie did them on Thursday – Marie, who had an abortion at nineteen and – well, I think I've told you about Marie already. It's better than the usual colour she chooses. It's called "Frisky Clover" from Rimmel. I'm really not sure how clover is capable of friskiness, but at least she's run out of winter garnet which was beginning to depress me.'

And as we chatter – to be fair, I do most of the chatting, but it is such a pleasure to do so, taking occasional spoons of the warm, sweet concoctions in front of me – I can take in the other people around us, and in particular two men at the next but one table, whose conversation has caught my attention.

I feel certain I heard mention of Sylvia's house, Lynton, just now. I am tempted to ask the two women at the table separating ours from that of the men if they might like to stop their ceaseless blithering long enough for me to hear what is being said, but of course there is no way of achieving this.

Rebwar seems aware of my interest, and does not speak at all. He has such sensitivity. Tomorrow, perhaps, I shall telephone my solicitor, and get him to draw up a new will. Rebwar is such a friend. One of the men is saying something about a break-in. All I can hear is one of the men say 'put the wind up her... any luck... too frightened to stay...' Sylvia did telephone this morning with a rather garbled tale of thieves not taking anything and did I think thieves would know that Louis's mother's fish knives were plate. She said she was on her way to synagogue, despite feeling dreadful, and would call the police later. And now the women at the next table have set up one of those interminable indignant I-said-to-her-I-said sort of conversations, and I can hear nothing else. Perhaps I misheard anyway. I look up once more, and one of the men looks over to me. He has a bright, friendly canine smile.

* * *

Sixteen

Mum and dad have gone to my sister's synagogue for *Yom Kippur*. Being married and now being mother to Miriam Candida, named after her husband's late mother and, it seems, a virulent venereal disease, my sister is more worth spending the high holy days with. I don't mind. I prefer it in a way, as it means I can pick Grandma Yes!?! up and have her to myself all day.

I called at ten this morning and she sounded awful. Someone tried to break in last night. It makes me feel sick to think what would have happened if they'd actually got hold of grandma. The house is so big, no one could have heard her and even though she's admitted aesthetic defeat, and has taken to standing some of her worse pots round the bed ready to hurl as missiles, it's hardly foolproof.

'Yes?!?' she'd answered the 'phone when I called.

'Hello Grandma. What's the matter?'

'Oh darling! It's you! Actually, you sounded like your mother then – but don't hang up.' She told me what had happened, and said she was about to go to *shul*. She didn't ask me if I was going. That's what I love about her so much. No pressure to conform to anything. She knows I know what day it is. Still, I know she was really pleased when I said I'd like to take her.

Grandma lets me drive, thank God. Reversing out of the long, Lynton driveway, the ancient Maxi stalls. 'Probably gone into withdrawal, sweetheart,' says Grandma, 'It's missing having its gears crashed.' Grandma is smiling at me, facing me full on, and her eyes are shiny, liquorice black with lashes to match. She mustn't have done any crying since she put her mascara on as there's no running, but she looks pained. Tired. I look up at the house when we reach the end of the drive, and I want to say how beautiful it looks, but I know Grandma can't live there much longer, and I don't want to rub it in.

'Yes, I know,' says grandma, reading my thoughts as if they were headlines. 'But nobody else seems to think so.'

'What do you mean?'

'Well, no-one's interested in actually buying it. And I need to sell it sweetheart. Actually, it's very difficult thinking about it. I'd rather die in it really.' And I don't say anything. I know the only thing in the world

I should not say now is 'oh don't be silly' or 'don't talk like that'.

'Can't you get that Dreggs man to pull his finger out sweetheart?'

And we drive to the synagogue.

'Oh, you know who that is?' says Grandma as we pass a silver raincoat with a wide-brimmed grey hat holding hands with a fawn gaberdine with a black trilby. 'It's – oh God, my brain's gone to compote. She's one of the Glassman girls. You know, her father had a chemist's on the corner of Bury New Road. You know – her daughter was at school with mummy. Lived on Palatine Road. Oh my god what are their names?' And grandma looks as if she might cry from frustration. I can't help her. I don't know grandma's friends.

When I was little, we knew all the hats and raincoats walking towards the synagogue on *Yom Kippur*, and there were plenty of them. But the community is getting older and thinner now. We arrive at the road where the synagogue stands. In years gone by, we'd have parked around the corner and walked the last three minutes. We're not supposed to drive on such a day. Except everyone did, and the synagogue started putting plastic traffic cones all along the side streets, which just made people more brazen and they parked on the main road right outside.

'Oh look, it's the hideous Shabalan twins,' says Grandma as I reverse the Maxi into a bus stop. Well, it's either here or three miles up the road. There is something spectacular in the ugliness of 'the girls' as they are still known, despite being almost sixty themselves. Grandma heaves herself out of the car and tries to out-stare her own reflection in the car window, to which she gives a look of unbridled contempt. 'I look like the Wicked Witch of the Bloody West,' she says, patting at her hair, the blonde of which has come out an intriguing silvery green.

'You look lovely,' I say, and I mean it. She has that beauty which gets better with age. An individuality and softness made all the more precious by the knowledge that one day, perhaps soon, she won't exist. I think about Blue's photographs. His fascination with the threatened.

'You've not said any more about your young man,' says Grandma, grabbing at my wrist as we cross the road.

'There's not much to say,' I lie. 'We haven't seen each other since that night.' We climb the shallow, marble steps and Grandma, with characteristic rudeness, which it is hard to blame entirely on her famed tunnel vision, ignores the proffered hands of the congregants on the door wishing us 'Good *Yom Tov*'. I say hello to the young man currently on guard duty. The risk of arab or neo-nazi attacks has been so long a part of the synagogue service on high holy days, I've begun to see it as part of the service, as if in ancient times, those congregants who were familiar with everyone would have been kept at the entrance.

Inside, young girls and boys skid across the marble chequered lobby floor while their mothers, many of whom I was at school with, but who have since metamorphosed into Chanel-suited dollies clicking on high heels with their big hair squashed under their big hats, try and shush them, but are really far happier strutting about the lobby than yawning their way through the long service.

They smile at me with their big mouths. 'Hi! How are You? You look terrific! Haven't seen you since...' And I help them with 'Last *Yom Kippur*' and they laugh and lift imaginary strands of hair from their faces with azalea coloured talons, and pretend that they were speaking about me only the other day.

And as they try and remember to whom they've given birth since last we met, their eyes are saying, 'So you're still single then? Shame. There must be someone. Anyway, thank God I'm not you.' And I'm smiling back as if this is the most fun reunion party I could ever have imagined, and I'm thinking I'm glad I didn't just arrive in a BMW with a personalised number plate and spend my Sunday mornings talking crap and jumping the queue at the deli. But I'm also glad that they didn't see me arrive in Grandma Yes!?!'s old Maxi, and I don't like myself for feeling this.

'Anyway, I'll see you after,' they say, the conversation drying like old breakfast cereal in a bowl. And I think, no you won't. I'm here for *Yiskor*, when the prayers for the dead are recited. Then Grandma Yes!?! and I will beat a retreat so we can enjoy our starvation headaches in peace. And I say, 'Yeah. Absolutely. Catch you later.' As I turn to look for Grandma, I see the unstoppable Edward Marcatta hobbling with the eagerness of a child towards the web of grandma's bottle green cape, and at the centre of the web, I can see that Grandma, her eyes as black widow as can be, is allowing her tunnel vision to block out the cricket like approach. 'Good *Yom Tov Seelveeah*,' he says, and Grandma swirls round like a musical box ballerina gone mad and completely obliterates the little man with her cape.

'Oh God, who's in there?' she demands as if he had deliberately got himself caught in the fabric. 'Oh, it's you,' she says. I think he must have a masochistic fascination with her. Somehow, I don't think he will become my step-grandfather this side of all our deaths. And we climb slowly upstairs to the ladies gallery, and Grandma Yes!?! sits in the seat she has had for a hundred years, and I sit beside her in my mother's seat.

We stare at the faces of the women, and the hats framing them and comment on them until there are no more comments worth making, and then lapse into nothingness. Downstairs, the hubbub of men punctuate their conversations about football and how much the wives talk during the service, and trips abroad, with occasional bursts of prayer.

I sit back, and think what they all mean to me. These people. This place. We sit close to a window. It is heavily coloured with ninety year-old glass panes which the sun lights up in amethyst, emerald and the pale pearl of dried honesty leaves. This window is dedicated by the children of Solomon Auerbach who died in 1909 corresponding to the year 5634, and to his wife Leah, who died one year later. The thin, black lettering insists optimistically that their names shall never be forgotten.

Over the years, I have read these little facts dozens of times, and do so again now, while all around and below me the chanting of familiar song and the endless buzz of conversation in a more decipherable tongue cocoons me. I wonder whether the children of Solomon and Leah would be happy to know that a girl – well, that a 37-year-old woman – whose upbringing was designed to prepare her to be a moderately effective Jewess, and who regards herself as such, despite her failings where aisles and white dresses are concerned, is keeping their wish alive.

Though I have no idea what Solomon and Leah Auerbach looked like, what they did, how their personalities showed in their eyes, or where they lived, they are not forgotten as long as I sit here on the very rare occasions that I do.

The rabbi raps sharply on the oak podium like an irked school master. He does this every time the market-day-like hubbub reaches new decibel levels. Those not too engrossed in conversation quieten, and the service continues. I look at grandma, so old and elegant, and I notice that most of the women around her are old and elegant also. There's a smattering of young faces too, but not enough to carry this group into another generation as a crowd. And far below us, in the sea of white *tallasim*, the men are the same. A few young fathers, but only those whose own fathers, little, high-foreheaded and charismatic, and able to sing in the rousing, minor key which makes the service seem so special, are still standing next to them.

Old Edward Marcatta is sitting now, unable to remain on his ancient little legs. Across from us, old Millie Grodski who spends so much of her time pressing her fingers into gefilte fishballs at the fishmongers in Didsbury is standing erect in white gloves and an absurd yellow net hat with half a bird sticking out at the side of it. She is talking animatedly to a big, blancmangey woman with a small veil over her fat face, who has turned her hearing aid down to better ignore her.

'Look at Millie Grodski,' I say to grandma, and she says, 'The one sitting next to her that looks like a cuckoo is Herta Fox.' And somehow I feel safe and comfortable with the name, which I don't know, but I'm glad Grandma was able to recall it instantly.

I mouth 'hello' to Caroline, whose seat is at the other end from mine. In her tailored, cream linen-suit, collared and cuffed in fake astrakhan, and a coal-shovel hat in stiff black, she looks beautiful and from another generation, and possibly planet, from me. Darlings One and Two are rampaging, snotty-nosed and weeping and "creating" as my mother would call it, downstairs with their proud father, and looking at Caroline now, it is impossible to see her standing like a puppet with its strings cut in the sports hall as she finds herself the last person to be picked for the rounders team over twenty years ago. She is standing with her own grandmother, Hettie Oppenheim, who I haven't seen for years. One day, Caroline will become Hettie Oppenheim. She has already begun the process. But who will I become? Grandma Yes?!? I suppose.

The congregation becomes silent and begins to creak to sitting position. At this part of the service, we remember those relatives who are no longer with us. Old Rabbi Landau used to read out the names of congregants past and it was the one bit of the service which always stuck in my mind. Not spiritual, but real. Genuinely summoning past eras to mind. Old Landau read them in the most bizarre manner, like teutonic football results, always putting the wrong stress on identical surnames so it sounded as if they were on different teams instead of being spouses.

Maurice Silberman, Riva *Silberman*.

Adolfus Katzenburg, *Amelia* Levenson.

That sort of thing.

Nowadays, it is read by a strong, clear and sensible voice from among the men grouped near the ark. The names wash over us, but I know that somewhere in this vast room, either in the ladies galleries or downstairs amongst the men, each name is evoking memories for someone. Just for that moment, read out in front of all these people, each name becomes alive again, and I feel such an intense surge of pride on behalf of those people who recognise the name – who are the parents or children or siblings of those names, it makes me want to cry, and I wonder if I am perhaps capable of spiritual feeling after all, or just to human response. It is the one and only time in the service when no-one speaks about anyone else's hat. No-one refers to football or business or the trouble they had with the hotel in Netanya. There is respect at that moment.

And then, as the last name is mentioned, everyone prepares for the unofficial exodus. *Yom Kippur* is far too long a day for many to spend in synagogue without a break. And we stand up, preparing to disappear until the end of the service.

'I'm not coming again,' says Grandma Yes!?! She says this every year. It's almost part of the service itself. Comforting. And as we move, very slowly, in the thick-set jam of women making their way to the stairway, I look down at the men, sliding their *tallasim* off their shoulders into little velvet bags. In their jostle to escape they look like a flock of birds about to migrate. I am about to look back to help Grandma who is lurching without much vision towards the exit, when I'm sure I catch the face of one of the men. It is a violently beautiful face. Perhaps I have been thinking about him too much, but in that moment before a navy pill-box with a cancerous pompom on it blocks my view, I feel sure that the face is Blue's.

* * *

'Lynton', off Spath Road, Didsbury, M20.

Bloody police seem to think they stand a better chance of catching my burglars if they're armed with my date of birth. They said they'd come round, but they didn't seem very impressed that nothing had been taken.

'We'll bring a leaflet all about victim-support counselling,' he promises.

'Do you have a leaflet about victim-support selling of houses?' I ask, and he laughs and thinks he's got a game old duck here. I've got a blinding headache. I don't know why I go. I don't pray. When they were little, I used to tell the girls to read the English – and then one year Suzie said, 'But grandma, the Hebrew makes more sense coz you can't read it.' Anyway, it's been lovely having my favourite granddaughter with me today. I'm going to sleep now. I'll break my fast with a dispirin in an hour or so. I'm just exhausted. I'll speak to you later.

* * *

Sidney Fleiss Memorial Home. Room 6.

I want to call Sylvia, who will be back home with a headache by now, but I am not alone and it is all getting rather wearisome. I rather feel I should tell her about what I heard at Bumbles. I feel quite sure of it. The day has all rather gone down-hill since Rebwar brought me back after lunch. Mr. Sappirstein, with whom I was locked in the lift not long ago, was sitting in my chair in my room when I was brought back. It was quite a shock seeing him there, reading a letter from Howard to me.

'Mr. Sappirstein. You are in my chair!' I declared. I felt rather foolish. Deaf Bear, Disabled Bear and Demented Bear. And Goldilocks is at home with a headache.

'But this is my chair,' insisted Mr. Sappirstein, who once spear-headed cerebrovascular disease in Manchester, and whose father – I've probably told you already – came from Konigsberg.

'Look', he went on, quite indignant to be disturbed in this manner. 'This is my book. Jeremy Paxman. That proves it.' And indeed, he is brandishing my own copy of Jeremy Paxman's book and I seem to have no more claim to it than Penny who has wheeled me in.

'That letter is to me,' I say gently. It is from Howard.

'Yes,' concedes Mr. Sappirstein even more placatingly. 'He says he is having a lovely time at camp, but that you haven't yet sent the postal order you promised.' And that did it. I never cry, and I am not going to now. How dare whatever passes for God make Mr. Sappirstein so hopeless that he sees fit to read letters from my son sent fifty years ago and kept by me. I am perfectly aware that I forgot about the postal order. I was sure I had sent it, but had not. And now I must try and forgive Mr. Sappirstein, when he does not require forgiveness as he has done nothing wrong. And I have. And I must have Sylvia come and live here before I become another Mr. Sappirstein and open other people's old post and think it my own.

Penny leads him from my chair. She is really very good. She does not attempt to tell him he is in the wrong room. Instead, she says that he has been moved to another room because the views are better, and he seems happy with this. I call Sylvia on the speed dial thing.

'Hello dear. Are you fasting well?'

'Oh Rhona! Actually, my head's in bloody agony. I told you I was broken into?'

'Yes you did, several times dear, and I heard the most interesting thing over lunch in the...' And I know from the great tragic sigh which follows, that Sylvia is not going to be receptive to what I want to tell her.

'Actually, I haven't had lunch and I really can't talk at the moment. I'll speak to you later. I need to sleep now.' And she is gone. Oh dear. She thinks I was insisting on telling her I have eaten on the fast day. But that isn't it at all. Sylvia has a granddaughter who works at the estate agents, but I don't know her. Besides, she won't be working today. I wish I had found out what they were talking about at that table in Bumbles. It really is most intriguing, and I can tell no-one. They will all think I am goading about eating on a fast day.

* * *

105

Seventeen

I am standing outside Maplehurst, and it is seven and a half minutes before Blue is due. I don't remember the last time I felt this excited. Better than his shock appearances in the fishmongers or bursting through the office door when I had chocolate stuck to the roof of my mouth. It's the liquid gurgle of anticipation. And it's better than a date, too. He's coming for a reason other than me. To photograph this house. No pressure to appear at the top of a sweeping staircase, an aura of white chiffon billowing from wherever it is chiffon should billow. Not that I've given it no thought. I picked up this suit in Affleck's Palace for fifty quid. It's genuine '40s, in Prussian blue wool with a boxy reefer jacket and really well-cut skirt.

OK, OK. I didn't actually know what a reefer jacket was either, but the girl in the antique clothes stall is a real war-era freak and looks like she's permanently about to burst into song, and she knows this sort of thing. She wanted to coerce me into a snood and a pair of tie-up brogues which looked like shoes for club feet, but I limited myself to the suit.

Mum said it was typical of me to choose an era of make-do-and-mend to make my hallmark style, and suggested I complete the look with grandma's peculiar old fox thing with its claws that used to frighten me as a child. But I haven't picked anything as a style as such. I think that's terribly limiting. I imagine the girl at Affleck's Palace goes the whole hog and lives in a time warp, but I just thought that it might appeal to Blue – endangered fashions, images of eras on the brink of being forgotten. Well, maybe it won't, but it's worth a try and the shape is actually pretty flattering, though I whisper so to myself.

As I was about to leave the office, Mr. Clegg asked where I was off to. When I told him, he said there was an offer in on the house from a developer.

'I mean we're still doing viewings of course, but these people are quite eager to get things moving.' It seemed a bit unlikely. The only diary entries for viewings on Maplehurst appear to have been cancelled, like the one from that South African couple.

'What do the developers want to do with it?' I asked.

'A sympathetic conversion,' said Mr. Clegg, his smile almost labrador this time.

'But it's in the conservation area. Won't they need permission? I mean the council won't let them turn it into flats. Not there, surely.' I feel a rush of frustration. Anger. I know just how Blue will feel. Mr. Clegg is only telling me because he thinks I've got a potential buyer.

'Oh, they'll need permission alright. And they'll need lots of tea with two sugars for the demo mob, but neither should prove a problem.' Mr. Clegg is looking distracted, as if he is miles away, reading some document. But it is a practised, unconvincing miles away. The sort of miles away that smacks of inches and complete awareness.

'I didn't know anyone was interested. I mean, it's been on the market a long time, hasn't it?' Mr. Clegg looks up, the labrador look evolving into well-fed alsation. 'Yeah. A long time. Too long. Owners want shut of it. Can't blame 'em.' Mr. Clegg's tie is too bright. His collar crisp as snow.

I think of the owner. Old Essie Shabalan who doesn't know if breakfast is something you eat or cuddle. Essie Shabalan who probably would be quite happy to see a skyscraper built on the site of her lovely old home that she shared with the recently late Joe. But then there is very little she would not be quite happy with. Those funny looking daughters might be behind it, I suppose, but they didn't strike me as the kind. Still, they've moved away from the area. Perhaps they don't care.

He's here. Striding down the road towards me. Pretending to be still too far away to have recognised me. Waiting to look up next door but one to where I'm standing and smiling that innocent-lech smile. And I feel so sensational, standing here looking like D-Day. And I say,

'You are fucking gorgeous. You know that? Of course you know that. The most magnificent man I've ever seen. How about heading back to my place, lifting that shirt – which is lovely by the way – over your broad shoulders and on past your very pretty head, while I undo that chunky belt and discover whether its a simple zip job, or whether I'll have to fiddle with buttons as I get you naked. Oh, and when you've come and gone, or come and come again, and I've spent the afternoon cheerfully coming myself, then we can get this house photographed and my world will be complete. Whaddaya say?'

And what I actually say is, 'Hello. Good to see you again. I'm afraid I've got some baddish news about this house,' and he says, 'Oh shit, can't we go in?' and I say, 'Oh yeah. We can. It's not that.' And I tell him about the developer's' offer and he responds in a way which mum would say means he obviously has a very poor vocabulary, and as so often, she would be wrong and would never know it.

'Where were you yesterday at about 1.30?' I ask, letting a smile play over my lips in what I hope comes across as playfully intriguing. I see again that moment when I looked down to where the men sit in *shul* and saw that beautiful face. And as he picks up his photographic equipment, and I open the stiff front door he says, 'It wa'n't me guv. Honist. I never killed no-one.' And I say, 'No, but really. Where were you?' and he says, 'Leeds. Headingley. A commission.' So. Looks like I was wrong. Of course I was wrong.

The house smells of an unopened packet of emptiness. Slightly stale emptiness. Blue begins photographing straight away, revelling in the abandoned charms of this huge old villa.

He lies on the black and white chequer-tiled hall floor. Focuses. Snaps. Crouches on the stairs, through the elaborate staircase spindles. Focuses. Snaps. Into the pantry and inside the wall-cupboards which are shaped with the same Ford Anglia slope as Caroline's heels. Focuses. Snaps. Me, looking at him through the leaded windows leading into the leaking conservatory which is full of browning ferns and a death-defying yucca.

'Beautiful,' he says, grinning at me, 'totally beautiful.' And I can't quite ask if the object of his desire is yours truly or rotting window frames.

Make sure he knows you're interested not just in him, but in what interests him. That was a quote from one of those women's magazines in the waiting room at Didsbury Medical Centre. The sort of article on finding/keeping/coping with a man, that I like to snort at, but can't resist returning to when I just can't bring myself to flick through *Amateur Gardening*, October 1994 or pre-death of Diana issues of *Hello!* one more time.

I am genuinely interested in what he's doing. His work is so exciting. So original. I'm not silly enough to start suggesting angles he might like. That's not showing interest in him. That's just bloody irritating. Instead, I opt for positioning myself where he has recently positioned himself to show I'm keen to see his pictures from his angle. Hopefully it looks a bit symbolic of trying to see life from his perspective. Anyway.

It's no mean feat straddling the bannisters in this skirt or crawling about in the cellars, trying not to disgrace myself by falling into the wash copper.

And yet with each undignified contortion I make in the name of showing my own interest in him, I'm not at all convinced that I am even remotely the object of his. I look at him now, standing with one foot on each side of the soap-green enamel bath, watching in awe as he clicks away at the Deco chrome taps gushing water in front of the vast black and green glazed tiles. The water seems erotic despite coming out an unappetising brown. I can see his thigh muscles, framing the antiquated bathroom and his beautiful bum as he bends forward to reposition a prehistoric loofah which must once have rubbed against Joe Shabalan's now non-existent back. And I think of what Caroline had said about 'all the prettiest ones'.

I rack my brains, trying to think of some question I could ask – something I could say which would clarify for me. Something about the age of consent or Liza Minnelli or the Pet Shop Boys. But only the most cringe-worthy clichés bounce into my mind.

'So do you ever go out in the Village?' I ask, absently picking up the disconnected receiver of the bakelite 'phone in the bedroom.

'That's terrific. Keep it there,' he says, and I can't help enjoying the keen interest of the camera lens.

'Well, I go out pretty often I suppose. Didsbury's got so many pubs and bars – and "Jem & I's" eggs benedict on a morning...' He carries on working.

'No. I mean the Gay Village,' I say, and suddenly, despite the fact that all shades of sexuality head for Manchester's gay quarter nowadays, I feel I've made a statement far too bald. I feel the heat of crassness burning into my eyes.

'I'm not too keen on it at weekends,' I say as Blue pulls back an unpleasant Wilton carpet so he can shoot a bedroom fireplace without the swirling maroon and pinks of the ugly pattern. 'Too rowdy and straight,' I add, trying to neutralise my previous words, but succeeding only in making myself sound as if I want to tell him I'm a dyke.

'Oh there!' he says, as we head downstairs again and he refocuses the lens to take in a box of servants' bells through the lattice-work of a carpet beater he found on the back of the larder door. 'I'm not really into all that. Used to be pretty good, but those shrieking dolly daydreams in their tiny skirts and tottering heels are pretty scary. They're rougher than the blokes.'

I don't feel I've found any answers from this. Aren't men supposed to find all that bare flesh alluring? Then again, would I want him if he did? Oh dear. Yes and yes to both questions.

'That reefer jacket really suits you, you know,' he says, determined to confuse me more. He knows it's called a reefer jacket. Is that normal? It suits me. He finds me, dare I think it, attractive in it? But then again, he's opted not to mention the limpid poolness of my eyes nor my skin as soft as satin. He's gone for my outfit. That has to be a bad sign. I'm not looking for a sodding sibling.

'Brilliant!' he says half an hour later. 'Can I thank you with dinner? Would next Wednesday be okay?' And the way he looks at me as he asks it makes me feel not at all like his sister.

* * *

'Lynton', off Spath Road, Didsbury, M20.

'Hello? I'd like to speak to Mr. Dreggs. What? Well, Clegg, then. This is Sylvia Lowenstein.'

I don't want to get my granddaughter involved in a complaint. Don't want the Dreggs man to blame her for bringing a pain in the bum into his agency. But I've got to hurry them up.

'I'm afraid Mr. Clegg's in a meeting at the moment. Can I get him to call you back? I don't think he'll be too long.'

'Who am I speaking to?' I ask. She tells me. Silly little girl's got one of those annoying voices like butter wouldn't bloody melt. There's probably a plastic ring in the nape of her neck which pulls out like a doll when she takes a call. 'Hi. My name's Charlene and I'm your friend but I never put you through.'

'Would you like to hold?'

'No. I'm not holding at peak rate. Please tell him to call me back.'

'And has Mr. Clegg got your number?'

I stare hard into the receiver and hope I'm transmitting a sense of my frustration.

'Well if he hasn't, it might explain why he hasn't used it once so far to make a single viewing appointment.' The girl is silent now. No-one's pulling the plastic ring in her neck.

'So he *has* got your number,' she persists after a few moments.

'Yes!' I hiss, and replace the 'phone. I sound angry. I feel angry. I don't sound scared. Looking around me, I see another bulb has gone in the hall light fitting. I can't climb up. The ceilings are too high. I don't sound scared, but I feel scared.

* * *

Sidney Fleiss Memorial Home. Room 6.

It is my birthday. I know this because Matron, who is new, has been in with best wishes and no bra. At least if she is wearing one, it's as unsupportive as Mrs. Solomons is currently finding her son.

'And how old are we today Mrs. Laski?' she asks cheerfully, tearing open the envelope of a large and lurid card from herself which I am sure she has only just licked closed.

'We are nine today,' I chirp. Sometimes I rather enjoy the presumption of madness. It will doubtless later be explained to Matron that I am not at all mad, but difficult, not to say devious, and that it's best to humour me and leave while I'm still speaking because otherwise one might never get to leave at all. It is unfair of me to toy with Matron like this, but it is difficult not to feel as if one is at school here, and what is school without playing up? Besides, as Matron rightly said, it is my birthday.

I share my birthday with Kitty Glass, but she escapes before the ritual humiliation of 'the birthday tea'. Kitty is dreadfully deaf, but otherwise the definition of sprightly. She always comes in on the morning of our birthdays to deliver a small gift – usually a piece of my favourite Caerphilly from the *Cheese Hamlet* in the village, and to taunt me with the fact that she will not be attending the tea. Instead, Kitty Glass will share the day with her boyfriend, a Roman Catholic lorry driver who, at sixty-eight, is some quarter of a century her junior.

'And many more of them!' she shouts, her voice like car tyres on a gravel drive. She has knocked, and I have called, 'Wait a minute I'm all undone,' as Siklunli was called away in the middle of buttoning my blouse, but deafness has rendered knocking rather pointless in Kitty's case.

111

'Ah Kitty! And a very happy birthday to you! It is ninety-three this time?' I ask and she shouts back, 'Yes, there'll be a horrible tea,' and I mouth 'ninety-three' again and she gets it this time and says what she delights in saying to everyone she meets nowadays, including first time visitors to other people in the home.

'Yes love, ninety-three, but I was good till I was forty-eight. A good girl I was. Made up for it since though!' and she launches into the gravelly guffaw which is familiar to everyone at the home and reminds me of my old Triumph Herald coupé not starting on a winter's morning.

'Yes dear. You've made yourself look like quite a prostitute since haven't you,' I say. I am not being unduly unkind. Something rather strange makes me enjoy saying such things. I say it in my usual tone and as I'm smiling charmingly throughout, so Kitty is quite happy and doesn't hear a word.

'That's right,' she says beaming. 'A good girl till I was forty eight.' I like Kitty. Nothing gets her down. Except this morning, she comes closer to me and her smile disappears for a moment. 'They've taken Neville off me,' she says. And I feel dreadful in my guilt.

Neville is an elderly snow white poodle belonging to the daughter of one of the inmates here, and Kitty was entrusted to look after him on the twice weekly visits. She would sit in the gardens outside my window, reading romantic fiction and smoking her cigarettes. Perhaps I should have said nothing, but poor little Neville standing by Kitty's handbag was quite grey by the time he'd been flicked with the ash from half a packet of Bensons. Kitty, riveted by the fate of the girl with the shimmering flaxen breasts and alabaster hair – or was it the other way round – of her novels, was quite unaware of course, but somebody had to tell the daughter. Ah well. She's getting her own back. Her boyfriend, Connor, (originates from County Wicklow, widowed, four sons and one daughter, lives in Stretford and has his own small haulage company and all his own teeth) is taking Kitty for a slap-up meal in Withington.

I, meanwhile, am fated to the birthday tea alone. The food is always lovely for these. Smoked salmon rolled up like cigars. Mushroom vol-au-vents with good crispy pastry tasting of butter. Even the potato salad seems less watery than usual. And there's always punch. Paper cups. Like a student party, except the overall effect doesn't really owe anything at all to the shindigs of our youth. The most embarrassing bit is the cake. Always six candles. Don't know why six. Somehow the six skinny little wax sticks in pink and white stripes like anorexic Brighton rock makes everyone concentrate on what age one has actually achieved. But everyone knows. It's a point of pride, in a rather silly way. It's brought into the most innocuous of conversations as if it were a career choice or a salary.

'Hello Mrs Koenig, how are we feeling today? Eighty-nine aren't we?' It's indecent. Of course, there's worse. The little auxiliaries working while they wait to get married insisting they can't believe we're not turning twenty one. We are treated like old dears, which of course we are, except we are the matriarchs. Meant for better. We married sensibly – for love, I suppose, but sighted love, not blind. We were to share useful, productive lives and have each other. But when death did us part, it's as though our lifetimes of commanding respect are wiped clean like an old criminal record, and the presumption that we were always fools takes over. Most frustrating, inequitable and not at all acceptable.

Neither the Chocolate Brownie nor the Victoria Sponge are having breakfast in the dining room today. They have both opted to eat in their rooms, which means I am alone at my table. This is indeed a birthday treat. Across the room, Essie Shabalan sits eating cereal in stoical silence. After I am wheeled in and Matthew (a little effeminate and not very bright) has disappeared to find my orange juice, Essie looks up at me and her face creases into a wide smile of enormous warmth. And I'm just thinking Poor Essie. Well, at least whatever is in her mushed up mind, it must be making her happy. She calls out, 'Rhona. Happy Birthday! I send you a kiss from me and one from Joe!' And I smile back, shocked at the thought of a kiss from Joe after all these years, and for a moment I can almost feel his silky moustache when he first kissed me with the late afternoon light shining darkly onto the chequered hallway of Maplehurst.

'You know he's died, don't you?' says Essie. Then she cranes her head towards me and whispers loudly through the otherwise empty room, 'I miss him dreadfully. I never knew how awful it could be, but I try and put a brave face on it for the girls.' And then she returns to her branflakes and I am left troubled by the notion that Essie Shabalan is not always shielded by dementia.

When I return to my room, I dial 1.4.7.1. just to see. And it is! Howard's number in Hemel Hempstead is read out, followed by the time of the call. Of course I know I am being foolish and unrealistic in being so pleased to hear this number. If anything, I should feel concerned, but it is so wonderful to know that that number has just dialled mine. I press '3' on the telephone with its big, easy-to-use key pad, to return the call.

'Hello Ma,' says Elaine. 'I just wanted to wish you Happy Birthday.' As this is the first time Elaine has ever called on my birthday except once to call me a manipulative bitch because the week before I'd asked Howard if he was happy with his life, I am not certain how to respond.

'How kind,' I say.

'Well, I'm sure you must have lots on today, so I won't keep you,' says Elaine through what I remember as thin lips, 'only I was reading an article in the F.T., I think it was, about pets and, you know, I just thought if you do want to consider one, well...' Elaine, who is, or was, pretty in her own, cold way wonders how best to put it. And I can sympathise with her. The role of concerned and loving daughter-in-law must be quite a trauma for her to pull off. Still, I will not assist her.

'Yes dear?'

'Well, it's just if you are at all interested, well, you know what they say "a shroud has no pockets" and all that.'

'But do you think they're such a good idea?' I ask, allowing her to battle on a little further. It appears she does.

'But I'm not sure the Sidney Fleiss would approve dear,' I say, and Elaine snorts and asks what on earth it has to do with them.

'Well, they need feeding and if they aren't house-trained they can be...'

'I'm talking about Potentially Exempt Transfers. P.E.T.S not pets!' she splurts out, and she has put a laugh into her voice because she thinks that will make it more socially acceptable than actually shouting at me.

Of course, I know perfectly well what she's talking about, but I have a better relationship with the Inspector of Taxes than I have with Elaine. Still, I should like to leave something to my grandson. It is so long since I have seen him, and he is certainly well past the age where his mother's antipathy towards me should be allowed as a reason for his continued non-appearance, but then he has been poisoned against me for so many of his formative years. I do not know him, but he is the one who will pass down my genes, if that can be classed as something to be encouraged. Elaine and I do not mention Howard at all. Both of us know better than to do that. So I say,

'I have considered my arrangements Elaine dear. You need not worry yourself about that. And how is my grandson doing now?' I do not use his name. It was one of Elaine's many unanimous choices which Howard, as with so many things, allowed to become considered as shared.

And Elaine says, 'Oh Blue's fine. Actually, he's moved north again.' And I know from her tone he must have returned here to his native city, but I will not ask.

* * *

Eighteen

It's Wednesday afternoon. I've spent the first half of my lunch hour idling around Didsbury's arty decor boutiques and my mind is full of dull steel and velvet, burr walnut and perspex and the six hours which spread like melting cheese before I am due at Blue's flat. This is a proper date, and I want to take something as a gift. Not a bottle. Not chocolates. The smooth, purplish tulipwood bookends are pretty gorgeous, but they're priced as wedding gifts. I begin to loathe all the flimsy femininity of everything in this last shop. There's a flight of plate glass shelves running to the ceiling, and all suspended by threads of silvery metal with little halogen bulbs spotlighting frail little monstrosities of feathers and crystal and tiny hearts painted in 22-carat gold onto papier-mâché figures, while an office fan causes a spray of hateful chimes to tinkle like cows coming home. I press lightly on one of the shelves, and it shudders slightly, the whole structure provoking images of cathartic vandalism.

'Oh thank God you've arrived – the twee-count in this place is making my nose bleed,' I say as Caroline appears at the door.

'I thought Didsbury was a bolt-hole from all that. I thought it was only people like me who swoon at sequinned hammocks made by prostitute lepers in Bogota,' she says, absently picking up a pyramid-shaped candle with gold stars painted on it.

'Yeah well, with all the new developments round here, there's a big call to fill all those new window sills,' I say and we wander out.

'Oh look,' says Caroline. 'This one's open till nine o'clock. Such a godsend if you need to pop out for that emergency cherub'.

* * *

We lunch in Bumbles. I know it is rather an old lady joint, but you can't beat the crumbles and custard, and it has begun to rain long, cold needles of water and somehow rain splashes are much more fun in a cosy old tearoom with steamed up windows and cakes under glass domes than in the samey wine bars.

'I just wanted a foccacia-pesto-goat's-cheese-sweet chilli-marmalade free experience,' I say, and Caroline says, 'Fine by me.'

And I ask her what she thinks it might be with Blue. If she'd meant what she said that he must be gay.

'Well, it's a bit hard to give an accurate diagnosis without ever having met the patient,' she begins, fondling her mobile phone inside her bag. I know she's itching to call home and check on Placenta (she's from Tenerife and this is the nearest Caroline has got to mastering her name). The Big Pink Finn, as predicted, is no more.

'Don't even think about it,' I warn her. 'I'm quite sure Placenta will have everything under control.' Caroline smiles. 'I know, you're right,' she says, which means she'll call home, but not for another forty or so seconds.

'Maybe you've just read him all wrong. Perhaps he's wild about you but he's shy. I think we've got men all wrong most of the time. I mean take Elliot. If I make a phone call to anyone – even to check if kitchen tiles we ordered five hundred years ago have finally made it from darkest Nantwich, he sulks. He'll get jealous if I'm not silently sitting there watching him watching the football. But when he swans off to the far east where you get naked girls with your chips, does he call his pregnant wife to see if he's become the father of triplets in his absence? He does not.'

'I know,' I say, wondering if I do. 'But you're married to him. You've learnt each other. At least a bit. You must have done. I just don't know with Blue. I mean, I almost want to ask him.'

'Ask him what?' asks Caroline, 'You mean if he's gay? Probably not a marvellous action plan. I mean I know it'd be a compliment to his artistic prowess, but if he is, you're on a hiding to nothing anyway. If he isn't, the suggestion's unlikely to bust his confidence-ometer. Hello? Hello? Yes? Pla...it's me. Caroline. Is everything...? Everything is. Wonderful. You're a marvel. Now do help yourself to the rest of the *tarte citronne*. What? The whole of it? But it was meant to feed eight – have they been sick? Oh dear. Well don't worry. There's some stuff that'll get it off in the... Oh, you have. OK. Well. I'll be home in an hour.'

I don't know how she did it, but Caroline somehow managed to reach for her mobile under the clothed table and speed dial Placenta for an update as if the phone were a knife left carelessly by a madman. Vomit induced by the stuffing down of multiple slices of M&S's luxury lemon tart into the darlings' juvenile throats is not, to Caroline, anything like as problematic as a moment's ducking in the bath. For the moment, at least, Placenta will not be going the same way as the Big Pink Finn.

'But didn't you always know that Elliot was interested in you?' I ask, visualising his comfortably unenticing features, and wondering how she had ever fancied him.

'One does not have to guess Elliot's intentions. He verbalises them into a dictaphone and I receive a memo from his secretary with his proposal for a further date. My breasts being first item on the agenda at our next extraordinary general meeting, climax relegated to any other business. Post-coital conversation is, needless to say, with apologies for absence.'

'You're not serious – he actually writes to you?'

'Well, no. I jest. But Mr. Intriguingly Mysterious, Elliot is not. You can't get much more straightforward than my husband.'

'Well Blue is hardly a definition of forward. I'm just hoping he is straight.'

'It's possible it's something else altogether,' says Caroline cheerfully. 'I mean, after Adam was born, Elliot thought that I should be given at least twenty minutes before I should be gagging for him to thrust forth inside me. I couldn't explain that an episiotomy is not an erotic stimulant. I had delighted in the idea that my industrial weight bra all sogged through with milk and a uterus the size of the Blackwall Tunnel was Mother Nature's way of saying that Elliot's ardour would have to wait. That while his call is important to her, his erection is in a queue and would be attended to as soon as some semblance of sex drive became available. Not so Elliot. Did the vision of me relieving pressure on my perineum with Habitat scatter cushions under my bum take his desire off simmer? It did not. I mean how can anyone be turned on by someone else's perineum after it's been in a brawl? I didn't even know what a perineum was until the midwife charmingly referred to my 'tender lower part'. Elliot seemed to find the whole thing utterly tantalising.' Caroline pats around her mouth with a paper napkin.

'Well, maybe cold chips and yesterday's lasagne looks good when you're starving,' I say, and immediately can't believe I have. 'I mean, maybe he just wanted to have...' Caroline laughs (fortunately).

'Yesterday's lasagne,' she repeats, 'Yes, well, I've been called many things...' We munch on, Caroline happily relating her antipathy towards sex after the birth of the recently vomiting Adam, and me

118

pretending that ignorance of such things has been a life choice of which I'm quietly proud. I'm actually envying her her tender perineum (whatever it is), and envying even more all the awfulnesses which I have so far been spared.

'Are you seriously trying to convince me that Blue not being interested is all for the best because at least it guarantees my bras will always stay dry?' I ask. Caroline says no, she is not saying this. Just that she could not believe Elliot was so raring to go while he could not believe that she was not bubbling with desire when he was, surely, as gorgeous as ever.

'But at least you had a reason. I mean, if he'd given it one point four seconds of thought, he'd have known why you wanted a Terry's Orange rather than him inside you.'

'Yes, that's true,' says Caroline, who has zipped a smile on for the waitress and is mouthing for the bill. 'But it doesn't explain why three months later when I thought that I would, after all, rather have sex than die, Elliot seemed less than ecstatic.

'I mean we'd had the battle about whether we'd feel worse with Adam eyeballing us from his cot, or whether we should try and do the deed with him as far away as possible at the other end of the house and risk him choking to death while we tried to remember what pleasure was. Anyway, *Your Baby And You* magazine said I should get re-acquainted with Elliot. But shaking your husband awake after the two a.m. feed and demanding to be 'reintroduced as his lover' left him as lukewarm as the yoghurt-scented sheets.

'You never said you were having problems,' I say, feeling that perhaps I am branded on my forehead with the sign of the dry bra, and am consequently not worth confiding in.

'Well, there wasn't much to say about it really. I mean it was difficult not to sympathise with him in a way. There I was doing everything *Your Baby and You* suggested, trying to eradicate the image of myself waddling about in the most humiliating article of clothing known to womankind – the pregnancy jean – and rediscover 'where I feel good'. You're supposed to be able to do that with your own fingers and a mirror, which I suspect only works if you're not quite right in the head. Anyway, Elliot's answer to my re-acquaintance exercises was to fall into knackered sleep.'

We stand up, and wend our way out of Bumbles. In the corner by the window, I see a couple eating lime curd cake and feel as if I know them. It is not until we are outside that I remember that they are the South African Carrs, who had been searching for their "ah-deel" house and had so liked the "blick end whart" tiled hall at Maplehurst. I'm intrigued to go back inside and ask them if they've found somewhere they like more, but perhaps that would be an odd thing to do. Besides, Caroline is taking her leave.

'I've got to go to the Sidney Fleiss and calm Grandma down. She's had another run in with Professor Muck — I think I've told you about her. Grandma's always going on about how awful she is. I'd love to meet her — probably will now — she's the woman she sits with for dinner. Something to do with preferring Outer Mongolia to Emmerdale. Do I need to break up a geriatric punch-up when I should be making myself stunning for a dinner date? I do not.'

'What dinner date?' I ask. Surely *Your Baby And You* hasn't recommended rebranding the mashed up mess which Placenta presents to all members of Caroline's family as a dinner date just to fool Elliot into believing he's special.

'Well, let's just say that while some may be eating out at restaurants nowadays, others can find that yesterday's lasagne, brightened with some fresh herbs and served up in the dark, can be just the trick.'

'Caro..., what on earth are you...?' But Caroline is swinging her legs into the Saab and in the darkness of the prematurely aging afternoon, her face is radiating irresponsibility of a kind I have never seen before in her. 'Have a lovely time tonight,' she calls through the opened window.

* * *

Sidney Fleiss Memorial Home. Room 6.

'Ah Sylvia! What a delightful surprise! And you have come at the most perfect moment.'

I cannot tell Sylvia why the moment is so splendid. Cannot reveal that I have just sent Siklunli off to the letterbox with a note of apology to the Chocolate Brownie. Yes, of course, I am perfectly aware I will see Hettie at dinner at a distance of just two plates of chopped fried fish, but we are no longer on speaking terms. I have been reduced to slowly scrawling a missive on one of the seven writing blocks I have on my desk. My fault entirely that I have so many. On the basis that no-one ever quite listens, I ask everyone with working legs if they would be kind enough to pop to Inmans, the stationers on Lapwing Lane, for paper, New Year Cards and gift chocolates. People must be listening when appearing quite asleep, as I have ended up quite weighed down beneath seven lots of everything.

I was quite unaware she had taken offence to a perfectly innocuous remark I made on Monday, but I did notice the zigzag vein at her temple was rather more pronounced than usual. Always a sign that the world has failed to smile while it was putting her first.

And then this morning, a letter on Hettie's old stationery with the address crossed out, to say she was 'very angry' at my 'attempts to humiliate her' in front of Maurice Gottlieb, who moved in here two months ago and still drives his old Daimler and is terribly popular with the bridge players.

It is all over nothing, as everything always is, but meal times promise to be even less pleasant than usual. I held what I could of my hands up and offered a 'mea culpa', but she replied rather oddly that she never drinks tea at that time in the evening. Anyway, it shall be a pleasure to tell Sylvia about it and have a real friend on my side. I must remember to tell Sylvia what I heard in Bumbles about her house. I think it all sounds very strange, and she should know about it.

'It's all terribly silly, but it all began because Siklunli was telling me about life in Mongolia, where her sister (two years older, harelip, but terribly clever according to Siklunli who is herself training in midwifery) – oh dear, where was I holding, as they say in synagogue – ah yes, where her sister lives.' I begin to relate this, and think how lovely it is to have Sylvia here. Someone who knows who I am. Someone who can look at me, and instantly see a woman who can be a real friend and who has feelings quite as strong as anyone else's, but was brought up not to show them and now lives where nobody's looking anyway.

'Well, Siklunli said her sister had sent a video recording about Mongolian culture, and asked if I would like to see it, as I had shown interest, and I asked Maurice Gottlieb, who is quite alone in the Sidney Fleiss in being able to work the video recorder, if we might watch it. I thought he might rather enjoy a brief interlude from re-runs of *African Queen* which matron has latched onto as a godsend for those in the nursing wing. She is quite adamant that the terribly sad moaning among the most far gone quietens perceptively whenever Katherine Hepburn appears. The Victoria Sponge likes to say that I'm rather keen on Maurice, (eighty-five, twice widowed, once divorced with hardening arteries and a penthouse in Bournemouth) which isn't true at all. He was a rather dashing young man in his tennis whites, and he still thinks of himself as rather the thing in his Tootal cravat, but that was a terribly long time ago. Ah well.

'And would you two ladies like to join our soirée,' he asked Hettie and Herta, with the same unawareness that allowed him to choose a wine-coloured shirt with an orange and tan tie.

'So I simply said that no, Hettie and Herta preferred to watch Emmerdale Farm. I thought I was diffusing an awkward situation as it can't be easy to admit to choosing a soap opera repeat over a unique recording of life in an unknown culture. Besides, they had only just been saying how much they wanted to catch the latest episode. Somebody or other (one can never tell with Herta as she will insist on keeping her hand in front of her mouth when speaking), is having a torrid affair – which is about to be exposed.

'Well! Hettie and Herta really did out-do themselves. Neither, it seems, care two hoots about Emmerdale, despite the two of them hot-footing it back to their rooms and missing dessert whenever we're running late and Hettie's missive to me this morning makes it quite clear that nothing could excite either of them more than learning about where 'Sick Loony's' sister lives, and they had said as much to her. Siklunli didn't know what I was talking about when I asked her about that, but I couldn't dare suggest they were lying when I saw them next. Oh Sylvia, you can't imagine two people less likely to be interested, but apparently, it was 'not my place' to decide for them what they might like to see. I do see their point, and have written this in my apology.'

I stop for a moment, to gauge Sylvia's reaction. In an ideal world, she would be my saviour and would storm out and bang Hettie and Herta's heads together and they would be meek and charming to me until the day we finally fall to bits over our lockshen puddings. But the world falls rather short of that, and she says, 'Oh life's too bloody short for all this'.

She is wearing lots of amber and jade beads and looks rather wonderful as she stares at me with those tragic silent screen goddess eyes. I do not admit to her that I have spoken with Maurice, and told him that Hettie and Herta would so appreciate it if he asked them again. I would like to think of them sitting through the entire two and three quarter hours of it, as I ended up doing quite alone last night, from the economic output graphs from 1978 to 1991 to the section about subsoil quality and its implications for farming. It was most informative, if tedious beyond comprehension.

'Actually,' Sylvia says to me now, 'I've been thinking about my will.'

She has, in her way, been listening to me, and while I know quite well that she only did so in order for her to begin her own piece, I can quite understand it. Why should she be interested in our nonsenses? I wouldn't be. But the tiniest things become the pivots of our lives here. I think again how unfair I am being encouraging her to leave her house for this, but she would have more freedom, and after the break-in she has not felt secure at all. I try and address myself to her concerns, which is about which of her two granddaughters to give which ring.

'One of them I never put on, and the other one won't come off, but I want to tell the girls which they're getting instead of waiting until I'm dead – and after the break-in, I thought I should do it before I haven't got anything to give.'

'Nothing was actually stolen,' I point out, but Sylvia has built that sad little episode into the great train robbery, and I rather think she feels things were indeed taken.

'My engagement solitaire's a better stone, and it's prettier than the cluster, which was Louis's mother's, but that's probably worth more,' she says. 'And actually, I was going to give it to Suzi, because she's always admired it, but when I went there last time, she said how pretty it looked, and I had this horrible thought that she's admired it almost every time I've seen her recently, and that she must be angling for it.'

'Oh Sylvia, I'm sure you're reading too much into it,' I say, though I'd be inclined to agree, and am impressed that she has seen this.

'Do you think so. Do you think I'm being silly?'

And I say yes, I think she's being silly, which is shortchanging her, but perhaps that is better than sowing the seeds of sadness that reality tends to reap. 'And of course she is married,' says Sylvia.

'But your other granddaughter may marry. And even if she doesn't, she's the one with whom you're closer aren't you? And marriage is no guarantee of continuity. Can be quite the opposite. I know we must all pretend we have no favourites, but we always do. One can only avoid it

123

by having only one, and of course there are drawbacks there too.'

I am about to amuse Sylvia with Elaine's telephone call about pets, but before I do, Sylvia says, 'Actually, she's very keen on someone at the moment. They're having dinner together tonight. Not Jewish, but she's quite smitten, and actually, I think there's more to life than picking the same. It's different for young people now.'

And I know that Sylvia does not believe what she's saying. Perhaps she is being kind to me, because Howard married out, but more likely she isn't giving me a second thought and is preparing to be the all embracing grandmother-in-law who will contrast so prettily with her daughter Shirley, who will be as sad as I suppose I was when Howard brought Elaine home.

We bluff – to others and ourselves. So eager to appear understanding and liberal to our young, in order not to push them further away, we feign happiness at all cost (and I wouldn't admit this to anyone except you, reading this). I think now of my friends, the Didsbury and Withington friends, who kept their culture around them like a perfume. Intangible, filling their homes with its invisible vapour, a sweet, evocative smell like warm marzipan which, in the days when we all visited each other for suppers or for coffee and cake, or book readings, was shared and known. Hardly any visible signs – a few old Jewish interest books, prayerbooks in living rooms piled to the ceiling with books on other cultures too. But piled with books all the same. We were modern, Jewish people, integrated into a thinking society. We were the way we were because we were Jewish, but we didn't want being Jewish to interfere with the way we had become.

But our children had not been born on the great strasses of Vienna. They did not remember the garbled Yiddish quests of our own grandparents to sit and to take more food. And some of our children held that vapour to their noses, and took it to their own homes. And some did not. Like mine. Like Sylvia's granddaughter is, perhaps, about to do. The vapour for her will be in her home when Sylvia visits her. And in her memories of her own childhood. And I suppose it will always intoxicate her, and bring a sting to the eye when she goes through her things in forty years' time, clearing out in order to move smaller. But sensitivity to a smell is not enough to imbue into another generation, and the best Sylvia can do now is to embrace the human and try and disregard the rest.

I am being shaken. 'Rhona, are you alright!?'

'Good gracious. I must have fallen asleep.' And I loathe myself for doing something so unspeakable.

'Don't be silly, you must be tired,' says Sylvia, and I can see her standing to leave, ready to lurch out and feel her way to her car. And I can't bear to think that I have had my favourite visitor, and have managed to drop off through it.

'Oh, don't go Sylvia. Please don't go.' And I can hear myself sounding quite pathetic. I catch myself. 'Sylvia, if you leave now, I shall have to sit with Hettie and Herta at dinner. If you stay, we shall eat well and have the company of Gita Kruk.' Sylvia does not know Gita, which is perhaps why she relents and I call for Penny to help me make my way to the dining room.

Gita Kruk, on whose jaw line one could file nails, has white hair lacquered to frost and a mouth permanently drawn downwards, making the creases on either side of her mouth like parrots facing each other. She has made a name for herself as an irascible old bat, though I find her highly intelligent, and when I have been summoned to her room for afternoon tea, I have gone with trepidation and pride at being asked. There is a glittering twinkle in her eye which I know to be her wicked humour, though Hettie Oppenheim says is the result of a detached retina.

'Rhona. Good evening,' she says, and she nods her sharp jaw over to me. 'Are you here for the simmering nightlife?' she asks Sylvia. 'Because appearances deceive. I only look like a beautiful blonde bombshell because they don't waste electricity on lights.' Sylvia twinkles back, I think rather energised by familiarity.

'Actually, I'm the striptease act who's on next,' she says, and Gita Kruk's face cracks open like the top of a ginger cake. 'I don't know if you believe in life after death,' she goes on to Sylvia, 'but what they served up yesterday would prove the doubters wrong – it was the most disgusting heap of shit I've ever seen. A julienne of inedibles on a bed of last week.'

I'm not quite sure that Gita, who is the only one amongst us to be called Miss, and who was once an architect in Berlin, is going to be quite the ambassador for the Sidney Fleiss I had hoped. I try and think what Gita and Sylvia have in common. I have always liked to forge links. You know, 'This is so-and-so who also collects Abyssinian butterflies'. Well, with Sylvia and Gita it is their resilience. Differently manifested, of course, but quite definitely there. It is what I admire in them so much.

'Mind you,' says Gita, who occasionally receives posies of flowers from an admirer known to us only as Lydia, 'It's still better than Muck-In-A-Truck that my friend gets.' I know that this is what Miss Kruk calls Meals on Wheels, which is rather unfair, but as she says, 'I've never been good at fair.'

After poached pears with a somewhat Bird's-inspired custard, Gita Kruk excuses herself and is wheeled off to read a heavy tome which I envy her being able to lift.

'I remember her from fifty years ago,' says Sylvia with one of her own special sighs. 'She worked as a secretary when she first came over. I remember meeting her for coffee at the Kardomah. She once told me how when the Germans ordered everyone to hand over all their silver, her father took the worst plate stuff to them, and then he took a little rowing boat thing into the middle of the river with the canteen of solid silver which they had had since the eighteenth century, and he and Gita threw it over so no piece of it would ever be placed in a Nazi mouth. I've never forgotten that. She was the eldest of five daughters, all murdered. Gita and that cutlery was all that survived the war. Still, she doesn't remember me.'

And I wonder if she does.

'Gita rather confounded the staff last week,' I say. I don't want Sylvia to think of sad times past, nor of being forgotten now.

'The inspectors had been called in. No-one seems quite sure from where they hailed, nor to where the results of their inspection would be returned, but it was enough for matron to panic over the state of the television room curtains. They had threatened to ask residents at random on their opinions, and on the day they were due, only the more charming and cheerful had been coaxed into likely positions rather in the way of people hoping to be picked on by market researchers.

The inspectors chose not to come that day, or the next and were, I rather think, no more than a shadowy menace by the time they did turn up. Oh Sylvia, it really was the silliest thing. First they picked on Essie Shabalan who had been briefly abandoned by the lift, but she told them she didn't live here and was visiting her own mother, who would have had to have been a hundred and thirty, but they accepted this. The only other soul apart from me – and I had been hidden away by the banana tree – was Gita Kruk. I saw a horrified matron scuttling behind the door to the cleaning materials storeroom in time to hear them ask Gita, 'And what do you think of the standard of food in the Home?' And Gita replied, 'Fantastic. Like a five star restaurant. Delicious.' And then she was asked about the standard of nursing care. 'Second to none,' said Gita. 'Like in a top class hotel.' So they went on with, 'And how about the facilities at the Home?' to which Gita smiled and said, 'It's like a luxury retreat – you could want for nothing. Everything laid on.'

Well Sylvia, really, Matron could hardly believe it, and I saw her wandering out after they had disappeared, and saying to Gita, 'Well Miss Kruk, you've really done us proud. I'm terribly grateful to you,' and Gita looked up at her with that tremendous jaw and said, 'Well, you didn't think I was going to tell them the truth, did you?'

* * *

And now, Sylvia has left. She has taken a taxi, as not only could she not find her car, but she suspected she would not find the road to drive it on in the dark. It is only once I am quite alone and in my bed, that I realise I have again not spoken to Sylvia about that conversation in Bumbles. I make a mental note to telephone her about that tomorrow. Ah yes. And to telephone my solicitor. Sylvia's dilemma about her will has made me focus on my own. As it stands now, it will not do at all. It is too much trouble to switch the light on and scribble my note, and so it sits in what remains of my mind. Like puréed soup in a colander, I'm afraid. There is no guarantee I shall retain any of it at all in the morning. I manage to turn my box of tissues upside down on my bedside table, hoping that their odd appearance will spark my memory tomorrow. From experience, I know the sight of the upturned box will remind me only that I had had an urgent thought the night before, but not what the thought contained. I go to sleep, thinking comforting and rather exhilarating thoughts of Rebwar's face when he hears from my solicitor how his life will change. How he will be able to follow his dreams.

* * *

Nineteen

Everything seems spiked with energy today. The air is cold in my throat, like custard poured down it straight from the 'fridge. It's Wednesday. Tonight, the only girl in the world has the world's first date with the most handsome prince. They are both clear-skinned, lovely seventeen year olds. Dinner will serve itself as they gaze into each others magical eyes. Silver cloche lids will whisk themselves from darkness to the candlelight. Invisible fingers will whisk them away, to exclamations as the girl – supple and glowing – spies brilliant fruit-hued ponds of buttery sauces like psychedelic moats around savoury castles of crisp devourability.

'Hello there. Anyone at home?' And Mr. Clegg is smiling quizzically at me, his eyes all border collie, as he cocks his head towards me and waves his hands in front of my face. I imagine in a mad moment, that if I were to throw the house particulars' stapler across the room, he'd scramble for it and return it to me in his mouth of lychee-white teeth.

'Sorry. I was miles away,' I say, feeling rather more irritated that my little morning fantasy has been shattered to shards by Mr. Clegg. I try and look sheepish, which is probably more appropriate than irked, and it occurs to me that it is strange that I should react myself as the very animal Mr. Clegg's border collie would seek to round up. And then my next thought – the fact that sheep really aren't sheepish at all, are they? is broken by Mr. Clegg saying,

'Well well! You're somewhere else altogether today aren't you! Are you ok?' And I insist that I am, and make out I've got a few things on my plate, and I have to concentrate hard not to start seeing plates of sensual food again. I'm not even hungry. Well. Not for food, and that's pretty unusual for me.

'I was wondering if you fancied a spot of lunch,' says Mr. Clegg, and I could swear he ran his tongue over his lip, or perhaps I'm just going mad.

'Only Trish's gone to see HouseBryte Homes as they're not happy with the opposition, I'm pleased to report, and Pam'll hold the fort. Anyway, we've hardly had a chance to talk properly yet, have we? I want to hear how happy you are.'

I smile, and twist a laugh out. The sort that's devoid of irony, I hope.

'How about Rouge?' he says. 'That's your sort of place, isn't it?' he goes on, cheerfully making me feel angry and isolated, and somehow a bit disliked.

Perhaps I'm overreacting, I tell myself. I mean, he's saying that he sees me as a relaxed French café kind of girl who likes to sip white wine and read the arts pages of the *Independent on Sunday* three days into the following week. No harm in that. But this is Mr. Clegg, and I can't help feeling what he really means is 'you think you're a cut above the rest, but you're nothing so special really. Just a regular chain-bar kind of girl too silly to resent paying over the odds for the perceived pleasures of listening to French crooners and checking your make-up in mirrors etched with advertisements for Gitanes'.

'Yeah. That'd be great,' I say. I wouldn't want to go with Mr.Clegg to "Jem & I". That's reserved for being with Blue. Mr. Clegg insists that, 'Please it's Andy'.

Maplehurst is more special territory with Blue. Even that bus stop outside the building site that was once Davrach. Mr. Clegg (no, sorry, it will never be Andy) tells me about his life. His dislikes and likes. Those things he likes to believe make him different from your average Mr. Smoothie. The to-be-absolutely-honests trickle like spring rain from his mouth of sharp, good teeth.

I am nodding and smiling like one of those felt dogs on the back window-ledges of cars, and occasionally I say something appropriate. He's learning nothing at all about me. Which is fine. His shirt is crisp and beautifully smooth, and I wonder if there is a Mrs. Clegg, and if it is she who makes sure the point of the iron slides all around the buttons and those cuffs, as strictly perfect as pillows on a hotel bed. Or perhaps someone comes in to do it. Or perhaps Mr. Clegg is a man who prides himself on doing these things himself, because, to be absolutely honest, he's not like the others.

'It's a bugger with the big houses at the moment,' he says, in between telling me how he isn't one for package holidays, him being much more an explore-on-your-own-and-sample-the-local culture sort of a guy.

'Is it?' I ask, genuinely surprised, as all the other agents in the village have signs saying, '*If you have a four to six bedroom house in Didsbury, we have buyers waiting*'.

'Oh yeah. I mean, those buyers waiting. Well, to be absolutely...'

'Yes,' I say quickly. 'Do, please be.'

'Yeah. Well. To be absolutely honest, what they mean is, the buyers of the big houses are waiting for the money to buy them. There's plenty of people like that. They want them, but they can't afford them.'

It seems a highly improbable argument, and as I imagine – purely out of intrigue, you understand – what Mr. Clegg would look like with the charcoal worsted suit trousers off, the tediously flamboyant tie flung over a chair and the blue and mauve striped boxers (ok. I'm guessing here) inside out on the carpet, I say, 'But you'd have thought people would at least want to come and see, like, my grandmother's house. I mean – even if they can't afford it. It's the sort of place you'd want to nosey round even if you'd no intention of buying it.'

Mr. Clegg stretches his legs out and recrosses them, and I think how like the birds of paradise in the big glass vase behind him he looks. The bright orange blooms, hard and taut, flirting with plump. Tapering, like Mr. Clegg's leather-soled Church's shoes, to neat, sharp points. And his body, stretched in the gym twice a week, pickled in beer nightly, oiled by football practice on a Saturday morning, and slumped in the office in between. A body toned and atoned, exercised and exorcised, muscled yet waiting patiently to go to seed.

'Well, we want to save your grandmother from all that,' he says smiling. 'I wouldn't feel right allowing people to just go round willy nilly. We like to do a sort of screening for our clients. Don't want her getting her hopes up with time-wasters.'

I don't know what it is, but something makes me feel very uncomfortable. I'd like Grandma to change agents really. I'm sure she'd be able to sell the house through someone else. A big, fat part of me hates the thought of Lynton leaving the family, but it would mean that Grandma could start properly living again – not always wanting to burst into tears and being frightened, but it would look so awkward now, to change agents. Where would that leave me?

'How is your grandmother?' says Mr. Clegg, his face a picture of concern. The very absurdity of his question, from a man who obviously couldn't care less – a man who hasn't actually ever met her, makes me feel cross.

'Better,' I say, 'Thanks'.

'Oh good. That's good,' says Mr. Clegg.

* * *

130

At last. I'm about to leave for Blue's, when the 'phone goes. I can never resist a phone ringing. Never understand how people can let them ring unanswered. I know who it will be. My mother. I know just what will happen.

'How are you?'

'Fine, thanks. How are you?'

'Oh. You know. Tired.'

'Oh. Right. Why?'

'Oh nothing. I don't need anything to happen for me to be tired nowadays. It's how I am.'

'Oh right. Well, actually, I'm on my way out.'

'That's nice.'

'Yes. It is. Hope so, anyway.'

'Anywhere special?'

'Yes. I mean. Well, yes. Out to dinner. Being cooked for.'

'Well, I won't keep you then. I wish someone would cook for me. You *are* lucky.'

'Why don't you get Dad to cook for you?'

'Oh, you know what he's like in the kitchen. I want someone to cook something I can eat.'

'Yes. Well, as I say, I'd better get going.'

'So who's the friend?'

'No-one you know. A photographer. A really good photographer.'

'That's nice. Well you have a good time.'

Pause, in which I hear a sigh, so silent it buzzes through the phoneline.

'I don't suppose you telephoned grandma did you?'

'No. Why? Should I have?'

'Oh, it doesn't matter. I'm sure she's fine. I know she is. I spoke to her just before.'

'Well, why should I need to speak to her?'

'You don't! Not at all. Just have a nice time. Are you going to a restaurant or is this your friend who cooks?'

'It's the one who cooks. What are you getting at about grandma? Isn't she well?'

'She's no worse than usual.'

I think of Caroline, and her conversations, or at least her acceptance of her mother's monologues, and how she would wait for a pause in the rambling to say, 'Mummy darling, it's been lovely, but I'm afraid I'm going to have to scream now', and her mother would say, 'Oh sweetheart, I so love having you to talk to. Your father's not interested in anything. I do wish you'd talk to me more.'

At least with Caroline, it was just a matter of her having to listen to lots of pointless wittering, but with my mother it's as if every 'phone call is a new chess move. Right now, she's moved her bishop and is waiting with that permanently furrowed brow of hers for me to do something silly with my rook. She's dying for me to beg her to tell me what the matter is with grandma. And if I were Caroline, I wouldn't deny her. I'd be straight with her, and ask her to tell me. But I'm not Caroline, and my mother isn't Caroline's mother, who wouldn't be playing these games in the first place. So I say, 'Right then, well if she's okay I'd better go then or I'll be late for my date.'

That did it.

'Well, maybe you'll remember to tell grandma all about your date tomorrow. Don't ring her when you get back tonight.'

'Who says I'm getting back tonight?'

'Well. If you do. She's going to bed early. She always does when she's got *yahrzeit*.'

So that was it! So eager to let me know my insensitivity, my mother has not reacted at all to the fact that I may not be coming back tonight. (Chance would be a thing of great fineness).

The anniversary of my gran'pi's death, when Grandma Yes!?! would light a memorial candle and put it on the piano in the drawing-room where, in the dark, the flame would flicker in its glass, casting burnt-butter light in erratic flickering shapes over her big, heavy furniture so it looked through the curtained window as if a black and white television had been left on all night. Still, there is no letting on now.

'Right, well I'm off then,' I say. Of course, I must now telephone grandma, but I let my tone run cold.

'Well enjoy yourself,' says my mother, not quite sure whether it would be best to bide her time and just move a pawn, or be more ambitious. Then; 'Perhaps you could call grandma from your friend's if you're not too busy,' she says. Check!

'Oh, I think I probably will be – too busy I mean,' I say. Checkmate!

'Hello Grandma?'

'Oh darling! how lovely to hear you!'

'Grandma, I just rang to wish you long life. How are you feeling?'

'Fine darling. I'm just fine. Oh it is lovely to hear you. Actually, gran'pi's *yahrzeit* isn't 'til tomorrow – but it's so lovely to hear you anyway.'

'Well. Just a quick hello, coz I'm out to dinner.'

'Oh! Well have a super time sweetheart, and don't forget what I told you – keep mysterious and you'll keep him.'

'I'll try,' I say. I want to call my mother back and tell her that *yahrzeit* isn't until tomorrow, but I suspect she knows, and I don't want her to know I bothered. Again the telephone goes. Mother again? My mood is fast losing its fresh, lifted feel, which is probably what she wants.

'Hello,' I say, with no question mark by it. I want her to know I can just tell from the ring who it is.

'Hi,' says Blue. 'Slight change of plan.'

* * *

'Lynton', off Spath Road, Didsbury, M20.

I'm just off to the Sidney Fleiss to see Rhona. She wants me to witness her will, which is like asking a leper for a hand, but she says I just need to sign my name. No need to see what's in it. I lock the front door and crunch my way down the drive to the Maxi which, now I'm approaching it, seems to be parked part over the lawn, which I don't remember doing. There's a figure at the end of the drive, just by the gatepost. It's too tall to be Edward Mar-Ratta, and I don't know if it's the sun which shines into my eyes through the copper beech, or if it's the tunnel vision which is like a fur hood all round my field of vision, but it's certainly a man.

'Yes!?!' I call out, leaning slightly on the car. My feet feel unsure now.

'Alrigh' love?' he calls back. It's a gruff, local accent. He's young. I don't know him.

'What do you want?' I demand. I could scream, but for what? He's just a young man on the pavement. But why has he stopped here?

'Can you see my friends arriving?' I ask. 'They're in a big car. A Zephyr.' Stupid, I know. I can't think of any makes of car at all. Only the last car Louis had before he died. I feel a bit sick.

'No. No Zephyr coming,' calls the young man. He's jeering at me, I can tell. 'No-one coming at all,' he adds.

'What do you want,' I ask again. Why can't Mrs. Thing from across the road choose now to twitch her curtains?

'Just admirin' your 'ouse,' says the man. He starts to walk towards me. I don't know what to do. My cape seems terribly heavy and I feel awfully blind. I feel for the lock and put the key into it, opening the Maxi's door.

'Thought you had people coming,' says the young man. He's quite close now. Not so young, perhaps. Blue jeans and black boots and a navy bomber jacket. I can hear myself repeating all this to the police, and then I wonder if someone else will have to repeat it to police in an attempt to find the killer. I think of Mrs. Oakway who's supposed to come on a Wednesday but changed it to a Tuesday, which is today, because her sister goes to the daycare centre on a Wednesday. Mrs. Oakway's cleaned for me for twenty years, but she's become unreliable. 'I don't suppose it matters which day you don't show up,' I'd said last week when she'd asked about changing days. Perhaps she's taken umbrage. If she were coming, she would be here now, telling me we're out of Pledge and making me feel secure.

'They're coming to see my husband,' I say. Defiant. Transparent.

'Don't think so,' says the man, quietly. 'Do you?' He's right up to me now. He's wearing a large, ugly signet ring with a green stone in it.

'Why don't you fuck off?' I ask. The sound is oddly shaped in my mouth. Feels like I imagine holding a gun the wrong way round, but the words come out clearly. The man makes an 'oo' face of fake shock. He, too, is leaning against the Maxi. 'I only wanted to tell you what a nice house you've got.'

'Well you've said it,' I say.

'You have. You have,' he says, and without another word, he swaggers back down the driveway. I twist into the driving seat. I put the key into the ignition, and put the bobble down on the door. I can feel hot wetness in my eyes, and it makes me angry. I'm angry too that I'm shaking. I don't feel I can drive. What will happen at the end of my driveway? Will he be there, smirking. I daren't go back into the house. It would be too easy for him there. He'd never let me get to the 'phone. Or perhaps he's just a bit mad. Perhaps he doesn't mean me harm. But he must. And how did he know I don't have a husband? I turn the key, and the familiar, catarrhal grinding starts up. Relief at that. A fresh gush of tears.

My hand in its leather glove pushes the gear-stick where I know reverse is, and I slide back, too fast, down my drive. The sound of the car, as always, is like a siamese cat in a brawl, until I hear the wing mirror crack and crunch as it hits the gatepost. I feel certain he will be at my window. That man. I press down harder on the accelerator, and wince as the whole side of the car scrapes across the gatepost. I'm crying now. So livid that after forty three years of not once ever touching them, I've now run the whole car down the side of them as if I'm a mad old thing who can't see her own nose. Yes, yes. I know. But it's not that. You know that.

There's nothing in the road, thank God, and I look at the stone pillars to survey the damage, expecting mustard paint on the white. But its as if the Maxi's in a monsoon. I switch the wipers to fast, but of course, that makes no difference. They squeak on the dry screen. I blink hard, and the windscreen wipers work.

I drive all the way to the Sidney Fleiss in first. The loudness, the grinding feels like punishment and it soothes me. I can't bear to think of Lynton being invaded with nobody there. I can't bear to think of Lynton being invaded with me there. I just don't want to think about Lynton at all.

* * *

Twenty

The slight change of plan means Blue and I are sitting in the smallest cinema at Cornerhouse. We are gasping for breath, as we had to run from the bus stop and we are a few minutes into the film already. A friend of Blue's apparently had two tickets to see this adaptation of an Edith Wharton novel and couldn't go at the last minute, and as a red onion *tarte tatin* had not tatined or whatever it is it was supposed to have done, Blue thought it would be better to take me to a movie, and then we'd get a Chinese afterwards.

I try and imagine how Caroline would react. She would have had none of it. First proper date should never be to somewhere where both parties are expected to sit facing in the same direction and unable to talk. And a Chinese meal isn't, perhaps, the French Restaurant at the Midland. But I'm not Caroline. I rather like the feeling of sitting so close to Blue, without having to think up bright and unusual things to say, with the knowledge that food is to come, and the happy unknown for afters.

'I've a good mind to write to Delia and ask her what she's playing at,' Blue whispers as his breathing evens out. 'I did everything she said. Everything. The bastard thing's been in the oven for ever. Have you ever known a cooking-retardant onion?'

'Shsh,' says a pinched-looking studenty face behind. And we sit in silence. Perhaps because I spend some time enjoying the idea that Blue has been endlessly cooking for me, even if it is just an onion with behavioural problems, I find that when I start to concentrate on the screen, I have no idea at all what the story of the film is about. It's very sumptuous. The camera ambles over endless interiors of velvets and silks and curly wurly silver ornaments like a visual take on a southern states drawl. I am vaguely aware that the action, such as it is, is taking place in turn of the twentieth century New York, and there's plenty on which the eye can feast, but my brain is really scraping at crumbs. I move slightly, very aware that my thigh is just against Blue's. Again, I hear Caroline say that he must be gay. Well, she hasn't said that, but here we are, with him at daggers drawn with Delia and this movie is hardly *Lethal Weapon Three*. He turns and throws a smile from his whole face. It's so beautiful and so tender. There's no justice if it isn't really meant for me.

I try and concentrate on what is being said by the characters. But they seem impossible to tell apart. Pretty women with half pheasants and a front room-worth of net curtains twisted into their hats coming out with bizarre lines to serene-looking young men – or is that the same man we just saw – and the men replying with what sound like *non sequiturs*. I feel such a fool. How am I going to be able to make a comment on it when it's over? I think of what Grandma said about being mysterious, but blind ignorance can rarely pass for mystery.

I debate nipping out with the pretence of the loo, and finding the Cornerhouse programme booklet which will at least give some sort of resumé, but it would be too much of a hassle from the front row of this tiny auditorium.

The words all seem simple enough, but nobody seems to follow through anything with a recognisable thought process.

Blue's profile is still. Pensive. For a moment, the two lead characters (well, the man and woman who appear the most often anyway) are discussing love, and it seems to make sense. Then the woman, who is squeezed into some exquisite satins, says, 'And if I agree to marry you, will you come with me to London?' and Blue leans across to me, and whispers, 'I thought he was her brother.' And I say, 'But she hasn't got a brother,' and he says, 'Yes she has. The one who inherited all the money,' and I say, 'That's not him.'

'Looks like him,' whispers Blue. Then, after a few more moments of silence, during which I feel relieved and happy that I was able to make a distinction between the two men, Blue leans into me again and says,

'Have you got the slightest idea what any of this is about?' And I begin to giggle and say, 'None at all,' and he begins to laugh, silently too.

'Isn't she already married to the fat funny-looking one?' he asks.

'No. That's her father.'

'Well, who's her lover then?' whispers Blue, and the most delicious quaking of hysterical rumblings come through his mouth.

'I think it's the tall one she keeps kissing,' I spurt, and a gush of laughter bursts out like wind.

The two of us are shaking, uncontrollable, and it is the most agonising and wonderful sensation of being completely out of control, and knowing that this is cementing a bond between us, and the duality of feeling something made firm by such helplessness is exquisite in its intensity.

From then on, for the rest of the film – we do not want to walk out as the visuals are alluring even if for the most part incomprehensible – we feel cocooned, protected by our inability to understand, I feel very close to Blue, and feel sure he does to me.

When it is over, and I feel a slight embarrassment that others in the cinema must have disapproved of our immature giggling, we head out into the city. The streets are full of young girls wearing bits of clothing like Tarzan's Jane and tottering on high heels, hugging their bare arms in the freezing night. The boys with them, in expensive shirts worn out, shout to each other with an aggressive camaraderie. I look at Blue, in his thick, loose woven sweater in emerald green, and I feel a gush of desire. A frustrated gush I need to stem.

We head off to Chinatown, and as we cross Oxford Street, he takes my arm, and I slip my hand down to his, feeling the cool skin of his fingers for a moment. He clutches me, but a Vauxhall full of young men has revved up close to us, and I cannot tell if it is an instinctive protective impulse, or anything to do with desire.

* * *

Sidney Fleiss Memorial Home. Room 6.

Sylvia looks perfectly dreadful. My solicitor, Merton Lewis, is here. Forty three, unmarried, converted to law from medicine at University College, London. His grandfather and Sylvia's father were brothers, but I believe there was a rift in about 1910 and the descendants have never quite been able to bridge it though none of them have the slightest idea what it was about.

When I told Merton that I had asked Sylvia to witness the will he said, 'Oh dear,' and when I told Sylvia that Merton would be here she said, 'Well, I'll sign my name and go.' Poor Merton. Arriving at the Sidney Fleiss is shark-infested waters. Everyone has their will lodged with him. He knows all the surprises and shocks to come.

I rather thought I would be able to make both of them laugh with this week's Jewish newspaper mistakes which Gita Kruk circles for me and has sent to my room. There are two that are quite perfect. A marriage announcement under Deaths and In Memoriam, and better still, a picture of Herta Fox with *sick racist graffiti artist* beneath it, while the photograph opposite, what they call a 'video still' of a vicious-looking young thug with a swastika tatooed on his neck is captioned *Herta Fox of Didsbury celebrates her ninetieth birthday with close friends.*

'And you're quite sure this is what you want?' Merton is asking as Sylvia sways in.

'Hello Sylvia,' he says, standing. I can't see her as she walks in behind my chair, but I'm pretty certain she's staring at him with what one can only call her rather unfortunate glower.

'Where do I need to sign?' Sylvia asks, 'Only I'm on my way to an appointment and I'm going to be late.'

'Just here, if you would,' says Merton. And I say nothing. Sylvia's appointment is anywhere that is not here, and that makes me a little sad as I would have liked to have talked with her.

'Merton dear, would you be terribly kind and ask in the kitchen if I might have some orange juice. I feel rather dry.' He is delighted to make his exit, and I can imagine him scurrying along the walls with his chin down, hoping not to be noticed by all those sharp beaks and dark eyes who have spent night after night rearranging their affairs in their heads, bequeathing less and less to those who didn't send cards on their birthdays or telephone to enquire after an operation, and more and more to those who did.

'Sylvia, I have made a list of things I have always liked very much, and would like you to choose something from it. None of these things are going in the will. They were going to, but then I thought I would be rather interested to know what choices everyone will make and I'd like you to have whatever you choose now. I have given you first choice as I've known you longest. If you hate everything on the list, I'll quite understand.'

And I hand Sylvia the piece of paper on which I have written in my spidery, impossible scrawl, the pieces I have from which she can choose. The will is underneath it, but that need not concern her. And I am rather glad that Penny (Patricia, not Penelope) has just knocked on the door and it is time to be taken in for lunch. I am pleased, as it means Sylvia need not feel on the spot about admitting she hates my little treasures, or perhaps she needs a few moments to choose between them while Penny wheels me round and fusses with my cardigan and my silly, dangling feet.

As Penny pushes me into the corridor, I see poor Merton, beaker of orange juice in hand, pinioned by Mrs. Grodsky who, as the world is being informed, now wishes to leave nothing, she repeats nothing, to her sister who didn't have the decency to ask how she was after her fall. Not once.

* * *

'Well, definitely the half duck,' says Blue, 'unless you don't like the pancake things.'

I want to admit to him that orgasms could only ever be seen as half-hearted substitutes for aromatic crispy duck pancakes smothered in intense, treacly dark hoisin sauce. But as we sit now, with the table of oriental teenagers playing on mobile 'phones behind us, and the rather more occidental strains of Diana Washington being *Mad about The Boy* wafting through the dim interior of the restaurant, I'm no longer so certain.

'I'm really sorry about not making you dinner myself at home,' he says as the waiter appears and starts slashing at the mahogany skin of the duck like a yob at a train seat.

'I don't usually use recipes, but I'd had the book for ages and it sounded promising. The onions are supposed to 'glisten with bejewelled beauty' or something. Maybe the oven's fucked – but I sliced the bastards in half and laid them flat last night, and after one and a half hours they were still sitting there like they were waiting for a bus, and when they'd been in about four hours and it was three in the morning, they had this thick, hard, black crust which no-one could describe as jewel-like unless Delia meant jet – and the pastry was like rosemary-infused conti-board.

'I think your time would've been better spent ripping my clothes off and taking me on the kitchen table and bugger the Spanish reds,' I don't say. Instead I say, 'Well, I'm very touched you went to all that trouble for me.'

He looks at me then, across the desecrated bird carcass and says, 'You're lovely.' That's it. And I'm about to make light with something like, 'Well, I am from the agency's deluxe list', but I stop myself.

'Where does your name come from?' I ask. I'm buzzing. He said I was lovely. That's good, whatever the rules are.

'Oh, silly story that. I was conceived when they were playing *Love is Blue* on the radio apparently. Cake shop assistants call me Love, and my friends call me Blue. I think my parents must have thought if I grew up to be really dull, it could be used as a conversation opener.'

I'm not sure how complimentary this sounds. I leave it.

'I'm really glad you didn't understand the film,' I go on, and he says, 'I'm really sorry about that too. If I'd had any sense I'd have got a video in. It'd have been more intimate to break our teeth on red granite pie watching *Brief Encounter* or something.'

The main courses arrive. Blue does all the choosing. Nothing too strange like fish lips and octopus toes and all those things that no-one ever picks. Just my favourites. Cashew chicken, beef in Cantonese, sweet and sour fish.

'Funny,' says Blue, as the waiter fiddles with rice, 'how we always think they like to be given our menu choices with numbers, but whenever you do, they look over your shoulder to see what the number describes'. His long fingers snatch a piece of crisp fish, and he pops it into his mouth and huffs at the painfully steamy heat as if he didn't realise that would happen.

'You know, I'd just watched that the first time I came over to your flat,' I say, thinking of *Brief Encounter*. He grins, the sexy smudges of darkness under his eyes widening.

'I watched it that day too. The Saturday morning. It's great, isn't it?' And I say, 'Yes, yes it is.' And with Art Garfunkel all but drowning out the twittering mobiles and with the cosiness of our corner table hidden behind an arrangement of false roofs of green glazed tiles, I want to ask him what he wants. If it's me. And if it's not, then what? And why not?

I remember Grandma Yes!?!'s advice, but my own mysteries seem unimportant. Impossible to project. I don't feel remotely mysterious.

'So what are you thinking about,' I ask. Yes, I know. Not exactly an originality award winner, but I feel like one of those fairground games where you keep slipping coins onto a slide and hope that it will push a great clattering of other coins off the edge. One of us has to make the decisive move.

Blue leans forward, his bare forearms coffee-brown in this darkness.

'I'm just wondering why you've molested the candle into an erupting phallus,' he says softly, and I look at the red wax obelisk between us. Its little flame is spurting from a bulbous head engorged with warm liquidity which I have been mindlessly fondling and kneading until a splurge of wet wax dripped down to burn the soft, fleshy valley between my finger and thumb.

'I can't imagine,' I say, and he bursts out laughing. I want to reach out and stroke him. Give him a squeeze. If I do, what could happen at worst. Surely he's not capable of being shocked. He must know. I want to kiss his neck, just behind his ear. It's the softness of his masculinity that is entrancing me. A smoothness of corners, as if the physical can be affected by the character. And then I'm brought up short. I picture him pulling away from me – softly, sweetly saying, 'I'm sorry. Look, I better be going.'

He looks at me then, and in broad Lancashire/Yorkshire borders says 'Well, ye've sin the phortographs. I've got some reet nice etchings if you'd like to give 'em the once over.'

We say nothing, just about, on the bus back to Didsbury. Hurtling past the cream stone university and into the jolly neon brashness of the Curry Mile at Rusholme with its endless Indian eateries, then the grungy calm of student-studded Fallowfield, until, with the bus almost empty except for an old white-haired woman in leather trousers and massive triangular earrings, the bus judders into the dark stillness of Palatine Road, the black and white stripes of Didsbury's neo-Tudor gables slashing past us behind scrawny branches bare of leaves.

'I've not known what to think. I mean, what you think,' I say as we trudge through the darkness towards Blue's flat.

'I don't know myself a lot of the time,' he replies softly. Then he stops and I stop. We are outside the development site of Davrach. A sales portacabin has been set up, with bright, toy-town looking primula set in terracotta bowls on a strip of turf which all looks neat and clean and utterly wrong amid the debris where the great house stood.

'Actually, that's a cop out,' he says. 'I hate people who pretend they don't know things they do know.'

Inside the flat, Blue settles me with a large folder while he disappears off to make coffee or something. I open the huge cardboard flap, and see myself in sepia through the spindles of the staircase at Maplehurst. Another of me looking about four inches tall with a backdrop of the black and white hall tiles. Another with the rotting wooden sill of the conservatory windows like a bar at my throat. It isn't me. It's more than me. The look in my eyes in these pictures is not the look I think people see. It's the way I see others. It's as if he's photographed me from behind my own eyelids. Incredible.

Blue saunters back in and he's taken off his sweater. He's holding what looks like a flying saucer.

'Catch!' he says, and hands it to me. Whatever it is is on a greasy oven tray and has a heaviness to it. It looks almost metallic, but more cardboardy. A papier-mâché version of the moon's surface.

'Do you want custard or cream with it?' he asks, grinning widely, and I look up from where I'm kneeling, and I'm smiling too, and I plonk the inedible looking onion disaster thing on the floor and I take the fingers of his hands and find myself launching myself at his mouth. I don't care what he thinks. How he'll react. It just must be done, and the oddest thought zips through my mind. It must be done on earth as it is in heaven. Mmmmm. I can taste sweet and sour, except its more sweet and sweet. He holds me, now. And I can feel what I've looked at so much, tight against me. I feel a sort of disbelief in the at-lastness of it all.

'White sauce please – like we used to have on Christmas pudding at school,' I say, pulling from his lips for a moment. I can't believe I've just come out with that, but I have. And he leads me into his bedroom. A light from an old window way beyond the cold, overgrown garden lets a bit of tiger's eye glow seep through the big, curtainless window in his room. He sits on the futon bed, and carefully unzips the side panel of each suede boot. They clop onto the painted floorboards. His feet in socks look warm, sculptured. He lies back, prone, his t-shirt riding up a little and for a snapshot moment, the pelvic peaks around the bowl of his stomach are lit by the weak light from the far off window, and I slide, fall, slip, pounce, collapse onto his warm, smoothly-angled frame, and in the near darkness, with my eyes too pressed into his skin to see anything, I can feel his smiling. His whole body is smiling and I pray to whoever is looking over us – as right now, somebody definitely is – that the phone won't ring. That he won't cough. That I won't sneeze. And as the minutes tick forward on his old, invisible alarm clock, he teaches me that half aromatic crispy duck pancakes with hoisin sauce are very good, but have their limits. And the 'phone doesn't ring, and we don't cough or sneeze, and it is perfection.

* * *

Twenty One

'Lynton', off Spath Road, Didsbury, M20.

I can't sleep. It's 1.47am and my mind's been doing a slow wash of delicates since I came to bed at half past nine last night. Now it's on spin, and the spinning never stops. I can still see that horrid man walking up the drive towards me. Leaning on the car. Telling me my husband isn't inside. Isn't anywhere. I keep getting up and walking to the window. I can see the gateposts from our – my – window. No-one there, but would I see if there was? What does he want? Did he break in the other night?

Rhona's wrong. I know she thinks I wasn't on my way to anywhere this morning, but I did go to the police. They offered me victim support. But I'm not a victim. Well, not yet. They seemed to like the idea of me being a victim and asked my date of birth again.

'It hasn't changed since the break-in last week,' I said, and they said they appreciate that it must be difficult for me, and do I have any relatives. That made me think of Merton Lewis. He's got the same face as his father. Anyway, I don't need relatives. Friends keep popping up, but relatives you can disown. But I'm not bothered about him. It's worse than that. Did Rhona tell you what she's got in that will of hers? I mean, I looked at her list of things, and she knows I've always liked the Lalique vase she has, but honestly, I'll probably be dead before she is, and what do I need with more things around me? I know she said I didn't need to look at the will itself, but it was impossible not to, sitting in my lap like that. I don't know what to say. I mean, I can't let her know I read it, but part of me thinks she must have intended me to. But then, she couldn't have known the girl was going to come in and start wheeling her off to lunch at that moment.

I mean, practically everything going to this young taxi fellow who bats his eyelashes at her. I think you're supposed to be sane to write a will – I'll have to ask my solicitor. But Merton must know what's in it. He drew it up. I can't speak to him. I mean, he wouldn't speak to me about it anyway. But then it's all so wrong. She's got all her investments, and I can't see how this fellow can deserve all that.

I've just had an idea. I'm miles from sleep anyway. I'll just look up, oh where is the bloody thing? There it is. Manchester South 'phone book. And I find the number for SupaKars, and write it on a pad by my bedside table. Tomorrow, I'll go somewhere by taxi. He can take me to Sainsbury's or Marks & Sparks... I suppose I can ask for an individual driver, can't I? Yes, of course I bloody can. I can do what I like.

* * *

I turn and lean into Blue's back. I want to shake him awake. Tell him how fantastic the world is. It's happened. So what now? Does it all slot into place now? I run my hand down the side of his body, loving the solid, tapering smoothness. As my fingers slowly open and close across the plain of his stomach, his hand grabs mine. He does it so it seems as if he's in sleep, but it is deliberate.

'Sorry,' I say in a small voice. I don't feel sorry, I just don't know what to say. He turns to me, and our faces are within inches. The light from that far-off window has been turned out. His skin is navy.

'It's just there,' he says. 'I'm not comfortable with hands round my waist. I'm just sensitive, that's all,' and he draws me closer, and kisses me on the forehead.

'Ticklish?'

'No. I mean, sensitive about myself.'

'But you're lovely,' I say.

'Well thanks. But I've always felt, well, there's too much of it. Fat.'

I take a moment to consider this. He can't just be fishing for compliments. Anyway, it's not the right time of day for saying charming things, meant or otherwise.

'Are you serious? I thought it was women who worry about that.'

'Yeah. Well. That's what women would have you believe,' he says, yawning in what I suspect is a way to make me feel he's relaxed when in fact a thread of tension is snagging between us.

'But you've no need to feel fat. I mean you aren't. I'm the one who's fat around here.' I want to sound funny. Light. Easy about myself, which is as unrealistic a proposal as it's possible to be. 'Come on Blue, look at all the anorexic catwalk models. I mean men don't have those pressures.'

'Look,' he says, 'please don't tell me that weight concern is a women's only club. It only looks that way because men's voices are never heard above the babble of women who think that men are only interested in slim women and never think about themselves. I mean, you've only got to look at the number of posters and ad campaigns featuring naked men. Look,' he says, and I feel I've hit something raw here, 'I really don't want to argue this one.'

'Nobody's arguing,' I say, and I can't believe we've achieved a row, fresh from sleep, within hours of going to bed together for the first time. We lie for a bit, the silence making popping and slapping noises in my head. I wonder if he's feeling the same too.

'I guess you're right,' I say, pleased with myself for being the grown-up here. 'I'd just always thought it was just me who'd want to back out of the bedroom mid-conversation so there was no full-on bum shot.' Blue laughs. I've diffused this one, and feel vaguely elated.

'Well, it's exactly the same for a lot of men, it's just society likes to pretend that men don't think about such things, or think it's nice or something. I've spent a lifetime trying to stare myself thin in the mirror. Having really sensible, light suppers of calorie counted fresh things and feeling heroic, until half past midnight when I'll pad into the kitchen and start spooning Nutella down me until I feel sick and hating myself.'

I lie on my back and think. Part of me feels a bit cheated. Men aren't supposed to feel like this. It isn't manly. But then, all those women's magazine articles about 'being comfortable in your own skin' are, to be fair, always written by women to please women and promote a feeling of sisterhood. It feels very strange. Blue saying all this makes him more like me. More compatable. Perhaps that's what I'm afraid of. Perhaps I don't want to be compatable. We should complement, not have the same concerns.

'Men get so used to being portrayed a certain way, we begin to believe it ourselves. That can happen you know.' I wonder if Blue is feeling he's created a tension, or if he's liking it. He goes on. 'I mean, when you listen to radio plays, and women do all the talking. You know, the real talking, and then the men bluff into the room and it's all "Oh sorry, have I interrupted something ladies? I just wanted to blather loudly about business or golf". If you hear enough of that, you think everyone's like that. We're not. That's all.'

'Actually,' I say, feeling that we are able to say what we want right now, 'I had been wondering, 'til tonight, if you might be...urm...gay.'

Blue smiles, puts on a deeply deep southern States hick accent and says, 'Well ma'am, I sure do hope I've settled your mind on that score', and I reach up and kiss his shoulder.

'I guess so,' I say.

'But what made you wonder that?' he asks.

'Well,' and I think of Caroline suggesting it, but dismiss that. 'I mean men don't normally know the sort of things you know. Don't have the same interests.'

'But that's like saying, "Well, women really want to talk about make-up all the time and don't like to know about current affairs". It's bollocks. Men are brought up to hide everything, and it gives women the idea that they've got a monopoly on all the things boys aren't supposed to notice. It's become engrained.'

'Tell you what,' I say, determined that this is not going to become the issue of the month, 'you promise to tell me when I'm having a media-assisted opinion, and I'll promise to block the way to the fridge after 10pm.'

'Make it 11pm and it's a deal,' laughs Blue. And as he crawls over me, pinning my wrists with his hands and his mouth closes over my neck, all I can think is that he is clearly contemplating me being around at 11pm on future evenings.

* * *

Twenty Two

Time does the only thing it knows how to do.
It does it for twelve months to the day.

* * *

Sidney Fleiss Memorial Home. Room 6.

Poor Elaine. She must have been hoping she wouldn't have to wish me well for my birthday again. If she were utterly honest, when I moved in here she would have made a card saying, "Wishing You Two or Three Happy Returns At The Most". But which of us are that honest? Not I.

The stone balustrades at the Marie Louise Gardens have been removed, nobody seems certain where they might be, the cheese served as an alternative to fruit really is perfectly inedible nowadays, and Gita Kruk died, in her sleep, after her usual four glasses of champagne, three months ago. She managed one final controversy by insisting on being cremated at Southern Cemetery, which is the second oldest crematorium in the country and really very beautiful with its carved pillars in warm, sunny stone. None of this cuts with the powers that be, of course. Traditionally, Jews are buried. Burning is not acceptable. It is nearly sixty years since her four sisters and her parents were burnt at Auschwitz. No-one bears her name now.

Hettie Oppenheim and Herta Fox, who, I think I am safe in telling you, are now registered as immortal, refused to attend although I pointed out that as a 'country member' of the Reform Hebrew Congregation, Gita was quite within the ambit of what was acceptable. I added at lunch that Gita's own philosophy was that environmentally speaking, becoming so instantly at one with the landscape was the only justifiable way, a concept of which I could only approve. Indeed, I remember when Gussu and I attended South Manchester Crematorium years ago, the walls were lined with the names of German Jews who had settled in Didsbury in the nineteenth century.

Hettie and Herta delight in the belief that I said it purely to upset them, but it's true, and I have stated it is what I want for myself. I imagine Elaine would be happy to secure my wishes today, if only the law permitted it. Besides, Gita left a statement of requirements in her bedside cabinet. Matron did not think the contents were quite appropriate for public consumption, but Siklunli photocopied it for me before it was removed – she really is a gem. Gita had written, 'Having spent a lifetime living amongst my own people, I'm buggered if I want to be buried amongst them for all eternity. Lydia, please see to it that I am not.'

Rebwar took me to see the little rosebush which has been planted in her name, and afterwards we went into town and had lunch at the wonderful old Portico Library on Mosley Street. Gita had been a member and used to take tea there among all the ancient books under the heading 'Polite Literature'. I didn't imagine I should ever be able to see inside it again, as there's about five flights of steep stairs, but Rebwar said that it was nonsense to be limited where there need be no limitations. He is quite wonderful to me. I loathed appearing at the fine old library in his arms, but he said, 'Mrs. Laski, pretend I am a fireman rescuing you from a burning block.' He knows nothing of his legacy, and of course he must not, though I must admit I would be so happy to see his face when Merton Lewis calls him.

Joe Shabalan's stone-setting, from what I hear, went off without disaster. I didn't go. Essie, in her madness, is quite ageless, and floats between being a child bride (which she never was in the first place), and the sadly perfectly aware widow (which she has been, on and off, since Joe died). I believe the hideous twins are having problems with Maplehurst which was about to be sold to developers, which seems rather a shame, but now there is some question as to planning permission as it's in the conservation area. According to the *South Manchester Reporter*, a meeting has been called because there are so many objections to the developers' proposals. I'm really not terribly sure what's going on, but when I asked one of the twins as she sat stroking Essie's hand and talking about nothing at all, she said that everything had been going swimmingly until someone who doesn't even live in the conservation area started drumming up support and scaremongering among the neighbours that it was the thin end of the wedge.

'Scaremongering about what?' I asked, but she became very tight-lipped and said everything would be a lot better if people didn't interfere. I think she must be under some sort of pressure, as she is kind-hearted if terribly plain, and if anyone would be the victim of scaremongering, one would have thought it would be her.

Mrs. Solomons – who you may remember was suffering from corns and an inability to accept that her sixty three year old infant son Philip has done what he could and more-than-that-he-could-not-do – enjoyed a brief lift in her mood when he separated from his wife of thirty eight years. She fell into decline again, though, when the couple were reconciled after a holiday in Eilat, and she is now busy causing the nursing wing staff to wish they had chosen other professions.

One thing that has not changed at all is Sylvia's position. It really is quite appalling. She is still in that enormous house and has had a perfectly dreadful year, but I'll let her tell you. I'm afraid we weren't on speaking terms for four months.

She telephoned me one morning – shortly after you last heard from her, to say that she had mulled it over in her head and she felt she could not stay silent any longer. She then began a whole tirade about people rarely being what they appear, and me being taken for a ride, and after she had ranted away round the houses for some considerable time, she admitted she had read the terms of my will and that she did not trust Rebwar.

'But you've never met him,' I retorted, feeling angry that I was having to justify him as if I were a teenage girl trying to prove her young man was a suitable date. Surely I should be entitled to leave to whom I wish, without interference from those who cannot know better. I suppose she meant well, but there is interference wherever I look. My decision not to have a particular cup of tea. My decision to take a sleeping tablet. My decision to have dinner sent to me in my room instead of having to suffer the incessant ramblings of the Victoria Sponge and the Chocolate Brownie's viperous swipes. Everything is questioned, as if it really affects anyone else. Whatever became of dignity? It is stripped clean away when it is assumed one's decisions are by definition arrived at by folly. There. I have said my piece. I have made friends with Sylvia anyway.

Still, I am now in a differently awkward position. I could not resist telephoning those estate agents she is using – the ones where her granddaughter works. I asked about Lynton, and was told that 'the seller may be taking it off the market'. I can't imagine why Sylvia would change her mind about selling, but it's impossible for me to tell her what I know. I can hear her now, telling me that after all my talk of interfering, I have no right to meddle in her affairs. She is perfectly right and perfectly wrong, but that is why there is never a right answer.

* * *

'Lynton', off Spath Road, Didsbury, M20.

Oh! I can't believe it's a year since I last spoke to you. I mean – I'm still here. It's awful. Oh, I don't mean I don't want to be here as in alive – although I sometimes wonder on that score. But I'm still here here. At Lynton. The central heating people say the whole system's on its last legs, and there's damp right up the wall in the back hall. The ceiling's got emphysema.

That appalling man came again. It's two months ago now, but I can't get it out of my head. I was making myself some lunch, and there was knocking at the door. Didn't use the bell. There's something very unsettling about someone knocking when there's a bell. In a house this size, how can anyone be sure of being heard with a knock?

The little MarRatta used to knock, but then he had trouble reaching the bell. Anyway. He doesn't come round any more. The only kindness of age is that it stops other people's legs bringing them to see me. Actually – and you must promise not to tell Rhona this – promise? I'm not actually entirely happy he doesn't come anymore. I mean, I always loathed the little man with his pointy teeth and that bloody twinkle in his eyes. But at least he didn't frighten me. Annoyed me, yes. Drove me to fantasise about slapping him. Irritated me. But he didn't frighten me.

I've never felt frightened. Was brought up not to be frightened. My father used to say that fear meant impotence, and we should all be potent in our lives. But somewhere along the way, I've forgotten the language of courage. Don't speak it anymore. It's gone like my school French. I can come out with strong sentences that sound like I know exactly what I want and am confident I can have it – but as with French, I can't follow what comes back at me.

I hate myself for it, but I can't bear this sense of fear. It's like a layer of dustsheets. It stops anything seeming simple and fun. Why can't I sell this sodding house?

When the knock came at the door, I thought it was the Bettaware catalogue people. They drop off their thick magazine all about plastic things for making easy all sorts of things I wouldn't dream of doing anyway. Devices for making marigold shapes out of slices of cucumber and holders for anything capable of being held.

I always keep the magazine untouched and the woman collecting it never seems remotely surprised. I wonder if anyone ever actually orders anything. Thinking about it, I could imagine Mrs. Over-The-Road getting quite excited at the idea of a courgette crimper.

Anyway. I opened the door, and at first, I didn't recognise him. I've stepped back since you last heard from me. Further back in my tunnel. My vision now shows only a disc the size of an old penny piece. And then I knew. Leering at me. The man who had come up my drive and made me scrape the car last year.

'Hello Mrs. Lowenstein,' he said. 'I thought you might be lonely'.

I mean. What could I say to that? It crossed my mind that he was about to plunge a knife into my heart. A lunatic trying to save me from loneliness. Strangely, it was one of the few moments I didn't feel any sense of fear.

'Yes,' I said, 'I'm sometimes lonely. What about you? Are you lonely?' I tried to sound cold. Hard. Brutal concern.

And staring into his face, I couldn't see anything beneath his collar. A dark grey polo neck. If I live, I thought, I'll be able to tell the police it was a dark grey lambswool poloneck. And the police, I remember thinking, will tear out to find the man, armed once again with my own date of birth. Then I saw his eyes had dropped from mine.

For a moment, I thought I should continue to stare at his eyes, though he was no longer looking at me. Then I followed them down, taking in more lambswool poloneck. I could make out a pale grey fleece jacket. Comfortable. Soft, I remember thinking. Open, but zippable. Practical. Something else for the police not to bother noting. And then lower than the jumper and the fleecy jacket, a pink penis sticking out like the indicator light on Louis's old Rover 75.

I stared at it for a moment. It was very strange. It was only when the victim support woman said that I must be finding it very difficult, but I must try to remember, that I realised that I had not even considered the possibility of rape. The pink indicator-like thing did not seem capable of rape, or much else really. I noted the foreskin, pulled back, and thought that this probably would not help narrow things too well for the police. I looked back up at his face.

'I don't think it's anything you need to concern yourself about,' I said. 'Actually, I have seen smaller in my time.' And I closed the door. I began to laugh then, as I haven't laughed in years. He hadn't moved, and I laughed silently at first, but then it was louder. I could hear it as if it were coming from someone else. I think I became quite hysterical, as I didn't notice him leave. But when I recovered myself, there was no one behind the stained-glass panes in the door panels.

The policewoman smiled when I described his pubic hair as not unlike the colour and texture of my scourer. I don't think she put that in her report.

* * *

The office at Anthony Holland & Clegg is quiet. It is three hours and twelve minutes until I can go home. That's 192 minutes. All I have to do is count to a hundred and ninety two sixty times and I'll be free of this silly place. And I begin. I know. Dreadful, isn't it? I actually count a minute of my life away. Only a hundred and ninety one to go.

Caroline is out, or in next to her answer machine and deciding that I'm not exciting enough to pick up the receiver for. I debate being unfair and blocking my number which might give her the impression it's someone more thrilling than me, but I don't want to hear the tone of disappointment in her voice.

Ever since that day she described herself as 'yesterday's lasagne brightened up with fresh herbs and served up in the dark', I've been trying to find out who she's been serving herself up to. But Caroline is the essence of discretion. I think she keeps things from herself sometimes. It's terribly frustrating. I keep guessing at possible friends, but she smiles and says,

'Do we discuss our sordidness over rocket salad with balsamic dressing? We do not.'

I have to say, I am deeply envious of her. She has someone about whom she can say 'my husband's just parking' – the same someone she can send down to open the door when the postman needs a signature too early on a Saturday. And then someone else for whom duvet battles are someone else's war altogether. Someone with whom sex makes her want to say things she doesn't mean – things that she would mean but would never say with he who doesn't bother to put his used underwear in the ali baba basket anymore.

So yes, I envy her. But I also feel a bit empowered, in an evilish sort of way. I mean, if I were a complete bitch, I could drop her in it big time. Easy. But my bitch-like qualities are far too tempered really. I just like the fact that she told me, even though I suspect she did so in a moment of weakness when she wanted to appear exciting.

So, no Caroline to break the tedium. No-one's been interested in Grandma Yes!?!'s house, which is pretty weird considering it's so lovely and things are supposed to be booming. She had some sort of break-in again a couple of months ago, only she wouldn't talk about it, which isn't like her at all. I think it's really getting to her.

We finally got the contract to sell the HouseBryte Homes flats at 'Windsor Court', the architectural abomination put up where Davrach stood. People genuinely do come in showing interest in the 'truly aristocratic phoenix rising from the ashes of this fine old mansion'. Of course, the sign's gone up, as it always does, saying 'only three remaining.' Mr. Clegg has that up the moment they go up for sale. 'Last few remaining' means none have gone at all. 'Only three' – that a couple have at last sold. 'Last one remaining' – that the cubby-hole under the stairs which was a storeroom on the original plans is all that's left.

It's all been young couples swooning at the exciting notion that they can choose their own kitchen tiles, not to mention a bathroom suite from the 'Regency' or 'Edwardian' range. Nobody's got an ounce of originality in them. They'd buy the dust on the Habitat show furniture if it were an option.

I just want to get home to Blue. We've been living together for nine months now. Just think. We could be parents ourselves. Except we're not. I gave up my flat and moved into his place, although the lease is up soon, and the landlady isn't renewing it.

'We could get a HouseBryte Home,' I suggested. Blue said something about corpses and the art of stepping over them. He's got himself all worked up over the fate of Maplehurst. Mr. Clegg has found a developer who wants to buy it despite all the neighbours being up in arms. And Blue's organised a meeting to get the planning committee to see what a disaster it would be if the place is pulled down. I've not said anything to Mr. Clegg about the meeting. I mean, he knows about it anyway, but he doesn't know about Blue and me.

Mum keeps asking when we'll get married. At first she seemed to have difficulty intaking air every time I mentioned Blue, but that was before the 'great discovery' last July.

We'd just had a Tuesday afternoon of Jaffa cakes and sex (I thought I was coming down with flu and took the day off work, but a naked man licking my nipples while Richard and Judy talked bollocks in the background seemed to work so much better than Lemsip and Nurofen whatever the adverts say, that I made a remarkable recovery).

We were talking about the chances of saving Maplehurst, and Blue said, 'It would really *krenk* me if the council approves the application without even doing a site visit.' And I was thinking about it, and I suddenly thought, 'he said *krenk*'. I mean, that's not like *shlep* or *chutzpah* – words that people think of as New York-speak.

And I said, 'Where do you know a word like *krenk* from?' and Blue said, 'Oh, my dad was Jewish. He used to say it.'

I felt a burst of excitement. Felt almost guilty for feeling it. I mean. I love him. It doesn't matter what our backgrounds are. Except that it does. Always has.

'So your mum isn't?' I asked.

'No. Far from it.'

'Did you know your grandparents?' I asked, and he started talking about his mother's parents who came from Wiltshire and I felt embarrassed because I was only interested in the Jewish ones. I can't help it. But I listened. Asked questions about the Wiltshire clan to show interest. Biding my time.

'But what you want to know is about my dad's family,' Blue said, kissing my hair. I felt about eight and caught cheating at school.

'Well?'

'Well. My grandmother's still alive, I think. My mum and she hated each other. I suppose I just grew up thinking of her as an evil cow. I can see now that prejudice is not unknown territory for my mum, but it's hard to break out of that now.'

'Wouldn't you like to find her,' I ask, trying not to sound too pushy. But I know I couldn't bear to lie in bed making love and munching all round the orangey bits of a Jaffa cake if I thought I had a grandmother out there who I didn't know. It surprises me with Blue even more – his obsession with the soon to be lost – the need to record the endangered present.

'Well, I do know where she is. I just felt, you know, it's been so long, and she's a stranger to me. She's in the old people's home here in Didsbury.'

My finger-tips felt cold. My mouth dry. I mean, you can't tell someone like me that your grandmother lives in the Sidney Fleiss and expect me not to react. 'Please,' I say to myself. 'Let me not be in love with the grandson of the *gefilte*-fish wielding Millie Grodsky.' Or worse still − and at this I feel my face burst into a sweat − what would Grandma say if the man I'm in bed with calls Edward Marcatta grandpa? But no. Grandma Yes!?!'s unwanted suitor does not have a grandson, I'm sure.

Blue's surname is Morton − but that turns out to be his mother's maiden name, and he preferred it. He kisses me on the lips, opening them with his tongue, and says, 'she's called Rhona Laski'.

'But you've got to go and see her,' I implore, as much as one can implore when someone's tongue is in your mouth.

'Maybe,' says Blue, and it sounds more like maybe not. Wait 'til I tell Grandma Yes!?!

Well. I did wait to tell Grandma Yes!?!. About twelve minutes when Blue slunk off to the bathroom looking strangely alluring in my old dressing gown which is mini-length on him. He won't walk about naked. Still has this strange notion that he's overweight, or at least 'prone' to it, as he calls it. I've told him that everyone's prone to being overweight. It all depends how prone you are to opening the biscuit tin, but he's so sensitive about it.

Anyway. Grandma was thrilled.

'Oh darling. Oh! I can't tell you!' I made her promise not to tell her old friend. 'It has to come from Blue. He'd be livid.'

'I understand darling,' said Grandma. And that meant she understood.

I told Mum.

She was silent for a moment, threatened to sigh, and said, 'But his mother's not Jewish.' Then she summoned all the exhilaration I know she was feeling beneath and gushed, 'Well, I suppose it's something.'

* * *

156

Still me. Still me. Sometimes I get carried away. Sorry. I was telling you that I'm still in this office and Trish has tuned into Insipid FM or whatever it's called. Ostensibly she wanted to listen to the news, but as she jabbered on about how expensive it is to have clothes taken in while Pam nodded with mute glumness, we all missed the headlines. I could make out that 360 people had been killed, but not where, and that something horrendous had happened on the Ivory Coast of Africa, but not what.

I tried ostentatiously straining my head towards the radio, hoping this might give Trish a hint as to my desire for her silence, but it didn't. And now in the middle of some awful slushy soul version of *Light My Fire* which could put the dampers on any mood, a very pleasant-looking man walks in, disturbing Trish mid lip-gloss-pout and asks if we have a big, late Victorian house with lots of original features and an owner who doesn't mind having her life invaded. They don't normally stipulate how they want the owner.

'Well, we have a beautiful house just off Spath Road,' I say, speaking loudly to cover my embarrassment at selling in Grandma's home so blatantly in front of Trish and Pam. They're not really listening though. Pam's slight smile now looks as if she's fantasising a horrible death for her skinny colleague. I hand the man the details.

'Yes. This looks lovely. What's the owner like?' he asks.

'Well. She's, urm, a bit mad. Very sweet. Marvellous cook. Actually she's my grandmother.' And I hear 'actually' come out exactly as it would from her, and feel myself once again sliding into my own future.

'Has she got new central heating,' he asks, and I say that no, it really couldn't be described as new. Not quite new. Urm, Perhaps very old is a better description.

'Brilliant!' he says. 'Like old geysers hanging off the wall?'

'Not quite, but you'd have to change it. I mean, the system does need replacing.'

'Oh, I wouldn't be changing that,' he says. 'In fact, if she had got a new system, we'd have to rig up an old one in the studio.' And then he explains he's from a film company and they're doing a T.V. advert for some kind of financial service or something and he needs a big old house with problems as a location. Still. Not all bad. It pays pretty well, and Grandma could maybe use the money to do up the worst bits, and that might make it sell better if anyone ever came to look at it.

He arranges to go and look at it. An hour later, Grandma Yes!?! calls me.

'Well, darling. Thank you for at last getting a viewing. Not over flattering that the feature he likes best is the conking-out radiators, but I think it'll be rather fun. You will come and be here when they're filming, won't you?'

And I promise I will. Next Tuesday.

Twenty Three

One of Herta Fox's grandsons has been killed in Israel. It is Martin, who I met, once, on *Yom Kippur* morning. It is a difficult thing, feeling intensely for someone one really doesn't like. But I can't help it. I want to be taken to see Herta, and to hold her hand. I want to be the friend I am actually capable of being. But of course, I cannot.

I could be much more use to Herta now than Hettie could, or just about any of the others. I think of Lionel, Martin's father – remember him looking at me conspiratorially at the thought of escaping going to synagogue. His son. Gone. Out of this world.

Funny how that phrase can mean 'glorious' when applied to a pudding, and unspeakably dreadful when applied to a son.

The Sidney Fleiss is, naturally, a hotbed of gossip, but it filters to us through the sometimes rather deaf ears of its news bearers and their perfectly clearly hearing relatives who seem to think that there comes a point in life when one wants to be lied to. To be protected from the truth. It makes me so angry when I hear imbecilic daughters of sixty declaring, 'Of course we haven't told Mummy.'

At first, they said it was a bomb on a bus. Someone said it was Martin and his wife and the six children. Then it turned out it was just Martin. The six children who were also killed were someone else's. I keep picturing his earnest face. It was not a face to which I could relate. I make no pretence about that. For some reason, I can picture Lionel, but only when he was about thirty, well before I knew him, and imagine him spraying a hosepipe in a summer garden on a toddling Martin. A Martin who had made no political stand on anything beyond not eating his spinach.

Herta is in her room. She was never able to recite the names of Martin's children, her own great grandchildren. I could. She disliked me for that. I want to be able to reach out to her. It is possible to embrace those we dislike, and perhaps it helps some of those feelings to evaporate. There is something disgraceful and obscene in this place – a place which treats us so well, we cause nature to misfire. Of course, Martin being killed is not nature, but every now and then, one of us grows so old, our children die before us of natural causes.

It is absurd. I think of Myrna Weinrich, after whom the camellia garden was named. She lived to be a hundred-and-two, and was sprightly enough to attend the funeral of her daughter, who died peacefully at eighty-three.

Herta is always going on about her family being her wealth. And now she has been burgled by terrorists. And just as the police did with Sylvia, everyone here keeps going on about Herta's age, as if that has anything to do with anything.

I will write to her. Right now. And I do. My hand is hopeless, but I concentrate hard. I feel like a child making some clumsy gift for a grieving grandparent. And as I write, I realise that I am not at all disliking her. We have become irritated with each other, because we are thrown together for no better reason than physical feebleness. Perhaps, from now, we will get on better. I'm sure we won't, but it would be good to think we might.

Rebwar has arrived. It is a really beautiful day. Citrus sharp. Herta is in her room, and family keep arriving for her like flowers. Hettie looks tired, and I dispense with Max and Trudi and their lunchtime jaunts today. Perhaps I am not going out with them as a tribute to Martin Fox.

'I'm just off to the park to do some thinking,' I say. And Hettie smiles back at me, and says, 'You have a nice time. It's a beautiful day.'

And I wonder if she knows just how often I do what I am about to do again.

* * *

Tuesday Morning. It's 7.35am and I'm at Lynton. Grandma is all bosoms and velvet slippers this morning. Some women have breasts. Others have tits or a bust. Grandma Yes!?!'s are definitely bosoms. Tunnel vision or not, her eyes are shining. It's terrific to see her looking so excited.

'Oh darling. It's so silly, isn't it? I mean you've no idea how much fun it is to have something gluing the day together other than lurching round the house trying to find things that shouldn't be lost. Do you think when the film's made, someone might see it and think they want to buy the house? Anyway – what is the film? I mean – is this what happens when you get too old to go to the movies – they bring them to you?' She's rattling on and there's an energy I haven't seen in her since before grandpa died.

'You'd better put some clothes on. They'll be here in a minute,' I say.

She knows perfectly well that the filming is for an advertisement for financial services and while the shoot will last all day, the end product should last about two and a half minutes. But in her mind, it's a feature movie, and I know this is how it will be sold to her friends. And why not?

I'm in the loo when the doorbell goes. By the time I'm washing my hands in the antiquated little corner sink, Grandma appears, still in her black Rayon dressing gown.

'The male lead's just arrived. He's gorgeous. Six foot two and covered head to toe in black leather. He's called Bobbodick. At least that's what it sounds like with his helmet on.'

I make my way into the hall in time to see the shiny black headgear being lifted off a fountain of spiky blond hair. 'Hi,' says the mouth beneath the hair, 'I'm Dominic. I'm a runner.'

'Hello,' coos Grandma Yes!?!, her head on one side in what I know she sees as coquettish. 'A runner,' she repeats, and I know she is visualising stair carpet. She offers to make some coffee, but Dominic says,

'Oh, they've got their own catering. Anyway. That's what I do. Coffee, tea, that sort of stuff.' It isn't exactly on a male lead's itinerary, but Grandma's not bothered who he is now. He wipes his feet with ostentatious concern on the mat.

I run off to the very-early-opening Late Shop for some semi-skimmed, and when I return, a big old Volvo is outside. Steve, the producer, is inside. I don't see him. Then, suddenly, there are nine more inside. Another three. Two leave. One arrives. Then four more. It's a strange feeling, all these polite, busy strangers in Grandma's house.

'I'll make some coffee,' I say, imagining everyone will be thrilled at my kindness.

'Don't set a precedent,' says Steve, who has a permed ponytail. He's obviously been a trainer at the television zoo for a long time. I nod conspiratorially. Mustn't let them know I've got a kettle or they'll all take advantage.

'Great house,' says a tiny lesbian to Grandma, who has clearly decided to stay in the black dressing gown. Grandma smiles again, and I can see her weighing up whether the little woman might actually want to own it. The lesbian is a man, I notice. Adam's apple the only sign.

At 8.16 am the doorbell goes again. Grandma swings open the door with the flourish of a Southern hostess welcoming guests. A vast bulge of woman in a purple anorak is weighted down on the steps.

'Fish,' she says glumly.

'Great. In here,' says Steve. A fish tank containing two goldfish darting in and out of an aquatic interior nightmare of glittering grottos is plonked in the dining room. Steve explains to Grandma that the character in the ad is accident prone.

'Has he got tunnel vision?' asks Grandma hopefully. I think she has what there is of her sight on a starring role. Steve ignores her pleasantly. 'So we've got all these framed pictures which domino onto each other and then the last one falls in the fish tank.'

Charlie (Charlotte) is introduced, but I can't tell what she actually does. Sporting a seven inch waist and turquoise leather trousers, she asks if there's a bedroom for the actors to dress in. And another room she can use as an office. Magda, who does make-up, needs a room for this too, and Grandma lurches upstairs gathering pieces of clothing that have been strewn over beds in unused bedrooms and wedging them firmly in other rooms where they will doubtless stay, in crumpled form, for months to come.

'Anyone seen Magda,' asks a string bean in a Motorhead T-shirt and suede pixie boots.

'Yeah,' I say, feeling very in with it all to know where she is. 'She's gone up to her dressing room.'

'She's not actually working,' he says with a sheepish grin. 'She's Simon's girlfriend.' We don't know who Simon is, but it doesn't seem to matter.

Outside, 2500 watt lights are standing on a massive tripod in the front garden. 'Do try to mind the fuchsia,' says Grandma, lurching out into the porch and clinging to the narrow column supporting it. 'Only it took four years to flower like it did last year, even though it's supposed to be a hardy variety.' Grandma steps inside.

'Blue's not been to see Rhona yet, has he?' she asks breathily.

'No. He hasn't. And you've not said anything, have you?' But I don't

162

need to ask. Of course she hasn't. The old piano can't be moved, but all the things which Grandma dragged upstairs the night of the first attempted break-in, and dragged down again in the months which followed, are now being lifted into the sitting room.

'Are these fish meant to be floating?' asks a Sloany voice coming through several bodies who are black leathering their way through the hall.

'Oh shit!' This is Steen, the half-Danish, half-Sicilian director. It seems one of the goldfish couldn't take the excitement. Magda is despatched to break the news to Mrs. Glum of the purple anorak. She seems a long time ago. I ask if it's strictly necessary to inform her so quickly, and Grandma pipes up, 'I mean it's not as if funeral arrangements need to be made.'

Steen agrees, but admits it isn't sensitivity to Mrs. Glum's marvellous relationship with her goldfish, but she does run the village pet shop, so she'll have his replacement ready with any luck. One goldfish having a gilt photoframe falling on his head isn't enough for the financial services commercial.

'There's a big man in a knitted v-neck mumbling to himself in the kitchen,' says Grandma. I look in. He's surrounded by activity, but he's reserved his conversation for the kettle.

Horace was the last goldfish. Another 'shit' from Steen. No more in stock until Wednesday.

'Actually, I've got some chopped fried fish in the freezer,' offers Grandma, and I look at her incredulously.

'No, darling,' she stares back. 'Only if the camera doesn't go too close, it'll look like a real one. I shaped them like that. It seems a shame for everything to stop.'

'Have you got a toilet roll holder?' Dominic asks Grandma. The one in the bathroom won't do, though. It needs to be 'one that lets the toilet roll rush'. I disappear into the kitchen, as I hear Grandma ask no-one in particular, 'Do toilet rolls ever rush?' The kitchen is full of polystyrene boxes. Nothing to nick though. Four crates of Volvic natural mineral water. 120 sachets of Options chocolate au lait with fewer than 40 calories per drink. I think, suddenly, of Blue. It's the meeting tonight, at 8 o'clock. The meeting he's organised to drum up support against developing Maplehurst. I can't imagine 8 o'clock ever happening.

There's an oil-drum-sized, catering jar of coffee open. For a moment,

I become my own mother. 'What a shame to leave the lid off. It'll all go tasteless.' The knitted jumper has now stopped talking to the kettle, and has graduated to telling the Kenwood mixer that 'we all know that accidents happen, so it's it nice to know that there is somewhere you can turn...' I suddenly feel hungry. It would be nice if there were great corporate tinfoil trays of chopped egg and cucumber triangles on variagated white and brown. Six crates of Lucozade block the way to the cooker.

I wander upstairs, edging past the monitors which are showing the surviving goldfish. At the foot of the stairs, Steen is sounding very in control, his lazy, slightly London accent with sequins of Northern European nuance calls out directions while Magda strokes his buttocks through his jeans. This seems to be her role in the film. She's a stroker. A director's stroker. She will appear as such on the credits after Dolly Grip and her husband Gaffer.

A very loud voice suddenly fills the house and makes Grandma jump.

'Buying a new house can be a pretty tricky affair, mark my words. That's why I chose to call Elite Financial Services.' The house is filled with this, as if it is the voice of God.

'Look darling,' says Grandma. She is huddling with everyone else around the screen in the hall. 'Isn't this fun?' she says, squeezing my hand. The screen fills with the glittery grotto, and Edgar, the surviving goldfish is two feet long and swims blithely into view. Then it's just the glittery grotto again.

'Put some more feed in the tank Jack, he's gone out of view again,' calls Steen. His left buttock is gently stroked by Magda, doing her job diligently. Sadly, Edgar seems already to have had breakfast. Anyway, he remains out of view. The actor's voice repeats the line about buying a new house being a tricky affair, and Grandma, seeing the room bathed in brilliant magnesium white light suddenly hisses, 'Christ! look at the dust on the picture rails. It's like a snow scene in reverse'.

'It's just as well that bloody goldfish is the star,' she says. Dominic suggests putting a couple of glass screens in the tank about three inches across. That would wedge Edgar in sufficiently so he couldn't disappear out of view. But the tiny lesbian man says that it wouldn't look right if Edgar was in a two inch space for his big concussion scene when the photoframe falls on him.

'After all, you can never be too careful,' says the actor. But it seems that Edgar the goldfish can. He seems to have some inner sense which prevents him being in the wrong place at the wrong time. He's indestructible. The little family photograph frames simply won't fall on him.

Dominic is making coffee for the crew. The sound man says that he'd prefer 'hot Vimto'.

'Hot Vimto?' mutters Dominic under his breath. 'Yer big blouse.' Dominic's black leathers and spiky blond crop seem a bit wasted as he stirs hot water on his Options chocolate.

'What's that contraption thing being wheeled in?' asks Grandma. She could be twenty or thirty right now. It's almost painfully pleasurable to see her looking so animated. The filming seems to have put her under a spell.

'That's a dolly.'

'Oh,' I say, 'so that's what a dolly looks like. So what's a dolly grip?'

'Him,' says Steen, pointing to a man in baggy jeans crawling after dolly. 'Can you stop that a sec,' he asks Magda, who seems to have progressed in a mindless, gum-chewing motion, to the back of his left thigh.

'OK. Stand by please. Quiet! Quiet!' The accident prone character is lying in the hall, his legs against the walls, his feet splayed. His forehead has a massive gash of pretend blood. The moment seems very tense. Exciting.

At that moment, the telephone goes, and Sylvia sways towards it.

'Yes??' she hisses.

'Ah Sylvia. This really is most strange. It's quite the most uncanny thing.' Grandma mouths to me 'Rhona,' and for some reason puts the telephone on monitor.

'I haven't telephoned you,' Rhona declares.

'What are you talking about? What do you call this?' asks Grandma. She sounds vaguely frustrated to be interrupted.

'But that's just it. I'm not even using the phone.'

'Well do you feel that we're speaking now?' asks Grandma. The crew are waiting, smiling at me with the most polite patience.

'Well yes, I suppose we are,' Rhona goes on. 'But it's Siklunli I want. She hasn't been to make the bed. It's been like this all morning, and I have Sybil Levine coming this afternoon and the place is a slum.'

'Well, you've not got Sik Whatever li, you've got me,' says Grandma, becoming exasperated.

'Yes, well, you must go. I mustn't detain you. You must think I'm quite mad.'

'Yes,' says Grandma absently.

'It really must be poltergeist,' Rhona goes on.

'Yes, well, I've got people here.'

'Oh. Who?' asks Rhona.

'Oh, about twenty people. I don't know their names. There's one in leather called Dominic, and then there's Edgar. He's a goldfish.'

Rhona is silent for a moment, perhaps weighing up who sounds the madder.

'But isn't it the strangest thing? I'm not anywhere near the 'phone,' she persists. 'I came back from lunch and dialled 1475, and saw that you had called earlier, but I wasn't trying to call you back. Not until after six.'

'It's 1471 actually.'

'What?'

'Nothing.'

'Well dear, dear Sylvia. I'm getting old and I'm rambling.' The receiver goes dead. And I imagine it strikes everyone who heard the conversation that not only did Rhona insist she was nowhere near a phone, but seemed quite at ease with the idea that her old friend was entertaining a goldfish.

Dominic is in the kitchen boiling up again.

'Three more coffees mate,' calls Steve.

'Are these for drinking or chucking on the floor?'

'Drinking mate.'

'OK, on their way.'

The telephone goes again. Grandma picks up the receiver and hears, 'Oh dear, this is quite, quite unimaginable. I was about to have some tea. I don't want to speak on the phone at all.'

'Well try not to then,' hisses Grandma, and replaces the receiver. Steve and Mike on camera are having a disagreement.

'Just spin the dolly round on its arse like I said.'

'What the fuck der yer think I'm doin' yer mong.'

'Don't fuckin' mong me lumpy bollocks.'

And then Steen calls, 'OK. Everyone. Stand by please.' And the

166

silvery tones of the actor burst out like the lyrics of a wartime classic, silencing the expletives.

At five o'clock, Grandma is looking tired. Everyone is in the kitchen. The actor is washing the rug on which we are pretending the pretend coffee was spilt.

'Fish coming through,' calls Steen. Dominic, his hands ghostly white from paint thinned with turps substitute carries Edgar out of the kitchen.

Steen looks at Edgar.

'Must be lovely being a fish. Tiny, tiny brain.' His face contorts into a pout. 'Oo look, a new piece of weed to look at. Oo look, a new piece of weed to look at.' Magda gives his bum a quick, reassuring stroke.

'Nice kitchen. Really like it,' says the actor as grandma makes her way in. She smiles, and delicately raises her hand to wipe away a loose strand of hair.

'Oh, thank you. Well, it's been in for ages, but I've always found it very good to work in,' she says, almost gushing. 'The servants' bells and everything are original,' she goes on. The actor seems to ignore her, but continues wiping at the rug.

'Nice kitchen – really like it,' he says again. I can see Grandma staring at him. First Rhona thinks she's not telephoning when she is. Now this man thinks he hasn't paid the house a compliment when he has. Only when he's said, 'Nice kitchen – really like it,' eleven times, does Grandma realise this is one of his lines.

'Oh, I feel such a fool,' she whispers to me, but she's laughing.

* * *

Marie Louise Gardens, close to Room 6, but far enough away.

The sun, at 3 o-clock, is like butter from the fridge. It shines into my face, creamy and cold. What a long time it has been since I have opened a 'fridge. I miss that. Choosing to open a 'fridge. Ah well.

It was difficult for Rebwar to lift the chair into the park's bandstand today. The council have built a metal grille over the openings, doubtless to stop midnight fornication or drug-taking or whatever it is people might choose to do in this unlikely spot.

There has been considerable activity here recently. From the missives scrawled over the seat, it would appear that while Julie is still fit, Karen is a slapper. From the handwriting, it could say flapper, but perhaps that is unlikely, given the setting. Indeed, Karen would appear to agree, as she has offered her mobile telephone number across one of the bandstand walls, with the offer of what she calls the best blowjob in town. Gaz, I learn as my eyes peruse the Accrington brick walls, between which the glossy black wrought iron foliage of the original bandstand looks so solid, is a dick.

I think Sylvia is losing her mind. It troubles me, as I should hate her to finally move into the Sidney Fleiss, and then find she's not there to talk to. She telephoned me this morning, and then swore blind that I had telephoned her. It was most odd. She then suggested she had a whole range of doubtless imaginary friends round, and one of these was a fish. I half hoped she was being funny, but she sounded quite serious.

She rang me three times in all, and then seemed to have nothing much to say, except that she was not telephoning me at all. In days gone by, I would have telephoned the doctor or someone, but really it seems impossible to get people to do anything on one's recommendation nowadays.

I have read in the local newspaper that there is a meeting, tonight, to protest about Maplehurst being pulled down to build yet more flats. The article was headlined 'Chelsea of the North – Threat'. It was difficult to tell whether Didsbury was being threatened by the building of more flats, or whether it was being threatened with being dubbed Chelsea of the North. I'm not sure which I dislike more. It is not at all like Chelsea. If it must be twinned with somewhere in London, surely somewhere a little more thinking would be in order.

Ah well. Poor Joe. He would have been so sorry to see Maplehurst being fought over like this. I can hear him reading his poems to me at the Kardomah as if he recited them yesterday. And I remember the first time I was taken to his home. It was in 1931. I can see that lovely black and white hallway. Perfectly square it was, and all the rooms coming off it were strange shapes. He said if he didn't marry me, he would stay a bachelor... but I'm repeating myself. I've told you this before. You are so very patient with me. I know I repeat myself, but sometimes there are things I think I have said before, and I've never said them, and then I get accused of not telling people things at all.

It is safer to bore people than keep them in the dark, yet boring people is surely the worst offence there is. It is really a very challenging job, growing old.

If I were in better shape, I would go to that meeting. I would surely see all sorts of people I know. But I don't really want anyone to see me, who hasn't seen me looking as I now do. Rebwar says he would be happy to take me. It is not during his shift, but he very kindly said he would take me 'as his friend'.

Sylvia made me very angry when she came out with all that about not trusting him. She does not know him. Why I am so angry, is that ever since she said it, I am quite unable to help remembering her words, 'But Rhona, he's taking you for a ride in more ways than the one you pay him for. Don't you see?' And she has proved quite unstoppable.

As Rebwar lifts me into the bandstand today, he says, 'I gave a lift to your friend.'

'Oh?' I said. 'Which friend is that?'

'Mrs. Lowenstein. She wanted to be taken to Sainsbury's.'

'And how did you know it was Mrs. Lowenstein?' I ask.

'Well, as we drove there, she kept asking me questions. At first, just where I lived, how long I have lived in Manchester. That sort of thing. These questions are asked by everyone who wants to talk. They mean nothing. But then,' and here Rebwar looks at me and asks that I do not repeat what he is about to say, and I promise. Does anyone fail to promise at such a moment? And he continues,

'She asked if it is difficult to make a living, driving the cab for SupaKars.' And I said, 'No, it's ok.' And she says, 'But is it not possible to make more money another way?' And I said, 'Yes. Of course. I could steal it, or marry a rich old woman and kill her, but SupaKars has less stress.' And then she said nothing else. And when we arrived at Sainsbury's I said I could come round and help her with the shopping, and she said, 'No, it's ok.' And I said I would wait for her then, and drive her home, and she said, 'No. I might stay a long time.' I didn't argue with her, Mrs. Laski.'

I really am rather cross with her. Surely Rebwar being so open with his joke about marrying a rich old woman proves he has no ulterior motive. And yet, Sylvia has made me think, and it is Sylvia who I resent for that. Why can people not keep things to themselves?

Before he takes me back, Rebwar wheels me around the park,

169

and I practise remembering the names of the trees – 'Crataegus Laevigata,' I say, 'Paul's Scarlet' – and a few moments later 'Malus Hugsenhensis'. I have forgotten the Latin name for sycamore. I know it begins with 'pseudo'. I remember wheeling Howard around this park when he was very little, just as Rebwar is now wheeling me, and we called the giant sycamore 'the pseudo tree'. The avenues of broad-leaved lime are still here, and there are lots of new trees planted, which is very pleasing. But people have started putting little memorial notes on them, and even flowers beneath. I do not want to see the Marie Louise as a Garden of Remembrance. It should be of life. Of the present.

'*Tempus Fugit* is written on the sundial,' I say, as we approach the block of stone. The dial itself has been stolen. There is a hugeness to the pleasure I take from this park. Chelsea of the North indeed!

* * *

Twenty Four

All the film crew have left now, and Grandma Yes!?! and I sit in the living room together, not putting the lights on, seeing each other just from the glow from a hall lamp through the open door.

'That was tremendous fun,' says Grandma. 'I did feel such an imbecile thinking that actor was actually complimenting the kitchen when he was reading his lines. Still.' She is smiling, and I think, not feeling any pain.

'I'd like you to have this,' she says, and hands me the envelope with the cheque in it for the filming.

'Oh, don't be silly. This is yours. Do something fun with it.'

'We could go out to town and buy lots of silky lingerie for you to wear for Blue and me to float around in, and then out to dinner somewhere absurd.' She smiles widely. It's not a grin. Grandma doesn't grin. Grins have hard lines, and she's all curves.

'I have to go Grandma. I've got this meeting to go to. You know, the protest to save Maplehurst.'

'Oh darling!' she says. 'I'd have liked to have come with you. But I'm too tired after today. Maplehurst!' she says almost to herself. 'You know you could have grown up there.'

'How do you mean?' I ask.

'Well. Joe Shabalan wanted to marry me, you know. If he had, we'd have lived there now.'

'You mean I could have been one of those terrible-looking twins.'

Grandma laughs. 'Well yes, but that's only because they didn't have me as their mother.' We smile in silence then. And a few minutes later, I slip out of the front door, leaving Grandma sitting where she was. I look up at the beautiful house which no-one wants to buy. The thought of it disappearing from the family, disappearing from the world's surface, if it goes the same way as the others; it's too much, and I don't look back as I walk briskly down the rhododendron-bordered driveway and towards the village.

* * *

171

The meeting is being held in Didsbury Library. It's an octagonal confection of liver-coloured brick and dirty white stone and makes up in its gothicky, quirky styling what it lacks in books within. It has always reminded me of Miss Haversham's wedding cake, though its claims to fame are that it was funded by Andrew Carnegie and it stands on the site where Prince Rupert stopped for a nice cup of tea on his way to the Civil War.

We're a few minutes early, and we sit opposite, in a café, watching people arriving.

'Should be a good turnout,' I say, spearing another slice of lemon ricotta cheesecake. Blue and I are sharing one piece, which means we're both pretending to hardly be noticing whose turn it is to take the next bite. I love him for that. For loving cake as much as me, even though he takes it out on himself with his weight obsession afterwards.

'Yeah,' he answers. 'But it all depends who's got the deepest pockets.' The tiny-waisted waiter brings more coffee. He's rather beautiful, with long legs in tight black jeans, a strangely alluring gold molar and a silky black ponytail falling over his shirt. He and his friends add authenticity to an atmosphere made French only by the panelling and gold mirror lettering.

'You can't put the great British public on a French stage set and expect to end up with anything approaching a gallic joie de vivre,' says Blue, noticing all that I notice. 'At best raucous shrieks and lots of mobile phoning. The new esperanto.' We watch people parking badly on double yellow lines and heading up the library steps.

'I mean look at that lot. All camel coats and replacement hips. They're not exactly the poll tax rioters, are they? They're not going to set fire to buildings and throw broken glass at the council.' Blue adjusts his camera lens, and focuses on people heaving their way past the war memorial and through the Gothic library doors.

'I don't know! Must be paying you too much if you can afford to fritter it away here!' And grinning at his own quick-witted bonhomie, Mr. Clegg stands before us with the collar of his nubuck jacket up and what must be Mrs. Clegg pawing at his arm. She has long, dark-rooted blonde hair which, combined with the cream, long-tufted expensive coat, puts me in mind of an Afghan hound. This canine effect, which I usually associate with her husband, is increased tenfold by the fact that as Mr. Clegg and I speak, she stares away towards the library as if she were a bitch on heat and the classic old building a dog with an appealing odour.

'What's going on there?' she asks. She points her nose back at her husband's face.

'Dunno,' shrugs Mr. Clegg, and I can't help feeling he must do. I am uncomfortably aware that he will recognise Blue as the unlikely looking man who came in asking about Maplehurst. He had been a perplexed mongrel that day, asking why Blue had been 'sniffing ' in the office. Now I can see him looking at Blue like he is an old bone, vaguely discarded out of lack of interest, but now joyfully refound.

'Haven't we met before mate?' he asks Blue, who has glanced at me and seen my eyes on full beam, trying to impart to him that he should say less than nothing. I think Blue imagines I've got a nervous disorder.

'Have we?' he asks Mr. Clegg pleasantly. It can only be a matter of moments now before Blue blabs about the protest against the Maplehurst development, and then I'll be implicated with him and there goes my job and do I care? Yes I do. It's the awkwardness I hate. The sensation of being perceived as traitor.

And then Mr. Clegg says, 'Got it! – Aren't you the fellow who did those pictures of Old Paris at that exhibition in London?'

'That's right, I did!' gushes Blue. He's delighted to be recognised. 'The Marais area,' he goes on.

'Yeah. I went to the Opening,' flashes Mr. Clegg. 'Mate of mine owned the gallery. Hoxton, it was.'

And Blue beams on as Mr. Clegg keeps bursting out with fragments of memory as if he can't contain them. They're both loving it and I can't help feeling, well, annoyed. A milk-pan spill of panic heats me like an oven door opening. Melodramatic, silly, but unmistakable. Jealousy pin-pricks me. Makes my wrists sweat. How the hell can Mr. Clegg dare to have a history (yes, well, it *is* a history) with Blue? How could he have met him before I did? And while a smile of apparent pleasure plays on my near-twitching lip, I take in the injustice and insanity of Mr. Clegg having ever been to an exhibition of anything. This is a man who calls Earl Grey 'muck'. Still, I suppose he can't help having a gallery owning friend, I reason. And then Mr. Clegg says,

'I loved that one of the religious Jew walking past the gay bar,' and Blue smiles in a foreign language. I get this image of screaming queens munching on *gefilte* fish and muscle Marys sharing *boreshkes*.

173

Blue says, 'Well, it really was like that. I mean, it sounds a bit hackneyed, but the Marais is full of authentic cliché. It's brilliant. I love life that's edging to the end. I mean, the old Jewish boulangeries and all that. They're more Rastas buying the cheesecake there than Jews.'

Ah, I think, he's off on his slipping-away-lives line. And I don't care about my job as much as sharing with Blue things that Mr. Clegg cannot.

'Talking of edging to the end, that gallery's gone now,' says Mr. Clegg, revelling both in his advance knowledge, and the sensation of development which he clearly finds sexy.

'What do you mean?' Blue asks.

'My mate who owned it. He's sold it. Knocked it down. The new building's already up. Flats going for £1.3 million each.' The thought of this causes Mr. Clegg's eyes to half-close and glisten like someone's performing fellatio on him.

'That's really sad,' says Blue simply. Makes me want to kiss him, until he adds, 'You should come to the protest with us. We need as many people as possible or they'll destroy one of the best houses in Didsbury and help ruin the whole village'.

Mr. Clegg looks like he's holding onto patience by a thread.

'Oh right,' he says, with a strange energy. 'And you going to lend support?' he asks me sweetly. I just nod and say, 'thought I would,' which sounds lame, even to me.

Mrs. Clegg chimes up then. If they don't make a move they might miss the first minutes of an all-important night of drinking in the Royal Oak. She has a gold chain round her neck telling us her name is Cheryl. I wonder if her telephone number and a plea for her safe return if found is etched into the other side.

* * *

'What is the point of a conservation area which doesn't conserve?' There is silence. Blue is standing, challenging the councillor. A tittered murmur of approval from the old tweed and camel coats. A faint rustling of chiffon scarves.

'I mean,' Blue goes on with a fire in his eyes, which look like sugar burning to caramel, 'If I owned a unique house, a house that can never again be built – and I wanted to know how it could best be conserved, and I approached the council, and asked what would be the best way to preserve its garden, and they said well, you could always try the authentic Victorian technique of concreting it over and commissioning an ornamental block of flats in the middle of it, would you think that was sane?'

More murmured approvals and a 'he's not wrong'. But Blue is right, these people are not going to pick up bricks outside and hurl them at the town hall windows in fury. They will tut. They belong to the Great Aquascutum-wearing, tutting mini-masses. The councillor looks flummoxed, and for a moment I feel rather sorry for him. After all, he's here, doing what he can, and none of the invited planners have shown up. If only he wouldn't obsess so with the drawing pin that keeps falling out of the hessian noticeboard by which he stands.

Blue is like a terrier now. Not giving up.

'How can you improve on a Victorian garden that's never been touched?' At this point, perhaps because he had given too much concentration to the drawing pin, or perhaps out of panic, the councillor says,

'Well, I mean, maybe if the proportions of the original garden weren't very nice.' That does it. The guffaw which breaks out causes him to find even greater fascination in the drawing pin, as if it were a Roman remain. He turns it in his hand over and over and over until it pricks him.

'So after a hundred years, the council thinks a mature garden isn't the right shape, and wants to right the wrong by dropping a block of faceless flats on it.' The councillor looks aghast. It's impossible not to feel for him.

'Oh, I think the design will be very much in keeping with the surrounding area,' he defends with a gentle, vague voice. I can almost hear him wondering if he's said anything else wrong.

Then a large old man with a face veined like dolcelatte stands, his red, sausagey fingers gripping the orange plastic chair in front of him.

'Can I just say,' he begins in slow, flat tones, 'that I'm eighty nine year o' age, and I've lived in this village for eighty six of 'em. It seems to me, Council 'ave made up their mind already on this. Them with the power aren't 'ere are they? No. So we're all blatherin' on, an' we all agree it's a disgrace, but we might as well be suppin' soup by ourselves at 'ome, coz it'll make not a blind bitter diffrence. Tell me if I'm wrong, Mr. Chairman, tell me if I'm wrong.'

Mr Chairman does tell him that he's wrong, with all the conviction of a sparrow arguing with a cat over a saucer of milk. A few more people speak. An elderly woman who sounds as though she is RADA trained, wearing a huge cameo at her throat, tells everyone that if Maplehurst comes down, it's the green light for anyone with a garden to build on it. A younger woman with an auburn bob and a Joan Bakewell neck says that knocking houses down in a conservation area is a contradiction. 'The fact that the council are 'minded to approve' the development without ever coming to look at it is just proof that the facts don't matter. 'It is mindless to approve,' she says amid applause. But Blue looks at me and we both know that the clapping is onto velvet gloves for all the sound it makes.

'We've been told that there's no demand for these big houses,' says an elegant woman with a South African accent, standing at the back with her husband, 'But we were very keen to buy this house, and were told that it was no longer available as it had sold to someone else – and that was over a year before these developers came on the scene. We tried to have another viewing, but were repeatedly told that was not possible, that the house was no longer available. I'd like to know why. We bought another house which we liked less in the end.'

Mr. Chairman says he does not know why, but that this – as with anything to which the answer would be really interesting – is a matter which she would have to take up with the agents concerned.

As I swivel round to look at her, I realise it's Mrs. Carr, who had said how 'ahdeel' the house was and how much she had liked the 'blick end whart' tiled flooring.

'That's funny,' I whisper to Blue. 'They said Mrs. Carr had cancelled her viewing.' I want to speak to the Carrs when the meeting finishes. But in the end, they have left before I make my way out. Blue and I walk back to his flat. I feel uneasy. Something not quite right.

We walk back along Barlow Moor Road, Blue's arm around my waist and mine carefully not around his. I've learnt! It's a shame. He's so beautiful. I feel so lucky. We pass great houses on their way down with KEEP OUT DANGER painted on their boarded-up porches. Other looming houses still used, but tarnished by multi-occupation abuse.

Beautiful houses still kept that way. Ugly, older faceless flats. Less ugly, newer, more twee flats. Before we reach home, we stare up at the Davrach building site. The new brick looks kinder, less awful in the dim sulphurous light of the street lamps. Like humans, and not like humans. Darkness takes away the ravages of age from people and of youth from buildings.

When we make love, now, and the warmth in Blue's fingertips makes my nerve endings jiggle with pleasure, and I can't get enough of him, however hard I try, I picture for a moment, Grandma's house. All the potential buyers who haven't seen it. And suddenly I feel very slow. Very thick. Very dim.

'Blue,' I say, pulling away to see him better. 'Blue, tomorrow, will you telephone my office and ask to view Lynton. Call at 10 o'clock, and I'll be out.'

* * *

Sidney Fleiss Memorial Home. Room 6.

The ulcer on my foot is so painful. But I will not let it show. Herta sat with us again at table this morning for breakfast, and she thanked me for my note.

Back in my room, I am feeling rather low. My telephone sits next to me, with its big digits which are so easy to push. But who is there to ring? I think of calling a number of people, but they are dead.

I must not become like the others. I must keep my interests. There was a lovely programme on the radio last night about early broadcasting. But no-one here listens to the radio. Well, not proper radio. They listen to some dreadful drivel. Quite astonishing. Penny has dressed me and done what she can with my hair. I have sent Marie away. She wanted to do my nails in some ghastly shade of pickled pomegranate or whatever she called it. Anyway. I don't want them done in anything.

I am feeling churlish and unlikeable, and it's better that people don't see me. I shall be very cross if Sylvia comes. She didn't bother telephoning to explain her strange behaviour yesterday. I don't want to see the park either. I would like to telephone the park officers at the council and ask what they think they are doing, turning the Marie

177

Louise into a crematorium garden of remembrance. But I do not know the number. The parks department is not on my speed dial, and anything else is too complicated. I could telephone SupaKars, but there is nowhere I want to go, and I suppose poor Rebwar should get an occasional day off from me. I am company for no-one today.

There is a knock at the door. 'Come in.' It will be Siklunli with those wretched tablets. I do not want to take them. I will not take them. Nobody has a right to make me, and I won't. The girl is clearly deaf. 'Come in, I say.' And the door opens. I loathe this chair facing the wrong way like this. I cannot crane my neck.

'Hello Grandma.'

Twenty Five

'Lynton', off Spath Road, Didsbury, M20.

I've just had a call from the Dreggs fellow at the estate agents. Somebody interested in the house! Actually, I feel a bit strange. It has never been this close. He asks if I will be in at two o'clock. As if I'd not be available for a viewing.

Those filming people left the house perfect. Actually, it's cleaner than it was before. If I could get a weekly film crew I could get rid of Mrs. Woman. Anyway. I feel rather wonderful. I step into the hall, and see the mould on the wall into the larder. But that's easy. A chair will cover that. Except it doesn't quite. I drag the lemon-scented geranium off the jardinière and plonk it on the chair. The leaves hang down covering everything nicely.

I drive into the village and buy flowers. Bright, light flowers. Yellow. Red. Pink. When I get back home, I leave the car in the road. The driveway will look prettier without it. As I'm locking the car, I have a sudden memory of that horrible man, but there's no-one around. It's hard to make my way up the drive, carrying the flowers, but nothing happens. Everything's fine.

I find vases, and place the flowers around. One on the piano. Vivid pink. One on the kitchen table. Brilliant red. On the half landing, sunburst yellow. I heard one of those programmes on television about selling your house. About getting the smell right. I should make biscuits. Yes! my wonderful cinnamon crisps. I start to search in the larder. I've got everything. Self-raising flour. The cinnamon's a bit antique. Solid, at first. There's no sell by date on it that I can see, but it cost fifteen pence which indicates to me that this is not new. Never mind. It smells alright. I've got butter in, and I microwave it to melted. It's very strange, cooking with tunnel vision.

I feel like a cameraman on one of those wildlife programmes with that Attenborough fellow who's found a Sylvia in her natural habitat – very rare nowadays, and is taking zoom lens pictures of her in some strange ritual which Sylvias only take part in every blue moon. The cinnamon smells of nothing really, but there's some allspice which is about ten years newer. That'll do.

179

I start to mix the butter and flour and spices, but because of the vision, I can see nothing around them. Still, I'm enjoying it. I try and visualise who the people coming will be. A young couple, maybe. I want them to like it. Want them to oo and aah at the beautiful rooms. And I'll apologise for the damp patches and the ancient heating system, and they'll say that it doesn't matter – that it's the nicest thing they've seen.

I'm quite excited. I pull off walnut-sized pieces of dough and flatten them slightly on the baking tray. I've not made biscuits for years. Perhaps it will be an older family. After all, at the asking price, how could young people buy it? But then young people get paid such a lot. Oh, I don't know. I don't care. No. That's not true. Of course I care. I couldn't stand it if they wanted to knock it about.

What if they don't like the stained glass. Some people don't. Well, I can hardly put them off. I've not been inundated with interest. And now the biscuits are done. They smell delicious. Antique cinnamon and period allspice wafts up from the oven. And they look perfect. A good omen. I lift them off their trays onto a cooling rack, and walk around the house pretending to be looking at it with a view to purchase. They have to like it. It's beautiful, for God's sake.

* * *

Sidney Fleiss Memorial Home. Room 6.

It is not easy, feeling this joy. I am winded. Punched with pleasure, but punched all the same.

I am sitting in my chair, my hands still on the moss green velour. Still facing away from the door. Nothing has changed. Not the pain from my disgusting ulcer. Not the wallpaper. Not the small, shocking pink capsule next to the little plastic beaker. The second of three to be taken before meals each day. Every day.

My hands still do not work. My fingers still swerve at their unsightly angle. Their nails need filing. But the fingers have just been touched. Not by Penny, lifting me into my chair. Nor Siklunli, helping me to the bathroom. They have been touched by a hand which, though diluted through the generations, was created in part by me. But his is a beautiful hand.

I will not call him by his name. It is a name that irritates me. He kissed my forehead as he left. Kissed it with lips which smiled like his grandfather's. Yes, it was Gussu's lips just then.

He's gone now. With a promise to be back. I didn't ask. Wouldn't. Couldn't. And in the strangest way, I don't need to know if he will return.

I said very little. Well, very little for me. And I heard myself, and thought that what I did say was mostly nonsense. Not insane. I am not insane. But he saw me after so many years – such a long time since I have been whole.

He remembered climbing the giant copper beech outside our house. He remembered lots of things like that. He has the most sensational visual memory. All his memories were visual. He did not mention sounds at all. Or words. His memories were vacuum packed. Tactful. We did not mention his father, my son. We did not mention his mother. We spoke as if it were quite natural not to refer to them. He told me of his photography. It was quite fascinating.

He had brought some photographs too. He did not offer to leave any here. Perhaps I'm glad. He showed me one set, and I said, 'Ah yes. I know that house,' and he was amazed. I enjoyed amazing him. I closed my eyes, and I told him what all the rooms looked like. Just the shapes. Funny shapes. He told me he is living with a girl. I didn't ask her name. He didn't offer it. But he said he was very happy with her.

When he left he said, 'Sorry it's taken me so long,' and I said, 'Oh. That's alright! Not so long next time though.' And that's when he kissed me. Afterwards, I took the pink tablet and I wanted so much to call Howard and tell him.

* * *

'There's a Scottish gentleman on the 'phone for you. Shall I put him through?' Pam presses my extension. 'I'm just putting you through now,' she says, and the Scottish gentleman's voice says 'Och Ay! Is it convenient for ye to speak?' It's the voice of the "We're-All-Doomed" Private Whatever He's Called from *Dad's Army*. I smile to myself and tell Blue he can say what he wants.

'Only I thought you might have the 'phones on monitor or something. Well, I called this morning like you said. I was Australian – moving to

Manchester. Told them what I was looking for, and they said they had nothing.'

'Who did you speak to?'

'Dunno. Slimy git.'

'Oh right,' I say. Perfect. The organ grinder.

'So anyway. When he said he didn't know of any six bedroom detached houses with lots of character in big gardens, I said I'd been up and seen some really great looking houses near a road called Sprath, or Slath... and then I managed to come up with Spath. Still nothing, so eventually, I made out my wife was mouthing something to me, which was she'd heard that Lynton was for sale.' Blue stops for a moment.

'Yes, and?'

'Well, he said it had been taken off the market. Owners reconsidering.'

'No Shit!' (Pam looks at me with a pensive frown. This is not part of the customer service patter).

'Yes shit. Anyway. No way could we view it.'

I sit and doodle on my 'phone pad after Blue rings off. Mr. Clegg is in the back room, and I can see the top of his head through the glass partition. He's talking to someone, but I can't see who it is.

* * *

'Lynton', off Spath Road, Didsbury, M20.

Ok. So I've eaten six of the biscuits. Actually, they're lovely. My hair looks terrible, falling down and too thin. I look like a witch. It didn't say anything about frightening people into buying your house on that programme. I wrap a turquoise turban thing round my head and connect it at the back with a small diamante pin. Slipping my kaftan over me, I survey the effect in my dressing table mirror. The kaftan is tan and turquoise, and with the tiger's eye beads, I'll do. I wander once again into the pottery room. I've got my best pieces out. Of course, the people viewing probably won't know anything about modern ceramics – but at least they'll see it's a house where creativity flourishes. Well, has flourished until recently.

As I make my way downstairs, I see the bright yellow flowers on the half landing sill, and because I'm not concentrating, for a moment, I almost miss the top step. My heart beats fast. Imagine falling down the stairs now of all times. Well, I suppose there isn't really a good time to fall down the stairs. Anyway. They're here!

I lead them into the living room. Cosier, more homely than the drawing room. Except they don't look in need of cosiness. They're not really what I was expecting. Actually, one of them is the Dreggs fellow himself. He's quite attractive, in a sharp-edged, trustless sort of way. He introduces me to another man. Big, thickset fellow. I've left my smile on my face and for some reason I can't quite reach it to take it off or change it. It just stays there, rooted to my cheeks, pulling my skin horizontally around my mouth.

I become horribly aware that I'm trying to be charming. A lovely hostess. But I can't pretend to be warming to this man. I just keep smiling.

'Would you like some biscuits. They've just been made,' and I'm gushing, I can hear it like I could hear the gushing down the bathroom wall when the cistern broke. Dreggs and this big man, who doesn't seem to have a name – well, I didn't take it in – politely bare their teeth. I don't feel I'm at home at all. I want my granddaughter here.

'Would you like coffee first or should I show you around the house. There are some lovely features.'

'Thing is, Mrs. Lowenstein,' says Dreggs, and he is speaking slowly and deliberately as if calling to me underwater, 'Mr. Hunter already wants to buy. He likes what he's seen.' I continue to smile. Hunter. Jaeger, in German. Why do I think of that?

'But he hasn't seen. I mean, he's only just come through the door.' I have a wild thought that he's previously broken in and seen all the rooms. A burglar just wanting to do a viewing. I think of the horrible people, some of them faceless, one of them with a face, and other parts, who have appeared here during the past year.

'Well the thing is, if I can be absolutely frank with you Mrs. Lowenstein – and I do think one has to be completely straight with these things,' says Dreggs, 'Mrs Lowenstein – may I call you Sylvia?'

'No.'

For a moment, this halts the horrid man. Then he goes on as before, 'You see, Mr. Hunter is very impressed with the position of your house. I'm afraid it's not the house he actually wants as such.' And for a moment, I try and imagine him lifting the house into the sky, like the house in bloody *Wizard of Oz*, but Dreggs' teeth are gleaming and he's nibbling on the edge of one of my biscuits.

'You see, Mr. Hunter is a developer. He wants to build a range of very stylish apartments here – you might want to consider one of them yourself, Mrs. Lowenstein – imagine – "Lynton Court".'

And I do imagine. I want to vomit.

'But I don't see how you could chop the house up. I mean, the rooms are big, but it would be so difficult to convert it.'

'Not convert it, as such, Mrs. Lowenstein. Demolish it and start again. A whole, exciting new concept. Luxury of the kind we mostly dream about. The planners are quite open to a new-build here. Would provide more homes in this very attractive part of the village.'

'What are you talking about?' I ask. I feel frantic. I don't take in the bit about planners. 'That you spend your time dreaming, and most of that is about luxury? Or most of the luxury in your life is in your dreams.' I don't know what I'm saying. I don't want this to happen. He talks on. I'm not really listening. Then he makes his offer. It stops my thoughts swirling. It's less than my asking price, but not a lot less.

'But people could live here. I mean, as one house. As it is. This is a very desirable house. I mean, I know it needs everything done to it, but...'

'But no-one – and I agree it is a very nice house, and if I can be absolutely frank, it's surprised me too, but no-one actually does want it, Mrs. Lowenstein. As a house, I mean. And with the year you've had, with all those problems...' Dreggs' voice trails off.

'What problems? How do you know of any problems?'

'Oh, your granddaughter told me. Bastards – excuse my language – breaking in and, you know, exposing themselves. It's ridiculous that people can get away with it. Someone of your... standing... well, you can't feel comfortable living here with all that going on.'

'I need some time on my own,' I say. They excuse themselves to walk round the garden. They don't even want to see the rooms. They're not going to bother with upstairs, because there'll be no upstairs once they've got it. I sit back and close my eyes. How dare they suggest no-one wants it. But no-one does, do they? And I think of the broken glass in the dining room that night. And the banging on the front door, and that silly pink penis sticking up like the indicator on Louis's Rover. Oh Louis. It's all your fault. Selfish bloody heart attack.

I open my eyes, and stare up at the cornicing. I know every crack in it. The plaster *fleurs-de-lys* in this room, the pineapples and pomegranates, almost a compote after so many years of emulsion around the light fitting in the dining room. Well, I've had them for so long, perhaps it doesn't matter now if they just go. No bloody way would I live in Lynton Sodding Court. But a flat somewhere. I do need that.

I heave myself up, and clutch the door handle to reach the hall. They are sitting on the stairs, mumbling.

'Alright,' I say. 'On one condition.'

'And what's that, Mrs. Lowenstein.' The bright yellow flowers above his head look glorious with the light behind them in their cut glass vase. I would like to smash the vase over the back of his skull.

'You call your skyscraper something else. But not Lynton.'

They agree. Of course, they agree. They don't care what it's called.

'Smashing biscuits,' says the thickset man.

It's only when they're halfway down the drive in their shiny car, that I think about it. I'm sure I never told my granddaughter about that man exposing himself. Sure of it.

* * *

Sidney Fleiss Memorial Home. Room 6.

As I get richer, another becomes poorer. It seems rather unfair, but I can say nothing at table to Herta about my grandson coming to see me. He appeared within days of her losing hers. Of course, she has others, but I could not expect her to be happy about mine.

And I cannot tell Hettie, as she would assume I was telling her so she could tell Herta, and it would look spiteful of me. This really is how they think. But also, I cannot tell Hettie or anyone else, because he has not really been rediscovered. He appeared. It's not the same. I have no idea why he chose now to come and see me. I am utterly delighted that he did. It has made me very happy indeed.

But I cannot say it has left me feeling satisfied. Rather, it has filled me with dissatisfaction. I feel a hundred times more let down than I did before. Am I being ungrateful? No. I don't think so. It would be splendid to call Howard. But then that would be unspeakably splendid even if I had nothing at all to say to him.

Of course, I could tell Sylvia, but we still haven't cleared up that nonsense from yesterday. I don't feel very moved to call her at the moment. I am waiting for her to call me, but she hasn't done.

Speed-dial Nine on my telephone with the big buttons is my solicitor, Merton Lewis. I press this now. Everything has changed, despite nothing really changing. I am not an impetuous old fool. I am not suddenly going to divert everything I have to my grandson. But through the night, and I did not sleep at all, I thought of his kiss to my forehead. Of that quiet apology for his absence. If he had been poisoned with arsenic and survived to live another day, he would not be apologising for it. So, he was differently poisoned. It is not his fault. The poison only works if I allow it to do so. I bear no grudge against him. And my will shall reflect that. More than that.

Rebwar has been a wonderful friend to me. He has been kindness itself. No-one poisoned him, and I like him. He must not be punished either, just because I bear no grudge towards my grandson. Both will benefit. I would like to ask Merton if I can refer to my grandson in my will without using his silly name. I don't see why not. There are no others. And as I wait to be answered, I think again of what Sylvia said about Rebwar. About her not trusting him. But that is only her form of poisoning me against him. She is like Elaine, and I, like my grandson. I should not allow myself to be poisoned. But how does one help it?

'This is Mr. Lewis's secretary. I'm afraid Mr. Lewis is away at the moment. He'll be back a week on Tuesday morning. Would you like to leave a message, or is there anyone else who can help you?'

'Yes. Would you tell him to call Mrs. Laski please.' That's enough. I don't need the secretary to know my affairs.

* * *

Twenty Six

Grandma's just called. She sounded very flat. Distant.

'Actually,' I say, aware again how like her I am sounding, 'I wanted to speak to you about something.' I've been looking through the file to find the address of the Carrs, but can't see it. We usually keep names and addresses to send future properties coming onto the market. Oh well. I don't even know if it's worth bringing it up with Grandma. Might just upset her.

'Actually darling,' she says, 'I've got something to tell you too.'

I set off for Grandma's. It's only a few minutes away, and I don't bother inventing excuses to Trish. I ring on the bell, and when she opens the door, Grandma lunges at me, clinging to me.

'I've sold the house,' she says. She's still clinging to me. She is looking rather regal, and not to say a bit odd. She's got a turban on and a sort of kimono thing which makes her look like an actress in her dressing room about to put on a wig.

'For a good price?' I don't know what to think.

'Yes, darling. I think so. Not far off the asking price.' And then she tells me what will happen to it.

'Are you sure all this is kosher?' I ask. I don't intend to say anything, but I can't help it.

'Actually darling, I'm pretty certain it's not.' She puts her head on one side, but not coquettishly – more haughtily. Her mascara has run a little, just a few tears, and some of her hair has fallen from beneath the turban, and she's swept it into the silk folds. She looks a bit like Quentin Crisp.

'They're bastards. You don't know how bastardish they are, actually,' she says more strongly. 'But I don't think I've got much choice. Just promise me something darling... Leave that job. We'll find you another job. Something. Anything.'

'Oh Grandma!' And I hold her very tightly, and I cry too. I feel very silly, unsure as to why she is tickling something across my core like a guitar string. 'Of course I'll leave the job. I'll leave it now. In fact,' I think, remembering my coat on the hook which I've never really liked and which attracts fluff to it anyway. 'In fact, I've already left.' And I break out in a smile.

187

'What do you know about them, Grandma?' and she tells me it doesn't matter.

'We'll just have to get this thing done. Let's not even think about it,' she says.

And we sit in the kitchen, and finish off the biscuits, which are crisp and buttery, and the smell of the cinnamon bursts through my nostrils, even though Grandma says it's very old.

* * *

Sidney Fleiss Memorial Home. Room 6.

'Ah Penny!' I say. And I am very pleased to see her.

'So, who's your handsome boyfriend Mrs. L?' she asks, as she shoves and pulls my arms into my cardigan as if she were a little girl with an old doll. 'I must say, you're a dark horse with your young gentlemen admirers.' It irks me slightly that she is patronising me, but today I do not particularly mind being patronised.

'That is my grandson,' I say. And Penny says, 'Oh very good', and it sounds as if she is complimenting me on my ability to make up an explanation so quickly and plausibly. I am almost tempted to say, 'but he really is,' but why should I justify myself? Perhaps she believes me. I do not care.

'Penny dear, could you go to the top drawer of my desk. Yes, just there. If you open it, you'll see some letters. Yes, that's right. Now if you go beneath the letters, there should be an envelope.' And Penny draws out my last will and testament, made by me on this day in the year and it shall revoke all former wills. 'Now Penny, would you fetch me a large beaker of water dear?' And Penny asks if I prefer Malvern or Perrier and I say it doesn't matter a jot. Tap will do fine. And then I ask to be left.

Merton Lewis will be back a week on Tuesday. Everything will be sorted out then. But I cannot wait. I want to start the process now. I have a box of safety matches in my bag, and with some fumbling, I manage to strike one. Quite a feat. It flares for a moment, and I allow it to catch the edge of the paper in my hand.

I can already picture the headlines declaring that *Frail Old Bid Sets Fire To Herself*, but I am very careful. I hold the will as far from myself as possible, and when the scraps of silky, black frailty trail into the air, and the band of narrow, bluish flame has crept along almost the whole piece of paper, I drop the final fragment into my wastepaper basket, and tip the water on top of it.

It is a lovely day outside. It was silly of me to have rowed with Sylvia. I can't remember what we rowed about. But I think it is time I telephoned her, and told her about my grandson's visit.

'Hello Sylvia. It's Rhona. Yes. I have some rather exciting news. What's that? Ah, well you tell me yours first. No. No. I insist. Mine will wait. It has waited long enough anyway. You have? Oh, but that's splendid! Oh, what a surprise! And just when you were thinking it might never happen. Oh well, we must celebrate. Why don't you come round, and I'll organise dinner and... what? Oh, well she can come too. Oh. No, no. That's alright. I understand. Well, let's do our celebration as soon as you've got a moment. What? Oh! Well, I'll tell you as soon as I see you. Now don't let me detain you any longer. Yes, of course we're friends. We're always friends. Goodbye dear. Goodbye.'

* * *

Friday afternoon. A week later.

It's hard not to remember the old man in Didsbury Library telling us that we were wasting our time. The councillors were minded to approve the demolition of Maplehurst. Nothing changed their minds.

I am melting two huge bars of white chocolate in a small bain-marie, and Blue has just kicked open the front door of the flat and is heaving stuff inside. He's covered in dusty muck. I pour the liquid white chocolate onto two saucers and bring them, with teaspoons, into our hallway. The place is littered with stained glass window panes, still in their frames with old, rusty stays dangling from them.

'What are you going to do with them?' I ask, and Blue stops for a few moments to spoon the warm sweetness into his mouth.

'No idea – but at least they're safe,' he says, kissing me. I lick my lips. They taste of creamy sugar and dust.

'Come on,' he says, 'I'm going back.' Workmen are already attacking Maplehurst with a vengeance. It's almost as if they know that if they don't make the building dangerous and requiring complete destruction, someone might come along and insist on saving it. When we get there, vans are lining the road, and the black space where the windows were are staring out like blind eye sockets.

'Alright mate!' calls a workman who has accepted from Blue five pounds for each pane of leaded lights. Everyone knows they're not his to sell, but if Blue doesn't get them, eternity in shards will.

'How much for the floor in the hall mate?' asks Blue. He never says 'mate', it sounds false and strange from him.

'Urm…well,' says one of the men, weighing up how much it would be to sell what isn't his. 'Depends if it'll come up.' They try, but each beautiful Minton tile, some ivory white and some jet black, crack as they try and lift them. Blue scampers inside. The front door is already off its hinges.

'Come on!' he calls to me. I feel like something out of the "Famous Five". It feels very strange being inside this house again. Last time, for the photographs, everything seemed so untouched and untouchable. As if the ambience had a power just by the duration of its existence. But the power was just an illusion.

It's unbearable. I watch the workmen yanking out the mahogany newel post from the foot of the stairs. It's like a rape scene. It is a rape scene. I'm so glad we have those photographs. I wonder where Grandma Yes!?! stood here, and where Joe Shabalan was, and whether they kissed, and what else they did, here in this desecrated house.

Blue emerges from the kitchen clutching the box of servants' bells. It's painted cream, but the front is all gold lettering. *Drawing Room. Master Bedroom. Library. Front Door.* 'Take this. Hide it somewhere,' he says, and I clamber back into the street, and wedge it in a hedge.

'It makes me so fucking mad,' says Blue. There's no soothing him. I don't try and touch him. He's still seething about Grandma's house. 'I mean how can they be so short fucking sighted?' he'd demanded when I told him about the sale to the developers. Grandma's house isn't strictly in the conservation area, though to look at Maplehurst, it doesn't seem to make a lot of difference.

We climb up the staircase, precarious now without the bannisters which have been snapped up by an architectural salvage company. Up in the bedrooms, it's strange to see the layers of decades. Terrible Novamura wallpapers the Shabalans had put up in the sixties and seventies. A pink bathroom suite in the attics with pink and black tiles like a mouth of decayed teeth. A poster of Ringo Starr on the back of an attic bedroom door, the whole room painted lilac. Memories of a Shabalan teenager. One of the terrible twins. How strange that they would not want to be here. To see the place one last time. But then, how not at all strange. How could they bear to see this?

At last, when the light is fading fast, we make our way back, me lugging the servants' bells box and Blue dragging a huge piece of panelling from the back morning room. When we get back, the remains of white chocolate is hard on the saucer, and we line all the stained glass panes up along the wall of the hallway, like refugees arriving in secret in a foreign country, unsure where they are and how long they will be able to stay.

* * *

Sidney Fleiss Memorial Home. Room 6.

I woke this morning and turned on my side to cuddle up to Gussu. Imagine! I haven't done that once – not once since he died. I don't know how, but I knew instantly that he wasn't there as soon as he was dead. I always sleep flat on my back. I did at home. I do here. Yet this morning, I wake to see the panic button and the photograph of my home, which I keep on a ledge.

I lay for a few moments, awake. And with my eyes closed, I imagined Gussu asleep, just beyond me. If I do not reach out – if I keep my hands where they are, warm and unused, it is as if everything is back where it was. And as I lie here, I wait for the silence of morning to be woken by Howard, who will bound in. I luxuriate in this, and Howard does indeed bound in, except he knocks first, which is most unlike him, and then when he speaks, it is with the voice of Siklunli.

I open my eyes. There is no point at all in keeping this up. But as I am spruced up and twisted into my clothes, I cannot understand why I should have these thoughts today. Gussu and Howard were not preying on my mind. I am embarrassed to say that I don't think I thought about them at all before I went to sleep last night. There was something terribly funny on the radio, and I remember laughing aloud. I was not thinking of them at all.

Rebwar will come and pick me up at eleven o'clock this morning.

But I'm not sure I want to visit the Marie Louise Gardens today. I will wait until the parks department rid the place of all those plastic tulips and scribbled messages wrapped in polythene remembering 'Mam' and 'Gran'.

Breakfast tastes rather good today. A tangerine is peeled for me, and I enjoy it with a peculiar awareness of how fragrant it is. How sweet and refreshing. I want to tell Rebwar that I have found my grandson. That they will both share what I will leave. But Rebwar knows nothing of the will which I burnt yesterday. Perhaps I should tell him. I feel fortified and confident today. I have not felt like this for years.

When he arrives, I am sitting waiting for him in the lobby in my best, hydrangea-blue jumper and around my knees, a thick, soft rug as grey as a dove's wing.

'You look very happy today, Mrs. Laski,' he says. He looks very handsome in a black slashneck sweater and black denim jeans.

'Ah, well, I woke up to a surprise!' I tell him. But I don't say any more. It sounds rather foolish now. When I am safely installed in the deep front seat of his Nissan Bluebird, he turns the key, but the car does not start. It whines like a cat with a cough. He tries a number of times, and then reaches beneath the dashboard, and opens the bonnet.

I wonder if it would be kinder to give him something for a new car. After all, when I go, he will be able to buy whatever new car he likes. Perhaps it would be more fun for both of us, if he had the new car now. I am about to suggest this, when he gets back into his seat, and tries again. The car bursts to life, and I think that perhaps I will not say anything about new cars just yet.

'Not the park today, dear, if that's alright,' I say, smiling at him. 'I rather think I would like to see my old home.' I do not know why I want to see it today. I have not been back for such a long time. Somehow, today seems perfect for it. It takes only a few minutes to reach. There is a pillarbox at the corner of the road. Howard used to run with my letters there, and I once saw him kissing each envelope as he posted them through.

'What are you doing that for?' I asked him.

'Oh,' he said, 'it helps them get there sooner.'

As Rebwar turns the corner, I know that No.3 is just beyond the bend in the road.

'Stop, please stop,' I say, and Rebwar pulls in to the kerb, which on this street is still proper stone slabs. 'Rebwar dear. Would you do me a great favour?' I ask. 'Would you leave me for a while. I promise not to drive off in your car.' And of course, Rebwar does. I sit for a moment, looking around me. At the yellow gold, swinging mascot which hangs from his rearview-mirror. At the polo mints in the little ledge behind the gear-stick. And then I close my eyes, and I am walking back home from the shops, and in a few moments I will be there. It is lovely, to walk back home like this again. I do not want to see the large sign in the garden, with the name of the Home for the Elderly that the house has become. As I sit here, in the warmth of Rebwar's car, the garden of my home is not a tarmacked turnround with white painted markers for visitors and staff cars. It is a sunken garden, surrounded by white, crunchy limestone, and there are irises and pinks and dahlias and antirrhinums and wallflowers shooting colours all across the ground, beyond the great copper beech tree. And I can see the copper beech tree from where I lie, in my bed, with Gussu away at work. I can see it swaying in the breeze in the reflection of the wardrobe door mirror.

When Rebwar comes back, I ask him to reverse the car into the driveway behind. It is important to me not to see the house now. And we return to the Sidney Fleiss.

'It has been a delightful treat for me,' I tell Rebwar, and I am grateful again that he understands me so well, that he did not even think to try and encourage me to see No. 3 and what it has become.

At the dining table, I try and tell Hettie and Herta about my day. Sadly, the period of near cordiality after Herta's grandson was killed hasn't really lasted. Tragedy cannot make silk where silk is not. The two of them sit locked in political conflict, each determined that the intellectual stance of the other is without foundation, each resolute that their opinion on matters of international concern is the only logical one. It is quite fascinating to watch.

'I couldn't eat the last piece Lionel brought me. It was stale!' declares Herta as an opening gambit.

'Well mine was very nice. It was moist, it was creamy and it was lemony,' argues Hettie as if repeating a political party slogan.

'Well if that's what you call moist, well, I'm very sorry,' Herta flings back. It's not exactly *Question Time*, but I'm quite mesmerised.

'It's ever since they went kosher. It's not been the same. There was nothing the matter with it before, and now there's nothing right with it.'

I feel quite confident Hettie would go to prison in defence of the bakery in Hale outside which their middle-aged children congregated on a Sunday morning before the religious mob took it over and ruined the recipes.

'Well I've told Lionel not to bother going again. I'd sooner do without, I said to him, I said Lionel, it's you I want to see, not your bagels, and they were so hard I couldn't break into them.' Herta's face is flushed and there is chopped fish bobbing up and down on her lower lip. I try and suggest she wipes it off, but she is quite deaf to me.

'If you don't want him to bring you bagels, that's fine with me,' says Hettie with great magnanimity, 'But don't tell me their strudel isn't the best you've ever tasted. So much better than Grunfeld's used to be.'

Ah, I think. This is a real war zone. Even I know that Herta's grand mother was a Grunfeld, and she has mentioned the now defunct family bakery on Cheetham Hill more than once.

'What would you know about Grunfeld's?' demands Herta, her head flung back, the bit of chopped fish slipping slightly to her chin.

And I feel very strange. Not unpleasant, but as if I am slipping inside myself, like I sometimes do when I'm in bed asleep, and jolt myself awake. Like a gentle falling feeling. I call out to them. I suddenly know I need help. But I know I am silent ('ah, for once', you are saying!).

'I'll tell you what I know about Grunfeld's if you really want to know – I wasn't going to say this, but now we're on the subject,' I hear Hettie say, though it has gone very quiet, as if she is now a long way away. And I am aware that I, too, want to know what Hettie knows about Grunfeld's Bakers, as it sounds as though it is not something Herta would want brought up now. But I'm suddenly aware that I'm not hearing anything. It is Easy. Simple.

* * *

Twenty Seven

'Lynton', off Spath Road, Didsbury, M20.

The funeral's at two o'clock at the Jewish section of Southern Cemetery. Not the crematorium. I thought – well, we all thought – that she would be cremated. She talked about it. Perhaps she forgot to put it in her will, or tell anyone. It wouldn't surprise me if she never had the slightest intention of being cremated. You know what she was like. Anyway. What does it matter?

I'm determined not to feel that I should have come to see her when she was so full of the sound of fun a week ago. It would have been so easy. She wanted to celebrate me coming to join her, and she had something exciting to tell me. And I never came to join her, and I'll never know what she wanted to say and we never celebrated with dinner. I suppose I let her down in the end. Except I didn't. The last thing she said to me, was that we were still friends. That we've always been friends. I can think of someone who'll be dancing on the tables when he finds out. No more Supa-Sodding-Kars for him.

I'm being picked up by my granddaughter at quarter to two. And when she arrives, I'm ready in my old astrakhan cape, and the hat with the big brim I wore for Louis's funeral.

'Hello Grandma,' she says as I open the door. 'Oo you look nice. Like you've ridden in from the Wild West.' I think she imagines that as a compliment, and we kiss.

'I've got Blue with me,' she says. She introduces us. He's very striking, and oddly dressed for his grandmother's funeral in a blue wool suit and a white shirt, open at the neck. I want to hold him, because my granddaughter holds him, and has chosen him. But I think of all the years that have gone by with Rhona waiting by the unringing telephone.

I don't say anything until we are on our way down Barlow Moor Road. I sit in the front, and he is in the back. I look out of the window as we pass the Davrach site and have to stop as a car pulls out. Someone's scrawled 'bollocks' across the banner saying that only three are remaining. It occurs to me I don't know where I'll live now, once the house is sold. I think again of that slimy sod's offer of taking a flat in 'Lynton Court'.

'Did you ever visit her since you were a boy?' I ask. Sitting in the front, I can gaze out of the window. I'm not expected to look back at him.

'Yes, yes. Just once,' he says.

'Not much really, when you lived so close.' I can't help myself. I can feel my granddaughter's fingers tensing on the steering wheel. She wants to tell me that his mother poisoned him and this is hardly the time to have a go at him, but for God's sake, he's not a little boy. He must have been able to see that she was an old woman with nobody left. I don't care what they think. For a moment, I'm glad that taxi man's getting it all.

'You're right,' he says. 'I do know it. There's no excuse.' That's all he says. I mean, how can I simmer in silence when he admits it. He doesn't attempt to say that his mother stopped him. We don't say anything until we reach the cemetery. It's freezing cold inside the prayer house. We stand around the coffin which is draped in black velvet. And I squeeze my granddaughter's hand. 'Do you know,' I whisper, as the minister tells us which page to look at, 'I don't think I've ever spent so long with Rhona without her saying anything.' Oh, my granddaughter has the loveliest smile!

There's a motley collection from the Home. Siklunli, who dressed her every day and Penny (not Penelope but Patricia as Rhona never tired of reminding us). I could go up to each of them and tell them precisely where they were born, what their career aspirations might be, and the date of their parents' divorces. I know them all through Rhona.

Rabbi Landau looks remarkably well. He is older than Rhona and I know she would have liked him to be the minister (assuming she hadn't pretended to herself that she didn't want a minister of any description).

'Rhona was not the sort of woman who came to synagogue every week because she thought that was what everyone should do. Oh no! Rhona was true to herself.' He pauses for dramatic effect. Oh, I'd love to be able to drive straight back and tell Rhona. What a clever man old Landau is.

'Rhona was not an old lady who sat knitting all day. Oh no! – but to those who gave her the time to explore her depth, her intellect and her understanding of human nature, she embroidered the richest designs which they could weave into the pattern of their lives. She brought colour, and she brought a sense of lightness, even though she knew her own shades of darkness. Oh yes!'

And so he goes on, and I look at Blue, and I realise that what he lost in not knowing her was perhaps his fault and perhaps not entirely his fault, but he is paying for it, and who am I to give birth to a new rift? He makes my granddaughter so happy. So fulfilled.

When I'm being helped back into the car, I notice that the car in front has a sign on it. SupaKars. And I see him get in. He's not given anyone a lift. He must have come here alone.

* * *

Sidney Fleiss Memorial Home. Room 6.

Sorry to shock you! You didn't think anyone was in here, did you? It's me. Penny. Yes, I'm sure I don't need to tell you – Patricia, not Penelope. I've telephoned Mr. Lewis, that's Mrs. Laski's solicitor, and informed him of her death. He's only just back off his holidays. I told him what she did the other day – how I'd found bits of burnt will in the wastepaper basket, and I'd asked her what had happened, and she'd said it was perfectly all right, that she wanted to write a new one.

They're always doing that in here. Honestly, the times I've had to call solicitors and get them to come back and forth while residents decide that they're not speaking to one or the other. I shouldn't be telling you this, but do you remember Miss Kruk? Oh, she was a one, I'll tell you. She had this ring – it had rubies and diamonds in it, and she must have left it to half a dozen different people at different times, and in the end she left it to her sister, who she hadn't spoken to for years, but one day she told me she'd given it to her friend. She had this friend, Lydia Someone. Anyway, I said to her, 'I thought you left it to your sister?' And she said to me – and I'm not telling a word of a lie – she said, 'Oh, I have left it to my sister, with a clause stating that if I should not be the owner of the ring at the time of my death, then my sister should receive all the yoghurt marked as mine in the Sidney Fleiss refrigerator at the date of my death. So you see, I had to make sure I'd given it away before I fell off my perch.' And she'd stocked up on Müller Lights just the day before too! Oh, we did laugh!

Anyway, Mr. Lewis said that Mrs. Laski had insisted on holding the original will. So, that's that. No will. I've just got to disconnect the 'phone and contact B.T. Very useful that 'phone. Big numbers. Easy to use if you haven't got much control of your hands, like poor old Mrs L. There's still the list of speed dial codes written on the receiver. Ah look! Bless! She's still got her son's number on it. She was always talking about him. I sometimes think she'd forgotten he'd died. Terrible that, to outlive you're own.

I don't know what she had in that will, but it's a shame for that fellow who's always taking her out. She told me, oh over a year ago, that there was a bit of money left for him. Anyway, I called the firm and told them that she wouldn't be calling again, and to let him know she'd died. I think he was quite attached to her. He sounded really upset.

I'll miss her too. She'd have loved to have heard what that Mrs Fox and Mrs. Oppenheim told me. I think they'd almost got to fisticuffs, and Mrs. Fox said she turned to Mrs. Laski and asked her if she'd ever heard anything so ridiculous as Mrs. Oppenheim's suggestion that her family's bakery had been closed down by the health inspector, and when Mrs. Laski didn't say anything, Mrs. Oppenheim had clapped her hands and shouted 'Told you so!' and Mrs Fox turned to Mrs. Laski and told her she would see her in court with Mrs. Oppenheim on a slander charge, and then of all things, Mrs. Shabalan, who's at the next table, leaned across and said, quite calmly,

'I think you'll find she's died.' Oh Mrs. Laski would have loved to have seen Mrs. Fox's face!

* * *

Blue asks 'So howdya fancy learning how to make the best soup, now you're a woman of leisure?' And I end up with the glamorous, fun bits, like chopping onions, while he poaches dried pears in coconut milk, plopping cinnamon sticks and half a lemon into the liquid and breathes in deeply as he holds the top of a bottle of mirin to his nostrils.

The pears poach away plumping out, and he purées them. I fry the onions and he measures cornflour into an egg cup, adding water 'til it looks like Calamine lotion. When the 'phone goes, he's mid stir.

'It's for you,' I say.

'What's the matter? You look like you've been...?'

'Onions,' I smile.

He comes back from the 'phone wordlessly. He's been quiet since Rhona died, nearly a week ago. I told him how sensible the Jewish mourning process is. Sitting *shiva*. People coming over with food all the time. Sitting on low seats. No time to think.

'Yeah,' he said, 'But I'm half and half. The low seat'd only have two legs. Anyway. Who are all the people who'd visit?'

I think about when Grandpa died.

'People just come,' I said. Stupid to bring that up, really.

So now he comes back to the frying pan and purées the fried onions in some dissolved stock cube.

'Rule One,' he says smiling, 'Forget all the crap about top quality ingredients being the most important thing. It isn't. It's about not treating bog standard stuff as if it's rubbish. It often isn't.'

The pear purée and onions bubble in coconut. Fruity, sweetish and hot. He pours the soup into two non-matching bowls, and spoons a dollop of sour cream on top. We stay in the kitchen, sitting at the brightly painted table.

'This is lovely. You know you've not taught me anything though,' I say, blowing. Slurping.

'Why not?'

'Because it's you. It's your imagination that made it.'

'Ah, but it's flavoured with your tears. You did the onions.'

'This is true,' I concede, laughing.

Twenty Eight

Hi. We've not spoken before. Not directly. I'm Blue. We're sitting in the kitchen at Lynton. Outside the sky is darkening and dense, the dimming light from the cold sun turning the leaded window panes into a patchwork of dirty satin squares. The eucalyptus sways silently, its bluey mass cold, too, against the crumbling garages I can just see from my chair. I'm sipping instant coffee and over my knee is the heaviest old Crombie greatcoat you've ever seen. In its silk lining, the initials L.L. are repeated like a wallpaper pattern. They overlap each other slightly so if you didn't know, you'd think it was just a two-tone pattern. I love it.

'Oh, I'd love you to have it – take it, take it!' insists Sylvia. And I look quickly at her granddaughter who smiles back and nods. 'Go on,' she says, 'Grandma doesn't need it in her new flat. You'll look gorgeous in it.' And I try it on in front of them. It's long – almost to the floor. I can feel the weight of its weave on my shoulders. I can imagine the two of us, me in this coat, she in the reefer jacket suit she wore that first time she came to my flat, walking down Barlow Moor Road together on a blustery October afternoon.

Shame there's no tearooms with a women's orchestra playing or we could really be in *Brief Encounter*. This encounter hasn't been so brief. We've been living together for nine months.

A few minutes later, the kitchen is dark. I'd asked Sylvia to turn off the light when they left the room. 'It helps me think, being in darkness.'

'Yes,' she said without emphasis. 'I like it too. Helps the world seem softer-edged.' A gentle, creamy light filters in from the hallway lamps, and a spear of sharp white from the fluorescent strip on the steps down to the cellars stripes the old, built-in wall cupboards, but the rest is bathed in shadow and makes me feel I can untangle my thoughts.

I'm in the one old easy chair and I can hear the two of them shovelling things into bags and boxes they brought from Sainsbury's this morning. It's a massive job, emptying this house. Every now and again, Sylvia comes in and asks if I've any use for bits of camera or a combustion stove rusted to glory in the garage. 'Really – I'm ok,' I say. I've offered to help, but Sylvia's piles of stuff defy logic. Books for

Cancer Research. Suitcases of clothes for *Marie Curie*, mountains of sheets and blankets for *Help the Homeless*. Just this wonderful old coat which I can see on its original owner, Louis Lowenstein, in a photograph on the dresser with his arm round a young, dark Sylvia. I think to myself that I'm living with the next Sylvia. She's definitely going to turn into her.

There's shrieked laughter every now and then as the two of them discover all-colour reminders of black and white memories.

'You never wore that!'

'I bloody did.'

'With nothing underneath?'

'Of course! What's wrong with it?'

'Christ, what did mummy say?'

'Mummy wasn't born darling.'

'Blue? You wouldn't have need of a hammock, would you?' Sylvia appears at the kitchen door. 'It's very relaxing in the summer.'

The terrible pots about which I've heard so much have been carefully wrapped in newspaper and boxed up. I've had to receive one as a gift.

'And don't bloody tell me that you're alright – I know you're alright. Just sodding well say "Oo! Yes Please! It's beautiful!",' Sylvia had said with a big smile as she lurched towards me with a strange object shaped like a fallen soufflé and glazed in a murky, silver-polish pink.

'Oo! Yes Please! It's beautiful!' I say grinning, and she throws her arms round me. 'I'm so glad you've happened,' she says, and abruptly strides away, clutching at door frames.

I'm not altogether sure how I want this evening to end. I'm exhilarated. Confused. The thrill and the ambivalence remain unshared as yet. Have to. Until I decide. There was a 'phone call this morning from Sylvia's second cousin once removed or whoever he is. Merton Lewis. He's my grandmother's solicitor.

She left no will, he said. Well, there had been a will, and it had been destroyed. Apparently she'd burnt it the day I came to see her shortly after I left. I feel sick with myself that I only saw her once.

When this Merton Lewis guy told me about her burning her will, I just hoped she had burnt any gift to me. Then I thought why the fuck would she have left me anything anyway? I certainly didn't deserve to be left anything. I asked him – I said 'Was I in that will?' He said that wills are public property after their makers' deaths – but as it was destroyed by the maker herself, it would never become public property, and he didn't feel she would have wanted anyone to know what was in it. All he'd say was that the burning hadn't been, from what he could see, any attempt to spite me. Fair enough.

And then he told me what her burning the will meant. In practical terms. To me.

'I'm exhausted,' says Sylvia. The two of them join me in the kitchen, and I make hot chocolate with the cocoa and brown sugar in the cupboard. There's no fresh milk, but there's a tin of condensed circa a year ago, and we use that. It's the thickest, fudgiest gunk you can imagine.

'I don't suppose you can make use of any of the shrubs, can you Blue?' says Sylvia. 'I mean I know some of them are pretty ancient, but it's such a beautiful garden, and those bastards are going to destroy the lot for car parking. There's some quite rare specimens – and the stonework must be worth a fortune.'

'We can try and take some out,' I say. I don't really want anything from the garden, but I hate to think of her knowing all that lovingly tended colourfulness will just be steam-rollered into nothingness. Well. I say will be. Might be. It's what Merton Lewis said. My grandmother left an estate worth around six hundred thousand. No will. No husband. No children. One grandson.

Fuck me!

I could make two people very happy indeed this evening. One of them could move to somewhere warm and cosy and close by and never have to worry about buggered-up cisterns and exploding damp patches again. The other. Well – I'd so love to see her face. I mean – nothing's signed with these developers, from what I can make out. Looking around me, I can't think of anything in the world more wonderful than actually living here. I mean it's just so – so unnervingly beautiful. And to save the place. To know that this is one Didsbury villa saved forever. Well. As long as I've got it. We sip our tremblingly sweet chocolate and Sylvia holds old letters at arms' length, trying to decipher the words written to her by people lost or dead.

It's a wonderful feeling, the potential to provide such happiness. But I'm not saying anything. Something is stopping me. Is it the same thing that stopped me getting in touch with my own grandmother for all those years? Is there something weak in me? A coward?

Making others happy. It would have been so easy with my own grandmother. Just a visit. Sitting on the edge of a bed talking about nothing. Letting her feel a young hand gripping her old one. Letting her know that not everything was severed. But I couldn't manage that.

Do I want to be saddled, now, with this wonderful house? Do I want the sort of money I'll never have again thrown into one basket? Into our relationship, which seems so good – but didn't it seem so good with my ex? But it's a great investment anyway. There'll always be new blocks of flats. There'll never be another Lynton. But is it me who is destined to own it? If this one's saved and those around it end up being pulled down, what's been achieved. You can't really fight these tides of change. They're stronger than the individual.

They both look so animated, relaxed. At ease. And I've never felt less settled in my life. It's not coming into a huge amount of money that's thrown me. I've not really focused on that yet. I'm looking at Sylvia, lurching from room to room in her billowing violet kaftan. So different from Rhona, she is.

God, this is strange. I've just had a really odd sensation. Sharp, like someone accidentally brushing against my crotch. Acute, shooting joy, registering as pain, that I've been let go of by someone I let go of myself so long ago. The sadness of it makes me feel dizzy. She was always just "Rhona" to me. My other grandmother was Nanna Agnes. Mum's mother. Calling her nanna made her just that. Beige as dead rose petals. Heathery cardigans and a real gentile perm – pure white and curled like butter in old-fashioned good restaurants.

Dad – and Ma – always called his mother simply Rhona.

I close my eyes, and behind the lids, Rhona is in her big kitchen full of cream-gloss-painted cupboards with sliding glass door wall units. Piles of books recommended on *Book Review* waiting to go back to the library. Letters from friends all over the place, spread out on the big deal table she'd had covered with formica. Letters all full of cuttings about things her friends thought would amuse her. I can see Harold and Vita, the marmalade and the tabby, snuggled in their baskets on the ancient Bendix washing machine.

What I'm seeing best, as I sink into Sylvia's chair and drift further and further away from the laughter coming from the attics now, are Rhona's friends who were forever appearing, their accents so Jacobs cracker crisp and tinkly you knew they'd been born somewhere else – Hungary, Austria, Czechoslovakia.

Short, boyish haircuts and pretty, high cheek-boned faces. No jewellery, or hardly any. A Mackintosh brooch bought on a trip to Glasgow with the "Fiends" of the Whitworth Art Gallery, as Rhona called them, or a simple brooch set with brilliant green malachite bought on a trip to Israel in the '50s to see sole surviving relatives.

My head's stored these faces for over twenty years. I was only eight or nine when we used to see Rhona regularly, before we moved to Hemel. Her friends didn't interest me at all then. I'd sit, bored by the endless meaningless references to places and people who inhabited their lives and never even had an away-day in mine. Rhona was a wonderful hostess, bringing soups and cheeses and oat biscuits to the table and the friends would appear with cakes and vacherins. They'd all divest themselves of coats and gloves in the hall, though Rhona's own raincoat was always kept on a hook in the kitchen. Whenever the doorbell went, she'd slip it on, and if it was someone she wanted to see, I'd hear the exclamation, 'Oh how lovely! And perfect timing too! I've just arrived home myself.' And if it wasn't, it was, 'Oh! And I'm just on my way out!' One of Rhona's oldest friends was rather unlike all the others. More given to dramatic stares and gasps than the others. More given to swearing in the way of her generation – an embracing, easy swearing full of bloodys and soddings. She made wonderful stuffed monkey biscuits which she brought in trays to Rhona's teas. She's still making them, all these years later. She defrosted a load of them tonight.

I remember better the arguments on the way home back down the M1. Lying in the back of the car watching as the motorway street lights blew sulphurous yellow sunsets over the car's ceiling and Ma and Dad bickering.

'Did you see her speak to me – even once?'

'Of course she did. You're being melodramatic and silly, love.'

'Name one instance. Go on!'

'Well – she asked if you wanted soup.'

'Exactly!'

Pause. Dad, hoping the milk-pan of Ma's fury would simmer down just by his own silence, lets her have the last word. Sometimes this worked. But not often.

Her psyche worked on an emotional electric hob, not gas. A

seemingly calm, still ring, slowly and silently becoming brilliant, glowing red with no way for the heat to subside except with time.

One. Two. Three. Four... they think I'm asleep, but I'm seeing if Ma will spit out something else before I get to – say – thirty.

Twenty four. Twenty five...

'Do you think it's normal to ask if I want soup after we've all had cake?'

No response from Dad.

It hadn't quite been like that. Rhona had discovered the soup she'd made and forgotten about in the big Pyrex tureen, and had made the offer to everyone as a sort of joke. Spinach soup after everyone had finished Bronia's magnificent *Sacher torte*. I lay – waiting for Dad to screw up. I knew he would and...

'She wasn't just asking you. She asked everyone. She'd forgotten the soup, as if you didn't know.'

'Ah! – so even that wasn't addressed to me. The bitch has only got one daughter-in-law, and the nearest she gets to speaking to me – when we'd come all the way from London – is a general question to the whole assembly. You're so weak!' I knew better than to pipe up and correct her from the back of the car.

We'd come up from Hertfordshire, not London, but Ma liked to add a few extra miles for effect. Ten past eleven always became after midnight, if it helped the cause. She mimicked Dad. Well, not Dad. Just a wet, sissyish voice. 'She didn't mean any harm, Elaine.'

Seems hard to imagine now that my sympathy was all for Ma. Kids don't see things in black and white – they just find ways to push the darker greys into solid shadow, and bleach the lighter ones. It's easier to love and hate without misgivings. I loved Ma. I hated Rhona for not making Ma feel welcome. I hated her for waiting 'til we'd had our chocolate torte before offering Ma the soup.

My head let me disregard all the facts I knew. I left it like that, my hatred. Let it congeal until it wasn't active, sizzling hatred. Just a hard shell. I thought I was being loyal. I just didn't think enough.

So what did I come to Manchester for? It wasn't the row with Ma. Well. Maybe that had something to do with it. But it was just a catalyst really. Fifth anniversary of Dad's death. We'd been to the crem at Golders Green, Ma and I.

We went together every year. Stared at the plaque. Commented on the litter. Never quite knew what to do. Always made me feel empty – hopelessly guilty that his name should have been an emotional trigger, but somehow I just couldn't feel anything much, except the need to be away.

I always felt when there's a body, there's something you can talk to. Never mind the rotting process – the unspeakable images of what goes on behind a closed lid. The mind can do away with natural processes. See a vaguely smiling, calm face and a body dressed for comfort in remembered, liked clothes. Dad would have been in his Norwegian sweater and cords and his old boots. But you can't do that with dust. Dust doesn't smile.

After a little while, I'd drive Ma into Hampstead, and we'd toast Dad in the way he'd have wanted – with apricot strudel at the wonderful "Louis Patisserie", a little Hungarian hideaway on the High Street with wood-panelled walls and an air of 1930s gentility. There, I could feel things again. Biting into the buttery pastry and the sweetness of the fruit, I could picture him properly like hearing him speak on a tape.

'I wish he hadn't been cremated,' I said this year.

'So did he,' Ma said, moving the unused ashtray onto another table as if its absence made our table even more smoke-free.

'Well why was he then? How do you know? He never said, did he?'

Ma moved her bag from one side of her to the other for no reason. The waitress came forward to ask if we wanted more coffee.

'No, thanks,' said Ma. To me, she said, 'Yes, he did. Well. He said he wasn't bothered for himself. Shall we have another strudel? Or something else?'

'So why was he then?'

'Oh – I just thought it would help – help you just to remember Dad like he was. I hate to think of him there. Under stones. Weighted down.'

We had something covered in marzipan and filled with pastry cream. He loved those. My tongue spatulaed some almond paste wedged between the prongs of the cake-fork.

'Not bothered isn't not wanting to be cremated,' I persisted. And in that moment, I knew I was pushing something. And for the first time, a light shone on the black and a darkness blotched itself over the white of my black and white childhood. I looked up at Ma, and saw her one eyebrow raised, lips puckered in studied patience. Hard. Waiting for me to challenge her. To tell her that she'd had Dad cremated because she knew that Rhona would not have wanted that. That it went against the grain to cremate – that Rhona, a country member, of an orthodox synagogue – Rhona who would advocate people to do what they wanted, but wouldn't have wanted cremation for her own son. I was forming the words, 'So it was just spite then? Nothing to do with me. Or Dad.' But I didn't say this. It felt said in the silence above the little china plates with the scrapings of cake on them.

'I'd better get you home,' I said. And she admitted everything with her own reply. Silently gathering up her coat and bag and umbrella. A little, brittle smile to the waitress for the bill.

* * *

Twenty Nine

I came to Manchester a fortnight later. I wasn't searching for my roots. No intention of finding Dad's old schools or friends – still haven't. No persistent need to embroil myself in a culture which is mine and which has lain dormant through my childhood, adolescence and into manhood.

I'd been commissioned, along with another artist, to provide forty photographs for an exhibition called *Suburban Flux*. An Arts Board subsidy was funding the whole shebang, including the venue – a huge white space in a disused chapel in Stoke Newington. The remit was to look at the changing face of suburbia 'from north to south'.

Sadie Damask, the deeply irritating installation artist who thought there was something modern and exciting about nicking bits of buildings where famous people had been murdered, was my "co-exhibitionist", as the contract called her. With the conviction that North meant Hendon and South meant Tooting Bec, she had disappeared off to see if she could prise a bit of garden wall from Jill Dando's house in Fulham. For me, it was a beautiful opportunity to capture the images I'd retained for so long of the ageing, threatened villas behind their mysterious gateposts in the suburb of my own childhood.

That day, in the second hand bookshop in Didsbury, I'd seen her go in. I'd just come out of the film shop near the "Cheese Hamlet", and she appeared out of one of the clutch of estate agents which are sprinkled like parmesan shavings all over the village. Her face looked exotic and familiar at the same time.

Beautiful, her features set in a sort of claustrophobic sadness that I knew I could melt into a grin given the chance. She had the sort of beauty that beautiful girls don't seem to have now. Slightly other-decade-ish. And then I realised why she seemed familiar. She had been in my bedroom. Was always in my bedroom. At the bus stop, on my wall. The girl in the queue outside Davrach.

My favourite picture.

When I took the shot, my eyes had been dancing between images of decaying woodwork, the warps of coloured glass petals, trying to fuzz the pillows of dusty rhododendron and bring the heavy, black iron tracery of the old balcony front into focus. It was only when I was developing the pictures that I saw her. Third in the queue after an old man and a young black guy. I couldn't believe I'd not noticed her before. Camera's eye blind, like taking a picture of something with glass or water and not seeing the whole perfect scene in reflection 'til it's there in print. Blown up.

Something fascinated me about her. And moved me. I just sensed I was looking at someone who wasn't repeated anywhere else. Part of the make-up of Didsbury. A threatened sight, now that the make-up of the village is being disturbed, destroyed. Now the samey chain bars necklace the high street, filled with people waiting too long for goats' cheese focaccias and not noticing that the reason everyone wants to live here is ebbing away on a tide of mass market mediocrity. OK, so I sound snobbish. Well. Good.

Waiting for a bus. Straight backed. Aloof, but not cold. Wanting – needing for someone to reach out and touch her. And when I saw her come out of the estate agency, I couldn't believe my luck. And following her into the bookshop, I didn't know how to speak to her. It was such fun sharing views on the orange-back Penguins. Both of us tentative, waiting each time for the moment when the other's face wouldn't register recognition. And then I didn't know what else to say. Couldn't make the next move. All the leaps I could think of were too quantum. If I said what I felt, it would have sounded like a line, or worse. So I went for double or quits. Risk never seeing her again. Call it male intuition, but somehow I knew our paths would cross again.

And they did. I saw her next between an ideal investment opportunity of eight bedsits that would easily be turned back into a single dwelling, and a single dwelling with outline planning permission to turn it into eight luxury studio apartments. Stupid, sad mirror images. And behind the hessian screens, there she sat. Too bored to notice me looking at her. I'd looked in all the agents' windows searching for houses to photograph. Harder than I'd thought. Nearly everywhere with potential had been given the Poggenpohl-laminate-Velux-electrically-operated-Amtico treatment. And there it was. A classic old house 'in need of complete modernisation'. Music to my ears. And there she was.

Sitting waiting for me to walk in. Just perfect.

* * *

Sodding bulb's gone on the cellar stairs. I'll get Blue to put another one in.

Actually, Blue's being very quiet this evening. It's making me feel very alive, waking up corners of this house which normally sleep in the dark, warm pouches of my memory. I'm being brave. I'm not going to go to pieces over this house.

I've had a wonderful life here. I've loved it. I'd like Blue to have something. Something big that I can see when I go and see them.

The piano, or the library bookcase. But there's something in the way he looks tonight. Tunnel vision is bloody awful, but somehow it can focus things that I'd never have seen when my eyesight was complete. Maybe I'm being bloody stupid, but I don't think he's going to stay. It makes me terribly sad. I look at my lovely granddaughter. If I knew she'd be happy after I've gone − really knew for certain, I'd not think twice about leaving Lynton. What does a house matter really?

'You're very quiet tonight Blue.' I take a few steps towards him. See Louis's Crombie over his knees. There's something about him tonight. Something he's not saying. And that poor girl doesn't see it. I'm sure. And I can't tell her. I hope I am, and know I'm not, wrong.

* * *

Grandma Yes!?! seems so alive tonight. It's fun and shocking, pulling all these boxes and bags out of cupboards and wardrobes. Like pulling the stuffing from an old sofa. It can all go back for a while, but it won't feel the same. I can't see Grandma Yes!?! in a flat. Blue is quiet tonight. He seems very interested in the old photographs, but perhaps that's because they're photographs. Things that have been the same for so long are all about to change. Soon, Grandma won't be in this house. And then, a little later, this house won't be here. I try and visualise Grandma Yes!?! Court, an exclusive development...

And Blue and me. We share so much. I'd love to grow old and wild with him. Let my hair go white and mad and slink around in kaftans and paint my toenails when I'm ninety-five and go barefoot to a retrospective of *Blue Laski − 75 years of Pictures*. Well, Blue Morton anyway.

When we were in the attics just a few minutes ago, Grandma asked me if I'd like the piano. 'It's a gorgeous piano. I'd love it. But maybe you'll have room for it in your new place,' I'd said. 'Anyway, I'd have to ask Blue. It would take up precious wall space for his pictures'.

'If *you* want it, have it,' Grandma said. She doesn't think Blue's here to stay. I want to ask her if she thinks he's going to leave me, but I don't want to hear her say it. Besides. I know I am — I hope she is — wrong.

* * *

Thirty

The two of them are sorting through a shoebox of letters now. It has obviously been wedged between other junk from the way the cardboard has concertinaed at the sides. "Cloud Nine" stilettos. The label's still attached. I can just see Sylvia forcing her toes into the triangular points all those years ago. Screwing in amethyst filigree earrings, twisting to see if her petticoat is showing at the back beneath the hem of her satin-max evening dress; patting the tortoiseshell grip into her hair, navy black then, like I've seen in her photos, and remember from that time, so long ago, in Rhona's kitchen. And Louis holding out her ocelot which she's happy to wear shorter than her skirt because it shows it's real (this in the days when it was insured for more than her engagement ring, unlike now, when it isn't insured at all and never goes further than over her knees while she's watching Coronation Street).

I'm guessing at all this, of course – but the guess is educated by what I've been told. An adoring granddaughter's post-coital chatter about her family. The lazy talk that paints so many brushstrokes when sex is spent for a while. I never met Louis. Perhaps he never held Sylvia's furs for her – but when she flings her cape around her now, I can see through her momentary trance that Louis is behind her, about to hold her shoulders and kiss the back of her neck.

God. There's a six bedroom house-worth of furniture and clothes and pieces of things that once fitted into other things which have long since been thrown away – and Sylvia is looking proud and excited because she's managed to fill one small wastepaper basket with a dozen screwed up letters.

'This is making headway!' she calls to me, raising the bin like a wine glass.

For every 1950s' receipt she chucks, there's a letter to keep. To read. To remember.

My lover, partner – oh, I don't know what I'd call her – her whole concentration is in these folded sheets of her birthright. There are love letters from Sylvia's boyfriends. Poems and photographs of young men smoking cigarettes and standing by cars with running boards, odd words scribbled at angles in the pictures, tatty corners.

But there's also the odd letter in Russian, with a translation in

212

English which Sylvia reads out loud. Someone called Chaya Feigl writing to someone called Raisel. Lots of repetition, not much content – but impossible not to be stirred.

My dearest sister Raisel,

We have not heard from you for so long. We hope you and your dear children are well. It is worse for us here. Mendl has been unwell and there is no food. I know you will understand, my dearest sister, when I say I do not want to ask you or burden you, but I have no choice, my dearest. Whatever you can send we will be so grateful. May you have great health and happiness and may you and your dear family......'

The rest of it has disintegrated.

'That was my grandmother's sister,' says Sylvia, screwing up her eyes to make out the curling script. 'She wrote that in 1931 – from Odessa – didn't know Grandma Raisel was already dead two years.'

'Why had no-one in Manchester written back and said,' I ask, suddenly horrified by the pathetic injustice of it all, seeing Chaya Feigl begging from the sister who had escaped from Czarist misery over thirty years earlier.

'I don't suppose anyone could write Russian or Yiddish by then,' Sylvia looked up at me, warming to my interest. 'My mother never said anything about my grandma having a sister in Odessa. I only found out when I found this letter after mummy died, and by then it was the mid 70s. We just didn't ask our parents about, well, anything really. And they never volunteered.'

She turns from me. 'That's your great-great-great-aunt!' she breathes passing a photograph to her granddaughter, who looks into the eyes staring out of the century-old photograph.

'Look Blue!' she says and comes and sits with me. The photograph shows a young woman who has not been overly endowed with good looks, but whose dark, slightly sad yet determined eyes are with me in this darkish room right now.

Two sets of them. There was mistaking them (as in 'it was not the case that there was no mistaking them') but if you chose to see the

213

bloodline reaching out across a century and a continent and umpteen political regimes and God knows what else – well, you could.

I look back at the sepia picture, taken before the deaths of the Romanovs, taking in the ample bosom itself reaching out across the century into this room in Didsbury, the velvet skirt forced into tininess at the waist, the midriff like an icing-bag tapering to a funnel, the pale hand resting on an ornate chair-arm, the elaborate painted background of trees and a lake, the oval cameo at her throat. I wondered what could have happened to that cameo. Was it bartered for food? Did it go loose as the throat aged and thinned with hunger? Was it stolen from Chaya Feigl's middle-aged corpse as it lay where it fell in the untold loneliness of the USSR?

Something makes me think of my Dad. Dad died fat. Not obese or anything, but lumps of it round his middle. Unused energy that now never would be. Like that last little lump of coal in the coal cellar of a house I photographed. He died fat, and with his story unsaid. Stored for a day when there'd be nothing better to do but to tell it. Unspoken words that now never would be heard.

I don't let fat sit on my body. It has to be like modern-day snow. I have to run it into slush and watch it evaporate. That's why I can't stand hands around my waist. Anywhere else, but not there. Not where I know, as the years pass, some slush will rest a while too long while I watch T.V. It will compact and turn to ice and stay. That's why I hate to feel fingers stroking on the nerve endings around my waist. I know she feels I pull away. I know I do. But it's all less profound than she thinks. Well. Less profound re. her, and that's what's important.

So what should I do?

I can make things different. Affect things. But I can't change the flow. No-one can. I could bring such joy to Sylvia. And cement the love I feel for the beautiful woman sitting there with her. Give Sylvia a great grandchild. One to carry on the cultural thread that's wound its way through the continents. The centuries. In Jewish law, of course, I'm not – Jewish, I mean. Passes through the mother. But I've got it in my veins. One arm. One leg. One eye. One ear.

But I wasn't brought up with it. I don't feel it. And no amount of immersing myself in it would help. I know that. It's like a friend of mine from school who converted when he married Marcelle Tontino, a Jewish girl from Elstree. But you can only convert your religion and being Jewish isn't just that. It needn't be that at all. I can see that.

He told me that while he used to be just Paul, the guy Marcelle was seeing, once he'd converted to Judaism – and learnt more than anyone in the Tontino family had ever known about rituals and rites, the practices and the prayers – once he'd become the only member of Marcelle's family to know when to stand in synagogue not purely by following everyone around him, but by being immersed in the order of the service – then he became 'Marcelle's husband – he's not Jewish, you know.'

'I guess Marcelle swapping Tontino for Bates gave the game away a bit too,' I remember Paul chuckling.

No. It's all about the things you grow up with. The way you're sad or what you find funny. It's the things that can't be taught. That's its tragedy, the inevitability of demise in a place like this. In Didsbury. Jewish life spilled here in trickles and an occasional gush from Hungary and Holland, Germany and Gibraltar. It came in cakes and concerts, in books and bagels. It settled, established itself, building the villas here, butchers, delicatessens (one to go to every Sunday morning, and one never to set foot in since that episode with the stale cream cheese). Exotic and Middle European names carved into the back of benches in the parks – *Maurice Kolner loved these gardens, 1894-1967.* Etched into the brass plates of doctors' and dental surgeries. In the granite of the Old Folks' home. In the little *mezzuzahs*, like chocolate fingers on the doorposts. On the tombs in Southern Cemetery. In the stained glass windows of the synagogues.

But these people weren't Jews before all else. Not like in the other communities. They attended book clubs and Hallé concerts and theatre and had neighbours with Christmas trees and ate spare ribs at Chinese restaurants because the word pork didn't actually appear on the menu.

The cemetery is still getting its new names. Sharp, black letters on white marble. It's newest is a simple stone – *Rhona Laski.*

The delicatessens have gone. The park benches are still there. Some of the doctors' plates, in amongst the Mohammeds and Singhs too. *Mezzuzahs* like fruit in jelly, beneath decades of gloss. The Old Folks' Home like a backwards glance at the old community, full of wives turned great grandmothers. I can still point my camera all over the place. Record. Capture. But it's getting weaker all the time. I could nudge the Laski lineage a bit further into the new century, and with

Rhona's money – and I'm painfully aware it's the result of her destroyed will – for me, perhaps, the best will in the world – I can save a big, lovely house. But I don't want to live causes. And I ask myself how many of my feelings for this lovely girl have to do with what she represents and how I respond to what it all means. And does it matter.

And now they've joined me, and we're sipping sweet, luke-warm chocolate and all the time the light is fading till the coloured glass in the front porch is all aubergine, olive and night-sea navy.

And I sit with Louis's coat across my legs saying nothing.

Warm and quiet and with all and none of the answers.

* * *

For a full list of our publications please write to

Dewi Lewis Publishing
8 Broomfield Road
Heaton Moor
Stockport SK4 4ND

You can also visit our web site at

www.dewilewispublishing.com

Booker Prize Long List
Winner of the Society of Authors' Sagittarius Prize
Jewish Quarterly Wingate Literary Prize Shortlist

Wolfy and the Strudelbakers

Zvi Jagendorf

£8.99 softback
192 pages, 152mm x 216mm
ISBN:1-899235-38-8

Set in wartime and post-war England *Wolfy and the Strudelbakers* is a comic take on the disaster zone of displacement and exile.

Wolfy lives with the 'strudelbakers' – his super-critical aunt and melancholy uncle – in the surrealistic world of refugees granted shelter from persecution. He is an expert at living in two cultures – the chaotic, dark world of uprooted people desperately hanging on to their Jewish religion – and the vitality, variety and temptation he finds in London's streets. Wolfy observes it all with a sharp eye; the bafflement of his English neighbours at the odd, secretive nature of his Jewish family and their comical habits as they reluctantly learn to stop being 'aliens' and discover England through blitz, evacuation, menial work, school reports, team sports and Christmas. For Wolfy everything is new and exciting. He is a success as a budding Englishman. He lives near Arsenal Football Club, practises ballroom dancing with the help of the BBC and, of course, he is getting ready for girls.

This wonderful episodic novel is an enchanting blend of humour and crisp observation. A mix that gives it a rich and unusual flavour – the flavour of real strudel: complex, succulent and full of goodies.

Eating Wolves
Alexis Scott

£8.99 softback
224 pages, 152mm x 216mm
ISBN: 1-899235-84-1

An hilarious first novel from an exciting new Glasgow based writer.

Eating Wolves is a black comedy set in contemporary Nice and Glasgow. It follows the exploits of two Glaswegian families on their budget holiday in Nice, as they struggle to come to terms with each other, with France and with the French. When they return to Glasgow two weeks later their lives have changed in bizarre and unexpected ways.

Sheila, Gavin and their son Alan are invited to spend a holiday with Madge and husband Stuart, totally unaware of just quite how shaky their friends' relationship is. Madge herself mainly wants to improve her French, whilst Stuart is biding his time until the end of the holiday and doing his utmost not to be left alone with his wife. Packed full of incident and bursting with neat twists and turns this is a wonderfully rich, funny and human novel.

When There Were Heroes
Elon Salmon

£8.99 softback
256 pages, 152mm x 216mm
ISBN: 1-899235-59-0

*A vivid evocation of what it was like to grow up in the
pre-state Israel of the 1940s.*
The Economist

Gideon Jerusalem is one of Israel's founding heroes. Like the Jewish state itself, he is a complex character rife with contradictions. Loosely autobiographical and drawing on the author's own family involvement with the highest echelons of Israeli political life, the novel tells of the emergence of modern Israel; of a destructive father-son relationship in which both succumb to the lure of different cultures; and of a fated love story.

Gideon's diplomatic posting to London in the 1950s intensifies the conflict between him and his son Philo, who does not quite live up to his father's high expectations. Alienation leads to a painful and belated mutual appreciation. Philo's impressions of Israel's birth have the clarity and detail of a child's innocent apprehension. As an adult, against the background of war and breakdown of a marriage, he views his native country critically but not altogether unsympathetically.

Homesickness

Helen E. Mundler

£8.99 softback
192 pages, 152mm x 216mm
ISBN: 1-899235-64-7

A brilliant novel... elegantly narrated... captivating and engaging.
City Life

Having exiled herself from England, Hestia lives an emotionally precarious existence abroad. At thirty, she has lived with boyfriends but never slept with any man. Wearying of the enchantment of virginity and its concomitant dissatisfactions, but quite unable to submit fully to a sexual relationship, she returns to London to seek out Daniel, the gay university friend with whom she is unwisely but inescapably in love. Daniel fails her, pushing her too far, too soon, into the arms of Sven, a mutual friend with, as they little suspect, a dangerous penchant for violence. When Hestia finds herself pregnant, she leaves for Canada to bring up her daughter, Ilona.

Ten years later, circumstances lead Hestia to persuade Daniel to adopt Ilona, and this is the story of the tender, stormy, often funny relationship between man and child. It is also the story of the yearning for home, for a sense of belonging and connectedness, which unites the trio at the heart of the novel, each in their own way continuing the quest to allay their homesickness, a concept which gathers cohesive power as the novel unfolds.

My Cousin the Writer
Paul Binding

£8.99 softback
224 pages, 152mm x 216mm
ISBN:1-899235-09-4

*A splendid new novel... rich and engrossing,
as original in its structure as in its content.*
The Independent

*A dazzling new novel... bursts with surprises both funny
and brutal... exquisitely crafted, comic but oh so agonising.*
The Spectator

*I had so much fun with My Cousin the Writer...
I know it's going to be a huge success.*
Anne Tyler

It's the Fifties, and every weekday all of Britain likes to tune in to its favourite BBC radio serial, THE PARKERS.

No wonder a young man at a loose end, and frustrated by his rejection for National Service, gravitates towards the makers of the programme – to its founder, the enigmatic Verity Orchard, her ambivalent husband Charles, and Cassie, daughter of 'Elizabeth Parker' herself. They all make claims on him – claims that will pursue him down the years into late middle age. And then there's his cousin, Ian...

Paul Binding's novel is a poignant examination of emotional and cultural confusion. Both funny and sad, it captures the ambience of a fascinating period of British life. Resonant with the intrigue of soap opera it is a novel full of character and characters, a post-modern journey through an England long-since disappeared.

Carthage
Peter Huby

£8.99 softback
192 pages, 152mm x 216mm
ISBN: 1-899235-29-9

*One of the most electrifying reads of 2003... the research is
voluminous and the historical accuracy impressive.*
The Mayo Times

In April of the year 146 BC, after three years of siege, the Roman army
took Carthage by storm. The people of the city were massacred or
enslaved and every single building was razed to the ground in a frenzy
of total destruction: a cataclysm of calculated cruelty and enormous
ferocity.

The destruction of this, one of the greatest and most opulent cities of
the ancient world, was Rome's solution to the problem of Carthage,
their final solution. For more than a hundred years only weeds grew
where the city had once stood.

Set against this background, Peter Huby's latest novel tells the inter-
twined story of seven very different lives; of men and women who
become inescapably caught up in the destruction; in the hatred; the
treachery and the cruelty. It is a chilling novel that resonates with
man's inhumanity to man, in its exploration of this genocide of the
ancient world and its impact on the lives of indiviuduals.